T0062519

Other Published Works by the Author

Parthian Stranger 1 The Order
Parthian Stranger 2 Conspiracy
Parthian Stranger 3 Supreme Court

Parthian Stranger 4 Enzo Bonn

Stewart N. Johnson

Order this book online at www.trafford.com
or email orders@trafford.com

Most Trafford titles are also available at major online book retailers.

Printed in the United States of America.

ISBN: 978-1-4907-3349-4 (sc)
ISBN: 978-1-4907-3351-7 (hc)
ISBN: 978-1-4907-3350-0 (e)

Library of Congress Control Number: 2014906822

Trafford rev. 04/17/2014

www.trafford.com

North America & international
toll-free: 1 888 232 4444 (USA & Canada)
fax: 812 355 4082

I want to thank, Breanna B. Gibson, for which none of this would have been possible, for believing in my work, as an artist, and for providing a safe place to do my work, I will be forever grateful. For my wife, Penny, you are the cog in the whole process, from the computer work, to then support, without your help this book would have been difficult to have been made.

CONTENTS

Chapter 1 My alter-ego Enzo Bonn 1
Chapter 2 Mike's in trouble 16
Chapter 3 Intimate moment with Enzo 30
Chapter 4 In the Gauntlet 38
Chapter 5 A night at the casino 53
Chapter 6 A dive to remember 71
Chapter 7 Attack on Scopus Tyrell 84
Chapter 8 Fun in DC being Enzo Bonn 97
Chapter 9 Daniel Nicoletti where are you ? 116
Chapter 10 Carly meets Jack again 129
Chapter 11 Jack, (Enzo Bonn) visit's King Huffa. 143
Chapter 12 A long ride to torture a well kept man 154
Chapter 13 Criminal cleanup 167
Chapter 14 Jack's a stud and the world knows it 182
Chapter 15 King Leon, King of the Gangster's 196
Chapter 16 The Shadow Project 214
Chapter 17 Celebrations of discovery 233

CH 1

My alter-ego Enzo Bonn

A few month's has since past from the funeral of our beloved friend Samantha. Jack took it pretty hard, even for those Miss World girls who were hanging around to cheer him up, but the last of them left, I just follow a routine, feeding both babies, Maria had her child, she had complications, that has caused her into a state of depression, she can't have any more children, she had a boy, he was called Oscar, born December 5th, Christmas here was cheerful in one regard and depressing on the other, the President of the United States was re-elected by a huge margin. Jack himself is depressed, even the special agents guarding us, knows, he needs a new mission, either the cabin fever is killing him or we all will force him out. Jack tends to spend his time with Alba, the two, do all kinds of things together, it's more of a brother/ sister relationship, she too is damaged, so she is healing as well, as for Alexandra, she is the workaholic she has over a hundred 900 numbers that brings in a load of money, my sister Kate moved in, for protection, she lives on my floor, occasionally Debbie would come visit, only to see Jack, she was once Kate's lover, but has since deciding that she wants to become a wife too, but she is few and between, for Jack spends a bulk of his days in despair even for her, no more games, it's as if he has changed, I feel were a broken family?"

"As of today, we have over 100 million of dollars, it's interesting, whereas we wives get a per diem, for 150,000 per year or about

12,500, per month, tax free for life, and half for the children, for their life, and Jack gets nothing, well that's really not true, he has Mark and Mike, and my brother Timmy, and Maria's brother Hopi, on the boat, continuing what Samantha and I started, with the criminal fishing program, whereas he gets still one million for every criminal he brings in, on Friday's they go out fishing, and on Sunday they come back, Curtis, my protector mentioned to me, that they were assigning a new girl to him, I guess we will meet her soon, especially since Blythe is still in Washington, for training, it's all because of the line that has been drawn, and the separation of the two units, Lisa has taken whomever she can get her hands on, much to Jack's disapproval." At the house, the door-bell rang, Sara looked at the front door monitor, but already knew it was a friendly, a lot has happen, since the gate was installed, now there is a security unit of officers, who patrol the grounds, and provide 24/7 security, she looked at the monitor to see a young woman, she watched as the door open, as Maria, let her in, she closed up her journal, and placed it in her safe, to lock it down, gets up, she wore as with the other wives the same outfit, tank top and shorts, however we are all coordinated, she thinks,

"I wear white, I do what I'm told, if that is what Jack wants then it shall be."

She made it down the stairs to see the extraordinary beautiful girl of Latino descent, or maybe Spanish, to say, "Hi, my name is Sara." She extended her hand, as the two touched for her to say, "Hi my name is Tatiana, I'm Jack's new partner."

"Sure you are" said Sara under her breath. To ad, "Let me show you to where he is at."

Sara, opened the sliding glass door, to the patio, where Alba and Jack sat, in discussion, laugh's and kisses. While Tatiana watched, she said, "Doesn't that make you jealous?"

"No why, she is just like my sister" said Sara, as she went over, bent, down, took Alba's face in her hands and kissed her on the lips.

"Stop showing off" said Jack as he turned to see, the new girl, to speak up to say, "So Lisa sent you?"

"Yes", she said, to add, "I hope, I will do?"

"For what?" asked Jack.

"Well", she said, "You like to work alone, but don't you have a team that help's you out?"

Jack shrugs his shoulders, then says, "What special talents do you have?"

She looked at him, smiles, then says "Do you want me to show you?"

"Sure why not, what do you have?"

She came forward, stopped to look at him then began to speak in her native tongue, then switch to another language, just as she changed to another, Jack stood up and talked in her native language back at her, as the two were literally screaming at each other, when Sara got between the two to say, "Enough you two, take it inside."

"Alright, sorry dear" said Jack, kissing Sara, for her to say,

"Enough of yourself, take the girl down to meet the rest of your team."

"Yes, Ma'am", said Jack, going along.

"You behave yourself, and leave the poor girl alone", she said kiddingly.

Jack led Tatiana, into the house, through the house, to the elevator, he allowed her as she stepped in, he kept his face towards her as he stepped in, and took it down to the bottom, the doors open, for Jack to say, "Ladies first, go ahead." As he caught her staring at him, for her to say, "Your brave, you don't wear your gun, do you even have your phone?"

Jack watched her lead, as she went through the lobby, as she came to the door, it was locked, she waited till Jack got there, it opened as he touched the door, he held it open for her, she was in the lead, onto the dock, where a well armed guy with automatic weapon, was at the ready, she looked up at the huge gun emplacement, the big boat, newly painted in blue and white colors, the rear read "Parthian Stranger", she continued to the boathouse, where the door opened by another guard, to comment, "This is some security, you have here", only to see Mike, standing at the door, at the ready, to say, "Jack, are you back in?"

"Maybe, she is here to convince me."

Mike looked her over, then smiled, then looked at Jack, who led her into his office, to say "Have a seat."

She sits down, and crosses her legs, showing off her nylons, for Jack to say, "Start talking "as he looked out his window towards the boat.

"Well let me begin, Lisa sent me here to see if you might be interested in helping me out?"

"How so, what do you mean?" asked Jack still not looking at her.

"Well I'm from Puerto Rico, and we are losing young woman at one per day or more by some pirates." "Why me, what about the local police?"

"There useless, to the tyrant running this operation to Russia."

"Russia you say, how do you know this?"

"I was undercover, till I escaped, let me tell you, there is no hope, except you?"

"How can I help you" asked Jack extending his hand.

"Well first off, your known in the islands as a feared man, and second, Lisa told me is that this is your territory, if your into woman like myself, then Puerto Rico, is your place, we know you just married the princess from the Dominican Republic, and you should have known about it."

"Not really, and why should I do this, to help you, looks like your free."

"But they have my sister, do you know what it is like to have your family in a tyrants hands?"

"Matter of fact I do, so who is this tyrant?"

"Some call him Escardo, or Mean one, some say he works for the pirate named Scopus Tyrell, or his son, Ellesa Tyrell." "Again how do you know all of this?"

Jack turned to look at her, she stood, and began to strip, first her shirt, to reveal her bra, then she slipped out of her shoes, to unbutton her jeans, she shimmied out of them, next she popped her bra off, and lastly, pulled down her panties, she stood nude, her clothes on the floor, her body, was scared, her ribs, were showing, marks across her breasts, burn marks all over her body, as she turned, to show her back, buttocks, and her legs, she stood defiant in his presence, to hear him say, "Get dressed."

Jack turned his back to her as she redressed, quickly, for her to say, "So will you take the case?"

Jack turned around to see she was still dressing, to say, "Hurry up, get dressed and get out of here."

She finished, picked up herself, as she exited the door, Jack let it close before he picked up the phone, and dialed up a secure line, to hear her voice he said, his code number and name, to say,

"What do you want, who is this girl?"

"Jack, this is Erica Meyers, we felt you needed a mission to get you going again, she is your new partner, with that she has a mission for you, why are you interested, did you see her body?"

"Yeah, what does that prove?, and how does that affect the U S,?"

"Well it's in your territory, and all the women are going to the European countries, how can you stand for all that slavery that is going on, and besides, didn't you say you want to do something new and adventurous, besides the President of the United States, needs you to attend the Summit of Spies in Switzerland at the end of the month."

"Really, he asked me to go with him?"

"Sure, it was invitational only, you and Ben, and hundreds of the best agents, the world has the offer."

"Well I guess you're right, I am getting somewhat bored here, so where do I go from here?"

"Puerto Rico, would be a good place to start, and the rest is up to you, somehow I think you'll find a way, you're like that you know, the President of the United States should be delighted to know your back on the job, for that I may just give you a million dollars, and I will have two credit cards, make sure you spend all of them this time, how is your team, need anyone?"

"Yeah how's Blythe?"

"You'll see her tomorrow, she should be ready for the trip, when will you be leaving?"

"As soon as I get my boat ready."

"No, you're not taking your boat, if you want a boat, I'll have one shipped out to you, I need you to fly out tonight, as we speak a plane, is readying itself headed for you, then on to Ponce, tonight."

"I'll be ready when you're ready I guess, I guess I'll coordinate with Jim?"

"I'll be there tonight, and I'd say we could catch up where we left off" said Erica.

Jack set down the phone, to see it was closing in on lunch, thinking either the buffet line at the hospital or Juan's sub shop, he felt around his pants for his cell phone, only to realize it was up in the bedroom, he realizes he needs to go get dressed anyway, he opened the door to see the young girl sitting by the door, for Jack to say, "I thought you left."

"How can I, I'm your new partner, so when you're ready, can we go?"

"How did you get here?"

"By boat, do you want to take it?"

"Is that how you were getting back?"

"We could, but I'm here to serve you, are you saying that you will take my case, and help out my friends?"

"Sure why not, how many does your boat carry?"

"Oh about six and some cargo."

"How big is it?" suspected Jack, looking at her.

"Not as big as your boat, but they say it's a high speed boat, travels about sixty miles per hour."

"Where would you be heading once we get there?"

"Ponce of course, there is where their headquarters is at." Jack opened the door to see Mark on the deck, of the Parthian Stranger, to say, "Can you have Mike, grab his gear, were off to Puerto Rico."

"Do I need to ready the boat for the trip?"

"Nah, its staying here, said Jack to ad, "Who will man the rest of the tours?"

"How many more do we have?" asked Mark.

"Were booked up for the entire month" said Jack.

"You stay here, till you can clear off the books and plan a vacation, then come on down there to where ever I'm at" said Jack.

Jack waves him off, as he walks along the dock, to the door, goes in, up the elevator, to his penthouse, where he steps off, he pulls off his t-shirt, and drop out of his shorts, and pulled on a white t-shirt, he pulled on his khaki stretch pants, he slid in two knives in the pants, next was his shirt, he buttoned up, then came his harness, he hooked that up, as he slid in his badge, and wallet, then his cell phone, he reached for the gun, he opened its case, he pulled it out it was hot to touch, he pulled up a loaded clip and loaded the weapon, put on the safety, holstered it, next was his shoes, part dress part running, all weather, lastly was his windbreaker, to conceal his weapon.

Jack rechecked his windbreaker for extra loaded clips, then opened the door.

His phone rang, Jack saw it was Mike, Jack answered it to say,

"Were back on, on our way to Puerto Rico."

Mike said "Who's the girl?"

"Ah, she is my new partner."

"Did you see that boat, I'm looking at it right now, it's a cigarette boat."

"So what are you saying?"

"Can I ride down there with you guys?" asked Mike.

"Nah, it has to be one of us, it would be like a secret mission of sorts, is that something you want to try?"

"Yeah, ever since the last few missions, I'd like to be the first in and do what you do."

"Are you sure, you're ready, it may be dangerous, are you armed?"

"Yes, and I accept the challenge whatever it is."

"Fine it will be you on that boat, and I'll see you tomorrow morning."

Jack closed up the phone and made his way down, the two double stairs, to the landing, Maria was in the kitchen, with Sara, and Alba.

Jack slowed his pace for Maria to see him first, she turned to Sara, it was Sara who came to him first, she hugged him as he held her in his arms, she felt his holster, as she whispered, "Are you finally on?"

"Yep, I'm going to take a look at what I can do, I'll be back soon."

The two kissed, Jack broke away, as he next held and kissed Maria, as she reciprocated, then he went to Alba, as he sat down on her chair's shelf, as he hugged her, while his other hand, was touching her right breast, the two kissed, as Alba said, "You be careful honey, I want you to be back as soon as you can, when you do I think I may be ready for you?"

Jack turned to say, "Sara can you call and have Alexandra come up. "the elevator doors opened and Tatiana stood there with Mark, as he let her go, and went back down.

Just as a helicopter, was heard outside, as it landed.

Jack got up, and went to the door, he opened it to see Erica, holding two cards in her hand, to say, "What does a girl have to do to get a drink?"

"Sure come on in", said Jack, ready to go.

"Where's your new partner?"

"Oh she should be on a fast boat into the gulf of Mexico about right now with Mike."

"And she was told to stay with you."

"Since when do I listen to you" said Jack and from behind him spoke a voice, "Right here", Jack turned to see she was there, as Maria handed her a water bottle, for Erica to say, "So are you both ready to go?"

"In a minute, I'm waiting to say goodbye to Alex." "I'll go check and see what's taking her" said Sara.

They watch her get into the elevator, as Erica said "Oh Jack I need to ask of you a favor, the President of the United States, has asked me to inform you that both you and Benjamin may accompany him to Geneva, to take part in the Council of Spies, on Air Force One, is that alright?"

"Ben can go with him, but I'd rather take my own plane, but really it depends on this next mission, where I end up but do you think I can take a guest?"

"Sure, of course you can have a companion, are you asking me to go?" asked Erica.

"Nah, you got Blythe, in there, that chopper."

"Of course, that was our deal" said Erica as they made their way outside, to the courtyard, where the still chopper sat, Jack opened the rear door, to see Blythe, with the headphones on, she saw him, but showed no recognition, as she went on singing to herself, as Jack let loose the handle he turned to see Erica who said "You look disappointed, thought she would be excited to see you, try again, all she cares about is being a spy, the best thing you can do, is give her, her wish, and let her be a spy."

"Sure, I think I will, he sees Alexandra at the doorway, with Sara pushing her forward, Jack approached her, and kisses her, she smelled sweet, then Jack waved goodbye, he got in the helio, as Tatiana was already sitting next to Blythe and sat down, across from Blythe, who instantly saw him, and gave him a hug and kiss, to say, "Thank you" in his ear, she nibbled on it, as she slid beside him, which put a smile on his face, as Erica got in on the other side, to a frown, as the chopper, started up, and in a moment it lifted off as Jack held Blythe in his arms, to a short distance to the airport, as it landed outside a hanger. Jack, Erica, Tatiana and Blythe exited, and through an open door, to see a familiar plane in the hanger, as Jim made himself available, to shake hands with Jack and say "Hi" to Blythe, she nodded back.

"Look we will be off in a few, let me show you what we have inside" he led them up the ramp, as the lights were switched on, in the middle was his Mc Laren, Mercedes, as Jim said other stuff, on the right is your main cabin, then around the corner is a galley, and you know the rest."

Both Trixie and Mitzi came up and gave Jack a hug as Blythe stepped back to give them some room, behind them was his new partner, the lovely Tatiana, who stood, to smile.

"In the front is your pilot, we have Bill Bilson, a commander of several hundred missions."

Jack looked in to see Mark at the controls, who smiled, to say as he pulled off his headphones, to say, "Don't think for a moment you are going anywhere without me, Guy came back for some reason to finish out the month."

"Nice to see you" said Jack as he looked at the two girls, then, saw Jim open the cabin door, Jack went out, to turn to see Blythe at the door to say, "Can I offer you company?"

"Sure follow me, as he went past his new partner, to his cabin, opened the door, and said, "Come in and close the door." Jim readied the gear, as he raised the ramp to wave good bye to Erica, who seemed a bit disappointed, as Jim clicked off the light, Mark started up the plane, Jim passed by Mitzi and Trixie who smiled back at him, he said "Please take your seats, we should be off in a minute."

Jim came in to the flight cabin, to take the reserve seat, to say, "Gear is all set, were ready to take off."

Brian, got in with a briefcase, as Mitzi helped Brian in and close the side door, as he went forward, into the flight cabin.

Trixie placed a pot of coffee on, as Tatiana took her seat, she spoke up to say, "How come I don't get a cabin, I'm his equal." Trixie turned to face her to say, "Who are you?"

"I'm Tatiana, Jack Cash's new partner."

Mitzi looked over to Trixie as the two smiled, as Mitzi came close to her to say, "You don't get it yet,"

"What, what is going on?"

"Listen Honey, you're a present for his pleasure only, if it weren't for Blythe it would be you in that cabin."

"No, I'm not that type of girl", as she began to cry.

Both woman stepped away from, as Mitzi whispered to Trixie, to say, "She is not in spy club, who is she?"

"Wait maybe it's a set up, you know she instantly shows up, means only one thing, she's a spy."

"For whom, go in and talk with your boyfriend Mark and see what he wants to do."

"Will do, have your gun ready" said Trixie, as she went into the flight cabin, to take a seat behind Mark, only to see Brian with the steel suitcase, to say, "Who's that for?"

"Our boss" said Brian holding it firmly with both hands.

As the plane taxied, Trixie slipped off Mark's earphone to whisper "We think she is a spy."

"Forget it, she is a guest of Jack's do you want to tell him how you feel, go back and leave us alone, it's not your place."

He slipped the earphone on, to guide the plane to the ready, then looked over at the new secondary pilot, Commander Bill Bilson, and got the ready sign, as it picked up speed, he eased it forward into the sky, as the rain came down. They were heading down to the islands.

Meanwhile somewhere in New Jersey, and heading over to long island, was Enzo Bonn and his partner Johnny Rogers, their flamboyant style of crime fighting made them a legend on the streets of DC, and now they had finally got the instrument to serve, their intended target, that of one King Huffa, a man who claims South Africa as his home, whose visa expired a year ago, and his dealings with and around known drug dealers, meant for the first time, they were given the Okay, to bring this man to justice, along with them was the New York's finest assault and cover teams, all in told, over a hundred men. Docked in a slip was the South Pacifica, registered South Africa, and the current home of King Huffa, its huge ship, had huge hallways, to accommodate the size and girth of this huge Black man, standing at 6 foot 9 inches tall and weighing in around four hundred pounds, on the ship were his lair of beautiful women, some wives, some stowaways, some slaves, as the alarm rang out, noise was deafening for his henchman to yell out, "They have crashed through the gates."

King stood and said, "Send in the slaves", he laughed.

Looking over at his counsel, to say, "Is it my right to defend our ground?"

"It is, your allowed to use all the force necessary to keep you safe, in accordance with the immunity protection laws, as set forth by the UN." Said Miss Jess Thomas.

The henchman came running back in, out of breath to say, "It's the New York police department, tactical team."

"So send in Rene, and have Jennifer on that 50 cal."

Down on the dock, Enzo cried out, "Fan out, as Enzo held his position, while Johnny readied their spot, and connected the loud bull horn, to the PA system, to allow Enzo, to begin, "Attention, Attention, were with the DC police department, King Huffa, we have a warrant to search your vessel, and ask that you come out peacefully, we will give you fifteen minutes to comply.", Enzo kept saying the same thing, the next fifteen minutes, but dropping a minute at a time.

King Huffa went to the door, to hear what was being said, only to turn and say, "What should I do?" to his Attorney.

"Nothing, you sure can't allow them on this boat, then you would be in trouble, No you need to stay put, and I'll go defuse this situation, as for your Slaves, have them at the ready, but don't fire a shot, till you hear from me."

"Alright I'll stay put" said King Huffa.

"Do you know if we have a bull horn?"

"No, not that I'm aware of, but I do have a intercom system that can speak outward, it's in the pilot house."

Jess comes to King and gives him a kiss on the lips, then an embrace, to say, "Don't worry I'll get you out of this intrusion." She went into the next room over, and the pilot of the ship handed her the microphone, as he turned up the volume, she spoke up,

"Listen, members of the New York police department, my name is Jess Thomas, Attorney, and I represent Mister King Huffa, if you will allow, I ask that you send your representative up here to serve that warrant, and so that I may validate its vilitily."

All was quiet on the dock, as a smiling Enzo, covered the bull horn to say to Johnny, "We got him now, wanna go?"

The Commander of the NYC stood close, to say, "I don't like this, he should be the one coming out?"

Enzo looks down at the Commander, to say, "He probably thinks he has Diplomatic Immunity."

"Oh its one of them, good luck", he said in reserve.

Enzo looked at the Commander, then to his partner, then decided, to speak, out loud, on the bull horn, to say "This is Enzo Bonn, I'm with the DC police, I'll be coming in", looking down at his partner, who nodded he would join him, then over to the Commander, who nodded, he would join them."

Miss Jess spoke up, "That will be fine, we will have the lower door open and I will meet you there."

Enzo got off the shipping container, and gathered up, his two other men, and the three walked towards the ship, at the base, was a group of women, all dressed in camo, and heavily armed, not the one of them looked all that attractive, actually they looked god awful ugly, thought Enzo, as they made it up to the platform. Enzo was in the lead, as the cargo hold, opened, there stood a smartly dressed blonde haired beauty, who said, "Hi my name is Jess Thomas, Attorney for Mister King Huffa, you know he has Diplomatic Immunity."

"My name is Enzo Bonn, and that there is Johnny Rogers, my partner, and that is Commander Scott, here is what I have", Enzo hands the document to the Attorney, who reads it and scans the document to say, "Yes, its legal, and I know the Judge, who authorized this, really, I don't think he is one of ours, alright come on in and take him", said Jess, motioning for the men to come aboard. Enzo was first, then Johnny, and taking up the rear was the Commander, standing inside was a tough looking guy, with a semi automatic weapon, on high position, and some other guy, who introduced himself as Kurtis, Enzo followed Jess, whereas Johnny was with Kurtis, and as for the Commander, well once the door was closed, Rene, shot the Commander in the back, from the silenced gun, he had, the Commander went down, and was dead. while Enzo and Johnny, were two flights up, and even climbing more, for Enzo to stop and turn to say, "Hey where's the Commander?"

Catching up with them was Rene, who heard him ask the question, to say, "He stayed back to await, your return" he signaled them to continue. Enzo caught back up with Jess, the smell of her fragrance was intoxicating, but it wasn't hers, as Enzo stopped at the door, and peered in, to see a full fledged orgy of women engrossed with themselves, he and Johnny were pushed on, as Rene, closed the door, to say, "You better catch up with that Attorney." Enzo and Johnny sped up, to her, as she said,

"King, I have the representatives from the DC police."

The door opened to see the huge man, who had a gun in his hand, to say, "Alright over there and hands up."

Instantly the two were surrounded, as their guns were taken, and held, while King Huffa and Jess conferred, till King Huffa said,

"Which one is Enzo?"

Enzo said, "It's me, and you under arrest."

"Ha, Ha, Ha, laughed the King, who said, "You're not on US soil anymore, you're on South African vessel, and now your my prisoners, take them."

"Wait, that order is a federal warrant" yelled Enzo, as he and Johnny were being pulled out of there, for the King to say, "So what this is my vessel, what does that mean anyway?" he asked his attorney, who said, "He has a point, a federal warrant means they could send someone from the FBI or CIA to collect you up."

"What point, he is on my ship, I have Diplomatic Immunity." Jess picks up the paper, to say, "This order means you're not following the President of the our United States request for your apprehension."

"So what, what does that mean?"

"Means someone may come to try to fill this order, from the looks of it, it's worth 20 million dollars."

"Ha, Ha, Ha, that is all I'm worth."

"What is your plans with the two policeman?"

"Oh you know the same, as the other one, plenty of torture and then if their lucky, they'll survive a killing."

She went to him, and pleaded, "Let me have them, and I can try to make all of this go away."

"Enough Diplomacy, they invaded my space, and trespassed, and now I'm going to hurt them for it."

"This isn't some drug dealer, stealing your product, this is going to have some consequence, as she tried to hold him back, he took a swipe at her, she went back into the wall, hit it, with such force, and slid down, for him to say, "Sorry luv".

King went down several flights of stairs, to a room on the other side of the ship, he entered to see both men were stripped of all their clothes, and chained up with both their hands and their legs, for the King to say, "Which one gets castrated first.?"

Both men were screaming, 'No, No, No, as Rene had a hot iron, as the King himself smiled, as he held Johnny's dick, and Rene, sliced off his balls, as Johnny went into convolutions, and expired. For both of them to stand back to say, "Whoa, that has never happen before."

"What a weak soul" said the King rethinking what to do to Enzo, to say, "Rene set that aside, and let's do that last, no, we need to take each toe first, then his fingers, then we will castrate him. Enzo held strong, but after the first toe, he passed out.

After King and Rene was through with them, they opened the cargo door, and pushed them out into the water, for the King to say, "That will teach them a lesson on who their dealing with, I'm King Huffa and I have Diplomatic Immunity."

Rene motioned for the King to say, "What of the troops?" "Send in our Slaves, let's kill them all."

Said a smiling King Huffa.

CH 2

Mike's in trouble

On the plane, both Mitzi and Trixie sat on one side across from Tatiana, to watch her as the plane experienced heavy turbulence, for the entire trip, Mark held the wheel firm, as he instructed Brian to open the briefcase, then read the coordinates, Mark punched them in, instantly a set of landing light came on in the darkness, he eased the plane down, slowed the airspeed, lowered the landing gear, and just like that he landed, into a driving rain, Mark guided the plane to the end of the runway, where the lights went out, as a line of lights were on, to the left he piloted into the hanger he turned the plane around and shut it down. Mark hit the button to have the ramp to go down. Both Brian and Jim were first to the cargo bay, the covert lights went on. The pair worked together, pulling the cover off the custom silver car, enstrapping the tethered ties as Trixie knocked on Jack's cabin door.

The door opened to see Blythe, for Blythe to say "He wants to see the girl" pointing to his new partner, Tatiana.

Mitzi escorted Tatiana to the door, for her to see Jack lying on the bed with his gun drawn, to say, "Come on in and shut the door." She entered, to stand right inside to say, "So you know, it sure took you a long time, you know the guy you sent on that boat is under our custody."

"Yeah, he knew that before he left, why me and why you, I admit I have no idea what your plan is but I think I'm going to keep you close, and see how all this plays out" said Jack.

"Good that's exactly what I hope you would do, you will see and I can show you how they do it, where they go and what happens to them, remember seeing how I looked I want revenge on them, especially on my brother."

"Who is that?"

"His name is Ivan, and part of his team is the Joker, who raped me, and then there is Rampage, Ivan's bodyguard, so will you still help me?"

"Sure why not, that's why I'm here, do lead the way, I'm in your hands."

"What do you want to see first, the operation or the facility?"

"Let's try the operations, how does it work" asked Jack.

"Well, that I can tell you, then show you, I can tell you this there is about eight to ten or twelve girls who are the recruiters, they scour the country, to capture and enslave the girls, and they have one of my friends."

"Go on, I'm listening" said Jack as he waved the gun at her.

She looked at him thinking she had a chance and missed out.

"I'm sure your thinking, you had a chance to take me down, at my house, or in the boathouse, or even now, but now that you're in your country, you should find the right time to have a shot or two, at me, well good luck".

"It's not about that at all, I'm here as a emissary, in hopes you will find my sister, her name is Alysia, she is just missing, you have to believe me, I think Miss Monica has something to do with it."

"How so" asked Jack with the gun still trained on her.

"Miss Monica recruit her and I at the same time, although she went on to somewhere else and I was imprisoned and whipped as you saw, shall I undress, to refresh your memory?"

"If you would" asked Jack, not kidding.

"Really I thought one humiliation would be enough."

"Before I could of cared less, but now, why don't you come close, after you remove everything, this time on the bed, he watched as she slowly removed her clothing, she stood on the side of the bed, close but still a ways away.

"Closer I want to touch you."

"No, I can't let you do that, it will hurt."

"That's the idea, so either you come close or your slumping dead body will do it yourself."

"What you will kill me, over this, fine, but if I start screaming?"

"Then go ahead" Jack said with a smile, as she inched forward, to allow his hand to touch her skin, she let out a whimper, he moved up her leg, to stop, he worked it around, to get under the scab, for her to say what are you doing?"

Then in one move he pulled off her scab, as she lunged into the corner.

Jack stood to say, "Give me one good reason, I don't end your life now?"

"I can show you how to get into Miss Monica's fortress."

Jack stood over her as he said, "And how does that serve me?" "Well there are over fifty of the finest looking girls held captive, and yours for the taking", she was scrambling for things to say.

"When I have one nude right in front of me now." "Thank you, well . . . ."

"That's just it, why don't you come up on this bed and convince me why I should help you."

"Surely" she said as she got up and made her way over to him.

Back in New York harbor, the next morning the police and investigators were all over the dock number 7, which once housed the South Pacifica, all that was left was over a hundred dead men, and two mutilated detectives, for Enzo, it meant a bag of his digits and balls in a sack, his eyes were permanently open, as the water also did no good to his body, decay had set in, as lead investigator Emma Rollins, lead the investigators around, to say,

"Something mighty powerful did all of this", as she led them over to Enzo. For her to, say, "He got it the worse, and there is a paper stapled to his chest, as the investigators said, "It's a federal order, send the body and that order to DC, it to allow his wife and children to say goodbye."

As for Mike, he was treated as if he was Jack Cash himself, he rode shotgun, at top speed, he was spent by the time the boat came to a stop in Tampa, Mike was refreshed from his overnight nap, the rest of the ride was pretty easy, as it was early morning they reached the private cove, at Miss Monica's castle. The men lead him up some stairs, being treated with a lot of respect, the two bodyguards, went up first as Mike followed, through a door, Mike entered the land of beauty, all around were women, mostly wearing little or nothing, Mike stood in the middle as they swarmed around him they spoke different languages and some words he figured out, like pretty, handsome and sexy, till a some what ugly girl stepped on the floor, and the girls fell to the ground, appearing like they were worshipping this ugly girl, she was dressed in white lingerie, even with all the lipstick and makeup, still it couldn't hid how hideous she actually looked, her hand outstretched to say, "Welcome Mister Jack Cash, your reputation precedes yourself, your far more handsome in person than in the paper, look around, at your disposal is fifty of the most beautiful women in the world, all for you, so choose who you would like to be with first or all at once?, you choose. Mike looked around, he twisted at his wedding ring, he now knew he was way over his head, each of the women, were truly so beautiful, he was thinking what should he do, and now regrets ever asking his boss to be first in, he now knew the big difference on being a spy and being in spy club, as he made a complete turn, he faced the ugly one to say, in a smart choice, to say, "I choose you."

"Flattery will get you everywhere, but I'm the hired help, no these girls are exclusively for you, try again."

That was strike one, against him, he was nervous trying to choose the ugly one, he looked around again to see a hot redhead, a deep dark brunette, which he pointed to, as they stepped forward." "Good choice Mister Cash, her name is Isabella, and she is not allowed to talk, so do what you will to her as you see fit, any other choices?"

Isabella was close enough to elbow him out of her view, to say, "No I guess not, one is fine."

"Good, then you two follow me, Mike followed close by as Isabella was behind him, the ugly one turned to face Mike to say "Did you really mean you wanted me instead of all those other girls?"

"Yes, I didn't catch your name."

"My name is Allegra, but thanks anyway, here is your room" Allegra opened it up, to say, there is fresh bottled of water in the refrigerator, along with other assorted drinks, you two have fun, so when Miss Monica arrives I'll let her know you're here." Mike enters the room, as Isabella follows, as the door shuts.

Mike stands in the middle, as Isabella pushes him back to the bed, as he falls back, she is on top of him, rubbing him, she unzipped his windbreaker, to see he had a gun, she disregarded that and went to work on his pants as the two kissed passionately, she unbuttoned her blouse, and threw it off, then unhooked her bra, to let her breasts out as she whispered in his ear, I want you inside of me, then we will talk business. Mike stops kissing her to look up at her half naked body, as she was still sitting on his under excited body, for her to say, "You were excited, now what" as she threw open his shirt, it all came to a crashing to a halt, she looked at his side arm, to say, "Who are you" as he pulled her close to him, she began to fight back, and with one swing it hit Mike in the face, to knock him silly, he tried to stop her, but she swung a second time, connected to his jaw, and he went down, and out. strike two. Moments later he awoke, or was it moments, as he cleared his head, he looked around at the dark damp surroundings, as he heard, "Mister, Mister are you alright."

Mike looked up at her, he felt for his weapon, it was gone.

"Mister we need to try to escape before they come and take you down to the punishment room."

"What's that" asked Mike.

"They will whip you, or other things, now can you see if you can escape."

Mike picked himself, off the ground, he pulled off his belt, he looked at the buckle that read Mike on it, to say "strike three", oh shit, now what, I can't even play off a good lie, let alone impersonate the boss, he pulls a file and a pick from his belt, to replace his belt, to hear, "Mister what is your name?"

Mike held his tongue, to say, "Jack Cash."

"Really, around here your quite famous, what did you do to get thrown in here?"

"I stopped in the middle of having sex with one of them." "Oh my god, really, that's what happen to us, we too were forced to have sex with someone we refused not to have sex with, so were all locked up, hey my name is Tami, why don't you try to pick your way out, this is an old prison system, with caves and secret tunnels, can you pick the lock, you know it's the old tumbler set."

"How come you haven't tried before" asked Mike.

"Take a look at my leg, I'm chained to the wall" she said. Mike went to work on the lock, it clicked, he pushed it open, he looked at her, then scurried away, past the rooms, to hear her, say "Don't leave us, free us."

Mike ran to a dead end, he doubled back, but the path was larger, as it came to a opening, as he stepped in the room, was all eight of those girls, as Tami came forward to say, "You don't get it Jack Cash, or if that's your name or not, we can all read clearly the name on the buckle says Mike, why would you wear, a guy named Mike on your belt, it's no standard issue spy belt, usually most spies would blow their way out, and free the girl, you didn't do any of that, do you know were playing a game with you, and you fail to want to play along, were just testing you to see who you really are, so we know now you're not the spy Jack Cash, do you work for him, if so would you trade your life for his, you look like a nice poor guy, if you had money you could afford . . . ."

"Enough Tami, the game is over" said a stunning brunette in a pushup bra to expose her nipples, her long flowing hair, covered them, as the girls disappeared, she came closer, to whisper in Mike's ear, "Shame, shame, shame, sources tell me the real Jack Cash is on a private flight down here with my girl Tatiana, all you had to do was say who you were and we all would have treated you the same or as a guest of Mister Jack Cash, she pulls out a piece of newspaper hidden in her bra, to begin to unfold it, she showed it to Mike, whom he thinks Strike four.

"So are you a thief, or no, you assumed the identity of Jack Cash, you two don't even look like him, so what shall I do with you, are you a wanna be spy, you know there is a published list of all eligible spies free to roam countries without a passport, but you have none, so were back to the beginning, I don't know who you are and you serve us no purpose, either you play our games, or don't in the end, everyone plays some type of game, either you're a player or on the sidelines, seems to me, you were once on the sidelines, now you want to play?, or would you rather lose, then if you can winners win and get out, while you my friend will be trapped here for the rest of your life, as a personal sex slave to me, how does that sound?"

Clubbed, Mike felt his head split open as he fell to the ground, he was conscious, as he could feel his clothes being pulled off of him, he thinks Strike five, if he was a cat he'd have four more lives. Stripped, and with her high heeled stiletto on his gear, he lay back in a daze, hearing? You shouldn't have hit him that hard, he could be really tied to Jack Cash and if he is, I don't want to lose my fortress because of a stupid move, now go get me a chair, and some rope."

Mike was hoisted up on to the chair, and strapped in, one guy threw a bucket of ice water on him, he was awake but still fuzzy, to hear, "So what is your name?"

Mike was silent, until a strike from a switch across his chest.

"Next time I'll have you stand and it will be below the waist line."

"Now who do you work for, is it Ben or Jack?"

Mike mumbled something.

"Good, telling the truth is a good thing, what you say will either keep you alive or not, are you an American?"

"Yes" Mike muttered.

"Are you rich?"

"No" muttered Mike.

"Do you work for the CIA or the FBI?"

Silence, from Mike.

"Wait, I sent Jack Cash a boat to travel here on, and low and behold it is you that was on it, evidently you're not him, so I ask you one more time, who are you?"

"Mike" he said.

"Good, now we are getting somewhere, so Mike, why were you on that boat, not Jack?"

"He asked me, well I volunteered to go in first."

"Did Jack ask you or did you volunteer, you seem like a guy who wants the accolades, that Jack or Ben gets, so what do you do for him?"

"Special Ops" said Mike clearing his throat.

"So your only support, I can understand that, I to have some helpers too, so where can I get a hold of Jack Cash?"

"I imagine he is on the island now." "Excellent can we give him a call?"

"Sure" said a dejected Mike, broken so easily.

Miss Monica pulled out her phone, to say "What is his number?", she dialed it up, it rang twice as Jack answered it to say, something as she cut him off to say "Is this the real Jack Cash?"

"Yes I hope my calling card didn't get him into too much trouble."

"Why of course not, he is safe for now, although he doesn't want to play any games, unlike you?"

"Sure I'll play a game with you, release him out your front gates, then let me in."

"I will under one condition?" "What's that?"

"That Tatiana comes with you, is she there with you now?" "She is, but she really can't come to the phone right now she is a little tied up herself."

"Fine I'll release him if you, release her?"

"Why is she of some interest to you?" asked Jack as he was putting two and two together to say, "Alright how about you and I play a game, you dress up all nice and pretty, in the sheerest of outfits" said Jack.

"And I will have dinner ready for you about four" said Miss Monica.

"And I will finish what I was about to say, I'm going to tie you up and torture you to climax."

"Deal."

Jack folded up the phone, as he continued to drill Tatiana from behind, as she was on her hands and knees, till they both came together, she turned to face him to say, "That was so sexy of you to say, the mere anticipation of what you're going to do to her is excitable, even for me" said Tatiana.

Jack got off of her, to say "Stay where you're at, till I get dressed." "Look I'm not going to attack you, we just made love some four hours of it, I'm exhausted, let alone you had that gun pointed at me the whole time, say how did you know those scars were a fake?"

"I just read a intel file on Miss Monica and her bunch before you arrived, what you failed to mention, was why and where, sounds like she had way too much fun with one of my team members, so now I must rectify the problem."

She stood up to show off her near perfect body, in all of its own glory, to say, "What do you plan on doing?"

"Oh you know, take her down and free the hostages, I doubt if there Is any, everyone knows she's the matchmaker to the rich and wealthy, young naïve girls for sale for a huge price, the girls like yourself willing to do anything and everything to satisfy their men, like you with me, yes I do admit I'm attracted to you."

"Believe it or not you're the second guy that has ever been in there, and you're the right size, as he was that huge, I like the really rich and wealthy men like yourself, however you're a bit different, you hunt and kill people legally, that gets me really wet, so are you going to do what Miss Monica wants you to do or are you going to keep me locked up in here, to use me as you see fit?"

"Get dressed, I'll watch, what do you want anything, to eat or drink?"

"To be here in your bed, that was my true intention, honest, I was extremely willing to do anything you wanted, I've been trianed by the best schools and now I'm ready to have a family, I'd love to be one of your wives, and together we could be a great team."

She reached out to him to hold him, the two kissed, she broke it off first to say, "I'll even spy for you, did you know you had some girl spies inside as we speak."

"What are you saying, is this a lie or a truth?" "Honest, I swear on my grandmother's grave." "Let's go, your coming with me."

"Were you thinking of doing both Miss Monica and I, of us together, you know she's into women as well."

"Can you keep your mouth shut, I may still silence you, forever . . ."

She made the motion of a zipper on her lips, as Jack opened the door, he saw the team assembled, to say, "Trixie and Mitzi, go to McCoy field, and see a Colonel Tim Lange, see if he will pledge his support", both of them smile, as they exit the plane.

"Mark, I need you to follow me to this fortress, where Mike is being held, Blythe you can go with Mark, and at the nearest University, let's find those behind these attacks."

"That's Langston, Langston University" said Tatiana. Jack turned to look at her, she shut up.

"As I was saying, go to Langston University, and pretend you're a coed."

"For you two, Jim can you call Erica, give her a SITREP, and can you have Miss Jodie Thomas, and her long range support down here, that leads me to you Brian, can you scout a place for which you and Jodie can give me support on the cliffs overlooking Sabana Granda, sits Miss Monica's fortress, overlooking the lake to the ocean, Esenada, is her place on the coast, the lake that surrounds her property is Guanica, be careful, her guards are patrolling that whole area", Brian leaves, as Jack motions for Tatiana to come along, along the back to the empty cargo bay, on the deck sat a shiny new car, for her to say, "You are really rich, this is a Mercedes."

"Don't touch, let me get the door for you", Jack opened it, she stepped in to sit, the seat adjusted to her automatically, as Jack closed the door, he said "Sleep", and went around, opened up the door, to see she was out, and it was clear, he sat, looked at the steering wheel, then the dash, he thinks to himself, "Start, and on to Esenada, please."

"No please here" said the car.

"What do I call you", said Jack to the car, who he thought was Sara.

"Whatever you like, I'm set up with any program, your current preference is a women, so I have a women's voice, how fast do you want to get there?"

"As fast as you can Sara."

"So would you like to call me Sara, is that after your second wife?"

"Yes, you remind me of her, safe and sound."

The car sped up, as Jack sat back to see at times, the car hit, over hundred, as it blew by traffic lights as controlled by Sara the car, while Tatiana slept, the car slowed as the road to Esenada broke into a tee, straight on the coast right to the towering fortress.

"Right please, the car made a sixty miles an hour right hand turn, up the road a ways, was the guard house and wall, the car slowed, as the window went down, the gate guard, looked down at him to say, "Who are you, are you expected?", while looking at the million dollar car.

"Tell Miss Monica it is Mister Jack Cash and Tatiana." "Where is she at" said the guard looking in.

"Asleep, she was tired."

"I'll have to wait till, oh alright" Jack heard another voice in the guy's ear, say "Let him pass. And park in VIP on the first floor."

"Your free to go, take the road on the right, it will take you to a cut off and down to a parking garage, stay on the first floor, and park in number 13 space, through the doors."

Jack looked up at the gate guard, to say, "By the way is there a guy in your shack that belongs to me?"

"Actually there is, his name is Mike, would you like to see him?"

Jack said, "Hold it here, and got out, he followed the guard into the shack, on a bunk near the front, he lay, his head encompassed by lipstick and heavy of women's perfume, he was beat up, battered, his eye was swollen, and a fat lip, he was just mumbling, Jack stood up, looked around, and then dialed Mark up, who answered "Yeah, just leaving the college."

"I'm at the gate, change of plans, have Jim fly onto the grounds, and fly Mike out" the phone went dead, Jack looked up as a huge Helio-copter passed by, for Jack to say, "What was that?"

"Oh that is Mister Tyrell's he is coming to pick up . . . ." "Hush Brant" said another gate guardsman.

Jack thought a moment what to do, and he knew, he said "Thanks, release him to a guy named Mark, he should be right behind me", Jack got in, and the car took off, in his rear view mirror he saw Mark get out, as Tatiana awoke, for her to say

"Hi there, I must have been tired, sorry I took a nap."

"No problem", then instinctively, he pulled out his phone, from the dash, and put it away. Jack saw the parking garage, the car pulled in, and found its place. The car stopped and shut off, a buzzing noise was heard, as both doors opened simultaneously, as Tatiana, got out, then Jack, who said "Lock down", then escorted her in, with his hand in the middle of her back she led him, up the grand entrance to the main floor, then it became very awkward, there standing in the middle with a huge metal suitcase stood a very large darker skinned man, with a full beard and mirrored sunglasses, a huge chain was around his neck that bore the initials MM, a nasty cigar was out of one side, his sleeves were cut, to show his massive arms, tattooed as normal sleeves, he was big and bad, and without words, as the two men were in a stare mode till Miss Monica, spoke up, "Down boys, there is plenty for all."

Jack noticed, the guy looking at Tatiana, with the way his head was positioned, he clinched his fists, yes he was getting mad, as his huge nostrils were flaring, then Jack thought, pull the gun out and drop him now, but held off."

Jack was ready to move when Miss Monica, got in the way, to say "How about you feel on these, offering her breasts up to him, while she motioned for her assistant to go, then a ugly looking girl spoke "Right this way you too, Miss Monica wanted you to have a private room."

She led Jack and Tatiana, who was quiet, into the room, for her to say, "Care for beverages, there is some in the frige, help yourselves", then she exited, for Jack to say, "What was that all about?"

"Oh nothing" she said nonchalantly, grabbing a drink of soda.

"Do you know who that big guy was?"

"Yeah he is a bodyguard who works for her, his name is Rampage, why do you ask?"

"Rampage that's an interesting name, are you lying to me, you know I can still drill you?"

"I love the way you talk, when and where, how about here and now."

"Nah, no thanks, I'm sure she will be coming through those doors, any minute."

Moments later it happen. She made her entrance, with both of her breast still exposed, for Jack to say, "Is that a fashion statement or are you still excited over that guy?"

In all this new commotion, Jack noticed Tatiana was gone, to say "Alright were even, you got your girl back and well I have my guy so what's next?"

"Well I believe you promised me a game." "That I did, what did you have in mind?"

"Well, while I take a bath, shave in all the right places, perfume up and slip into that sheer nightgown for you, I want you to run what we call the gauntlet, a series of passages against my guards, if you get out alive, well then you shall have me, anyway you like, if not, well I get your head, your body and those privates for me to consume at my leisure."

"I don't know It seems a high price to pay for my life, for me to take down all of your guards."

"No I didn't say that, I have over two hundred here, and No only twenty will be allowed down, oh and one more thing, take off your holster, I really don't want anyone to get killed, fair enough?"

"Sounds fair, but I want one more thing."

"Name it" as she seemed excited by what was going to happen soon.

"A parade of the remaining girls to be available to me tonight, say at least ten?"

"What I'm not enough for you?"

"You are, but I like to sample the best myself, Mike had his chance, I won't allow an opportunity like this to pass me by." "Consider it done, now the holster, don't worry no one can touch your gun, so what do you have to lose?"

Jack pulled off his jacket, and pulled off his holster, and set it down, on the table, then instantly it disappeared into the floor and was gone."

"Now Jack we are even, through that door is where you start, it will be open till the next door you see says finish, open that door, you'll see me on the bed, waiting breathless for you, now go", she watched as Jack opened the door, and went down the stairs, as the door slammed shut."

CH 3

Intimate moment with Enzo....

The Coroner's office at Metro DC, was over ran with bodies, but two of its own, sat in a private room, whereas guest of the two fallen detectives lie in wait, battered beaten and mutilated, there evidence was hardly seen as the coroner, reconstructed their physical body for all those to see, both had been embalmed, and a autopsy performed, as they just received word that misses Bonn was coming down to identify her husband. In the hallway the Captain, consoled the young wife, of the decorated detective, by saying, "He was a good man."

"I know he was a good man, I have been preparing for this day ever since I agreed to be his wife."

"Allow me to take you down."

She shook her head, as another detective held onto her children. She was a strong woman, as she kept her head up, as they made it to the coroner's office. The Captain, held the door open for her, as she went in, first to see Johnny, to give the sign she was a Catholic, to say, "What have you two been doing to get yourself like this, as she allowed a tear to go for him, and then went over to her beloved man, who looked pretty, and almost as if he was asleep, she touched him, to feel how cold he was, she saw that his eyes were taped shut, scars that were familiar to her, and even lifting off the towel, to see his junk, only to notice something was missing, his lively hood, for her rage, to well up inside of her, she let out a scream, "What happen to my Enzo?"

Instantly the Captain and the Coroner rushed the room, to come to her aid. The coroner held her arm up to stammer, and say, "I'm sorry I have them over here."

"What are you doing castrating my husband, isn't it enough he is already dead?"

The Captain was trying to restrain her, as the Coroner said, "They came in this bag."

"Who does this?" "Its not who, its . . . ."

The Captain took the lead, to say, "Calm down, Kristy, we know the who, but not the why."

She pulled away from him, to say, "And why are my husband's eyes taped shut?"

"He was severely beaten, battered and mutilated." "There is more, what else?"

"All of his fingers and toes."

"You got to be kidding me, who would have done this?" "Really only one man, his name is King Huffa."

"So why aren't we getting him?"

"That's just it, He has Diplomatic Immunity", said the Captain.

"So go get a warrant, I want retribution and avenge the death of my husband, you got that Captain?"

"It's not that easy, we think he fled the country." "So send someone after him."

"That's out of our jurisdiction." "Then who can I call?"

"The CIA or someone, as he hands her a card, of a special agent, Samantha Kohl, CIA, to say, "I think she is second in command, I imagine she could help you, but other than that good luck." The Captain stayed while Kristy cooled down, said her final goodbyes, wept some, and went out to say, "I need some air."

She went out into the back, to a courtyard, and placed a call, she reached someone, who said, "This is Miss Kohl, how may I help you?"

"I want to know who I can get to help Me?" "What is the nature of your call?"

"My husband was just murdered by a guy named King Huffa, can you help me?"

"Sorry for your loss, did it happen here in the US?"

"Yes, in New York City."

"Then it's the jurisdiction of the FBI, if you can wait I'll give you their number."

"Wait, but he fled the country."

"How do you know that?" asked a curious Samantha.

"The investigators said that his ship was gone."

"So your saying, the man escaped via a ship and is now steaming somewhere, that is the case for either the Coast Guard or Homeland security, do you have any proof when all this occurred."

"Yes, have you not heard of the massacre on pier 7, that happen last night?"

"I have in fact, heard of that, so your husband was one of the victims?"

"Yes."

"'Well let me have someone else call you back, is this the number to reach you at?"

"Yes, I'll be waiting." As Kristy pulled out a cigarette, and lit it up, and took a big drag, only to hear, "You're not allowed to smoke in here" said a police woman.

She took it out and stamped on it, and went off to hear, "Now your littering."

"Hush up, her husband was Enzo, the guy that got it last night."

"Oh I didn't know."

Kristy went back in, to see the Captain, who led her to his locker, as she entered the squad room, to see all the other detective, they cleared a space, to allow her to pass, she entered the restroom, and to his locker, whereas, the lock, was cut off by another detective, and he opened it up for her, inside was a gym, bag, she began to throw his dirty clothes in it, only to hear, "He used that for a stakeout.", she nodded in agreement, also there was a bat, and under the clothes was a box, she sat down, as she opened the box, and inside was cash, loose bills, some needles, and some polaroids, of naked girls, and then one who was repeating, over and over again, a tall beautiful nude woman in fishnet stockings, who wrote on the back, “To my dear Enzo, I will always love you.” She saw the date was just before the time they got together, and she calmed, and at the bottom of the stack, was a book, small in size, with numbers, like a bookie, number, that she turned to. It showed the last number of being yesterday, and of the balance, over a millon dollars. She sat back down, to began to cry, to say,

“Enzo what have you been up to?”

She dialed up the number, as it rang, and rang and finally it was received, to hear, “Barney’s pizza.”

She hung up, and took out a pen and wrote it down, and continued to search further, only to hear, “The captain would like a word with you” as she gathered the rest of his belongings and set it in the gym bag, and went out so several who were waiting, went in.

Kristy entered the Captain’s office, who waved her in, as he hung up the phone, to say, “I got some good news for you”, as she took a seat, for him to say, “There sending over a lead investigator, her name is Lisa Curtis, she said, for you to either go home, or stay, till she gets here.”

“I’d prefer to go home and make arrangement for Enzo.” “Suit yourself, I’ll call you when we hear anything.”

Some time had past’d, and a black Suburban pulled up, and Ramon and Lisa got out, and was led into the Coroner’s office, for her to say, “Who’s in charge here?” said Lisa in her command voice.

“I am, I’m the coroner, Elizabeth Jennings, and you are?” “Lisa Curtis, CIG”, she shows her, Lisa’s credentials.

The coroner gets up and leads Miss Curtis, into the staging room, only to see a picturesque woman, who turned to see Lisa, who said, “Sorry Miss, do you need another moment?”

“No, I think I’ve said my goodbye”, said Daphne.

“Who are you” asked Lisa.

“A friend of Enzo’s.”

“Sure you are” said Lisa, to add, “Do you have a name?” “Whose asking?”

“Name is Lisa Curtis, I’m with the Central Intelligence Group, and you are?”

"My name is Daphne, Nicoletti, and I was . . ."

"Yes I know a good friend, so when was the last time you saw Enzo?"

"Two days ago, he usually comes over on Wednesday nights."

"So how did you hear of his passing?"

"Oh someone from the precinct called me."

"Ramon, get her number and her address, so Elizabeth tell me what we have here?"

"From what I uncovered, she spoke in a lower voice, as Daphne was led out, to continue, "Both men, were tortured, beaten and mutilated, for cosmetic reasons, I reattached the toes and fingers, but forgot to do the testicles, which appeared to be sliced up, like if they were going to fed them to someone."

"I get the point, and other than Miss Nicoletti, and who were some of the other visitors?"

"His wife was here earlier, and now she must be gone, but you can check with the Captain, upstairs."

"I'll do that thanks" said Lisa, motioning for Ramon to come to her. As she went back to look over the body of Enzo, she said, "Ramon, if this guy had a goatee and a mustache who would he resembled?"

"Your guy, Jack Cash."

"Your right, same height and size, well except down there, interesting."

Meanwhile Kristy, hopped in a cab, with children in hand, and went to her parents house, whereas she dropped off Frankie, and Clarance, and on to the west side near the precinct, to see Barney's pizza, and told the cab to wait for her, as she went in, to an empty joint, she had Enzo's book in hand, and saw the name Keith inside the book, moments later, she saw a guy come out, as he said, "Hi Miss what can I do for you?"

"I'd like to see Keith?"

He looks at her, then carefully says, "He is not here?" "Where is he at?"

The guy looks around till another older guy comes out from behind, to relieve the younger one, for him to say, "Barney, this young lady is looking for Keith."

Barney begins to wash a mug, to say, "So go get him, don't keep this lady awaiting, then for her to hear, "Care for a mug of beer?" She looks him up and down, to say, "Sure, why not."

Moments later, she was slurping down, some ice cold beer, and sat at the bar, when a huge guy came out, and spoke softly, saying, "How may I help you, Miss?"

"I'm here to collect Enzo's earnings."

Instantly, he said, "Hush, and grabs her arm and pulls her back through the door, and opens a door to the right, and pushes her, with beer in hand down the stairs, till she comes across a huge gaming operation, in the basement, to a counter, and a chalk board, detailing all the day's games, as Keith goes behind the counter, to say, "So you are probably the wife?"

"Why do you say it like that?" "It's your first time here, right?" "Yeah, but, what . . . ."

"Precisely, most players bring their girl friends to the action, as you can see, we have everything down here, so what's your pleasure?"

"I want to cash out?"

"Why do you want to do that, Enzo is one of our top earners."

"He has past" she said quietly.

"What was that, I didn't catch what you said."

She looked at him and said, "He is dead, do you hear me now?" "Yes, keep your voice down, as he kept eying her, as he pulled out a ten key to say, "All in all he has a dividend of 200k." "No, it says here he has over a million two, your cheating me out of a million dollars."

"Whoa, calm, down, how did you come up with that figure?" said Keith.

She holds up the book, to say, "I have it all here." Scrambling, Keith says, "Enzo bet big last night, and lost." She shot back, at him, "On what game?"

"Geo Wash versus Howard."

"What crap is that, he would never do that?" "It was a sure thing."

"Nothing is a sure thing, if I know my man, he wouldn't bet on Geo Wash, regardless of who they played."

Then everyone in the back was coming forward, as one of them said, "Do we have a problem here?" said the guy to Kristy.

"This man has my husband's money and won't pay up." "Is this true Keith, who is your husband?" asked the older more sophisticated, looking rich guy.

"His name was Enzo Bonn."

Silence was everywhere now as the older guy said, "That is really low of you Keith, Enzo has been a friend to you and all of us, and what happen to him is a shame, but Miss you're not getting his earnings." They all laughed, as Kristy went to the door, only to be held back, by another, as the older rich guy, steps out of the shadows, for her to see him, he had a patch over his left eye, to say, "Let this be a lesson to you, don't ever come back and expect to live, just because your Enzo wife, doesn't give you privilege, we will give that to our friend and his true love, your money will be with Daphne Nicoletti, of the Nicoletti family." They let her go, as she got out of there. Only to hear one of them say, "Yes that was too bad for Enzo and Johnny, now we can gamble away all of their money."

Confused and frustrated Kristy, saw she had in incoming call, she ignored it, it just kept on ringing, till finally she answered it, to say "What do you want?"

"Hi my name is Lisa Curtis, and I'm investigating the death of your husband, do you have a moment?"

"Yes, I'm in a cab."

"Great, why don't you come back to the morgue, and we can talk."

"Be there in a moment."

Lisa was all over the body, as she told the coroner, to keep the body a secret for now, as she waited until then Kristy arrived. Lisa said, "Hi, I'm Lisa Curtis, we spoke on the phone, so you're the wife?"

"Yeah, the one who know nothing." "What's wrong everything alright?"

"No, it isn't my husband is dead, and some guy has all of our money", she broke down and began to cry. Ramon comforted her, as he led her to a chair. While Lisa stood in front of her, to say, "I'm deeply sorry for your loss, and from the looks of it your husband went through some trauma, what would you like me to do?"

"Get retribution for all of this?"

"Who, and by what means?" asked Lisa, looking at her.

"I don't know send in some agent?", or something like that."

"What we have here are a number of things, we have criminal, we have civil and we have jurisdictions, to contend with." "They said he fled the country?"

"Now we have that country and the UN to contend with, so where do you think I should start?"

"Go after the guy?"

"Which guy, the one who did this to your husband, or this Mister King, or his Attorney?, which shall it be?" asked Lisa.

"All of them I don't care, I just want to know I have revenge on those that killed my husband."

"From the looks of it I'd say he was a dirty cop, and I say that in the most respective way, I have so far uncovered more of what he was supposed of done, to what he really did, and then there are the ties to the Nicoletti family, not to mention his mistress, the one being that of Daphne, the daughter of Daniel Nicoletti, so my question to you is why did he marry you, two years ago, and not Daphne, my guess is that he wanted out, and they wouldn't allow it, so I ask you again Miss Bonn, what do you want me to do?"

"Find the man who had his hand in killing my husband?" "Fine, it will cost you a million dollars" Lisa said calmly. "What, where and what, you're our federal agency and why would it cost me a million, I don't have that?"

"Are you sure, according to your families financials, it says your Dad is worth 2.7 million, go ask him for it."

"Wait, how do you know that?"

"That's what we do, we know" said Lisa. Gathering up the papers, and stuff, for Kristy to rise and say, "Alright, I will ask him, what assurances do I have you will find the one who is responsible?"

"What are you asking us, you want some sort of proof, like . . ."

"Like what he did to my husband, I want it videotaped and all digits and toes, in my hand with his ball sack. Said Kristy with a sinister look on her face.

CH 4

In the Gauntlet

Back at the fortress, Jack was anticipating his next move, when instantly, the rooms walls went up, and big screened television sets showed his every move, as Tatiana and her father both stepped in, for Scopus to say, "Who is this man, is he the real Jack Cash, kill him."

"But him and I have a deal" Miss Monica pleaded with him.

"You and your games is gonna get someone of us killed, he is defenseless, so arm your guards and kill him now, don't let me pull in my death squads to do you and him in", then turns to his daughter to say, "If this man does survive, make sure you marry him, as planned, then you kill him."

Mister Tyrell was leaving the room, when a desperate Miss Monica said "If you do this then were over and I will tell him all about you, then not only will you have him but every American breathing down your neck."

He stopped in his tracks to look at her, to say "You wouldn't, remember I have your son Jacob, if you think you will do that then I will kill him and literally eat him, flesh and bones, then I will go after your daughter and your secret ex-husband, tomorrow I will have my son and his henchman come visit you, to watch over you, if this Jack Cash is still alive, I'll have my son do the job, as for us, your treading on thin ice", then he was gone, as the two girls stood by each other, for Miss Monica to say, "I screwed this all up." "You,

I have to marry the most wonderful guy I have ever met, and kill him myself."

"You have it easier, at least he has no one holding it over your head."

"Yeah, but that's all I am to him a pawn, to get him further along, to use me and abuse me as he see fit, especially since he was my first."

"Oh my dear girl come here, let's hope Jack survives, we may have to work together to take that mean man down ourselves."

"Well in my father's defense, I would still love him more than any other man, so I still will follow out his orders."

"Then you are brained washed, my young friend." "Yes, I know, I am."

Jack was on the move, down into a room similar to the one he left, along the walls were frames for doors, some had reflective mirrors, others led to passages, he knew he was underground and that she was watching him, as camera's were all over the place, he knew this was decision time, as the game was on hold till he decided to go one way or the other, just as he walked by a door frame he sensed something wrong, and moved to his left to miss the swing of a large club, he turned to drive his foot into the guy's knee, to hear a pop, sending him down in agony. Jack picked up the club and then tee'd off on that guy's head, realizing that the bat was too heavy to carry around he discarded it, as he decided to take the south way, he quickly, felt the floor shift, and down he went, through a trap door. Down a slick chute, he was actually going faster, from the pitch, that he used his feet as brakes, to slow him down, as well as his hands by trying to grasp hold of the roof of the clay tunnel, he slowed to a stop, as the end opened up to the cavern below the fortress.

Jack stood with his feet lodge in the sides as he steadied himself, he looked below, at a giant pit of something moving and bubbling, he swung his leg over, onto the edge, and onto the clay cliff, looking over he saw a chunk of concrete left over from the construction of this ride, so he worked it out, lifted it up and heaved into the goop, it sat on top, then it was sucked in for Jack to say, "Quick sand, now that would have been some trouble, he looked down to see he his watch, especially remembering when the guy visited him to deliver that new watch that can shoot fifty feet, and stick into any surface, so he spun the top and aimed, and off it went, it wrapped around a pillar, and it began to pull Jack out off the edge, as he swung over to a wall, he scrambled on to it. Jack turned his attention to what was at hand, as he unhooked the line and retracted back in, he was on the move, similar chutes were all over down there, over twenty such, and then there were these massive pillars evidently holding the fortress up, I guess some would call them Caissons, but they go down into the quicksand and up to the ceiling, if only I had some C-4, he stopped to really think about this, what would I need, well its dark down here, night vision goggles would be nice, a flexi rope, a riggers harness, crampons, and a flare gun, well I'm sure there is something else, wait how about something if I were to fall into quicksand, like a breathing device, or something like that, he looks up to see another huge pillar, and a rung ladder, on one of its side, somewhat concealed, in the shadows of the huge H frame, he quickly climbs up it nearing the top, he listens for voices, he pops up the floor door, and looks in to see the room empty, he climbs up into the room, then goes to the closed door to hear in some Spanish language that get all the men were gonna kill us an American."

The game is definitely changed, Jack pulls two credit cards from his wallet, pops off the corners and slowly opens the door, it creaked open to several gun shots towards Jack's direction, he waited, to see if they were going to follow up, nothing, so Jack was on the move, at ever shadow he stopped, he held both cards as he would a knife in different hands, thinking "Jugular, and Femoral, high and low."

He was at the ready, as victim on victim, met the slash of the card, and the card won, as it only took two dying bodies to convince the guards they needed heavy firepower, so a big gun appeared, rattling, was spewing heavy rounds in that little space, Jack froze, against the painted steel, then he knows what it was in the pillar, after the rattling gun winded down and out of ammunition, a new path, was available to him, as he dove through the bullet ridden wall, a guy appears to say, "What the hell", pulls out a gun and takes a shot at Jack, who dives, and rolls to evade the man's attack, Jack quickly gets to the overweight out of shape guy, to deliver a kick to the knee, sending him down, to lose control of the gun, Jack picks up what appears to be a 45 cal Russian made gun to say, "Who are you and why are you trying to kill me, I thought this was all a game of fun, it is until someone gets hurt?" said Jack.

Meanwhile inside the control room, Miss Monica, and all fifty girls were watching, alongside was Tatiana, smiling as she saw Jack begin to fight back, improvising and gaining control, for her to say "Looks like your losing, Miss Monica, how many men do you think has ever survived the chute to be here today?"

"None, that isn't surprising, he is who he says he is, a super spy, that was to be expected."

The girls all cheered on as Jack crashed through another wall, to add, "At this rate he should be at the finish line in oh I'd say ten minutes or less."

"That doesn't matter, to me the game is over, he lost, he cheated, and he is killing all of my best guards, I should have listened to Scopus, I'm gonna send everyone, he is starting to piss me off."

"Really that's what you wanted to play a game, with people's lives, little did you know he is slick as a panther, and more deadlier that a cobra, you don't know what you got yourself into, he will be disappointed to see that you're not there, he will come looking for you" said Tatiana with concern.

"Why such the concern, it's almost like you have feeling for that expendable guy, guys like that are a dime a dozen, he'll just use you, abuse you and then when he is done discard you", said Miss Monica.

"So is that your decision, you're staying here, well then I will go down and meet him with his gun", said a confident Tatiana.

"No you're not, get her Allegra, and take her to the hole, let's get mister boyfriend some bait, Scopus was right, we do need to kill him."

"You're going to regret that decision" said Tatiana, as she was being taken away.

"Regret it, I already forgot about it, let's watch girls and see how our guards take down this suppose super spy, you'll be seeing him soon enough" said the vicious Miss Monica, then she clicked on the intercom speaker, to say "Listen up, we have an intruder who has just raped one of our girls, he is armed and extremely dangerous, kill him on sight, his girlfriend is in the holding cells, wait till he gets there and kill them both."

Jack looked up at the camera, with a snarl on his face, he cut the feed line to the camera, his sense of direction was good, he pulled out his phone, to pull up where he was at, which way he went and where he was now, and the phone put a little map together, and yes he had been going in circles, he clicked on his phones tracker, a bleep close by came on, the bleep looked close by, he searched the wall, to find any triggers, a eye, anything as he remembered reading a pamphlet on mazes, the trigger was at least five feet away, either across, above or below, using his phone, he turned on a metal detector, the walls might be stone, or wood, he was looking for a bar or chain, to locate a spring, in the floor, just like a land mine, you hold down for three hundred count, and walla law. the door slid open, he went in to the room of Immense treasures, gold's and silvers, it was a treasure trove, old swords, boxes upon boxes, of ancient artifacts and probably from shipwrecks or Pirates, there was blood, on some pieces, he picked up one or two with blood on them, as he stepped further the door slammed shut, in the middle looking up Jack saw a reverse table hanging down, then followed down to the pile, where his jacket and holster were, Jack tossed the Russian gun, as he felt the energy as he strapped his holster on, next slid on his windbreaker, he put all his blades away, to admire the treasures trove, he pulled out his phone, and began to take pictures in a complete 180, then noticed some steps thinking it must be going up, to the room above, as soon as he reached the door, he opened it, then it closed shut, then a familiar voice spoke to him.

"The game is over, your surrounded, as I am speaking, a odorless gas is being released, you have thirty seconds before all the oxygen is forced out of that room, good luck."

Jack was already moving, he placed the jacket over his head, he then tore the bottom of his jacket, to reveal a rope of C-4, he used his camera to pin point the door's action, he located a pin on top and one on the bottom, he placed a piece in both locations and inserted a blasting cap each, turned away, set the frequency and it blew, and the door came crashing down, Jack was on the move, he could hear, "You need to reverse that he is coming." "You want to do it" said Miss Monica.

Jack was at the edge of the room, to say, "Girls, all over here stand against that wall, hug it, you the ugly one."

"Names Allegra."

"What are you doing, let me see your hands."

"I'm shutting off the gas, and turning on the exhaust fans, look my hands" she showed them to him, Jack had his weapon out, the pearl handed specially gun was seen and evident to all, who he was, for Allegra to say, "What are you going to do with us?"

"Your going into government custody." "On what charges?"

"Charges, I don't need any reason, I'm a international Bounty Hunter, empowered to capture, detain, hold ransom and kill if I so chose, by the order of the World Council, of International Corruption, so I say for you to place your hands behind your back."

She did as she was told, as he zip tied her up at the wrists, for her to say, "What are you going to do with me?"

"First I'd like you to tell me where Tatiana is?" "Why do you know who she really is?"

"Yeah, she's a spy" said Jack.

"No you got that all wrong, her father is . . . ."

Smack came a punch from a stunning brunette, to say, "A girl can only take enough of her shit."

"What's your name?"

"Isabella, and I can tell you I'm with spy club, so I'm here for anything you like?"

"Good, thanks, can you find or know where Tatiana is?" "Yes she was taken down into the hole."

"Do you know where that is?" asked Jack.

"Yes, but can you spare any weapons?"

"Sorry you can't have this one, it will kill you" said Jack.

"Fine what about where you came from?" "Yes I threw out a Russian 45"

"I'll go down and get that one" he watched her leave to say

"Alright girls get your stuff you have five minutes before were out of here" the girls scattered, some crying some laughing, others just bolted, Jack pulled out his phone and dialed up Jim, to ask "Where he was at and if he could come to his location, giving him the coordinates, and to ask him what is his ETA, then he stepped into the hallway as girls past him, out of the corner of his eye, he watched the monitor, as Isabella, was visible, as the guards let her pass, thinking if it were I we would be in a shooting match now, there on the move, as the girls started to assemble, in the lobby. Around him, he motioned for them, to exit out the front, as Jack held onto Allegra, as the rest of the girls exited out. He turned to see Isabella and Tatiana together coming up to him, Tatiana was smaller, Isabella said, "The guards were fooled hook line and sinker."

"Good let's hope for a long period of time" said Jack still holding onto Allegra.

Most of all the girls made it to the landing, he said, "Alright girls I need you to hid in those bushes till you see a plane land in this front field, realizing he needed to get back to his car, Jack thought it would be nice to command the car to come to me", he waited nothing no response, so he said, "Listen you girls stay here with these girls, I'm going around the building."

"So am I" said Tatiana, right behind Jack followed by Isabella, behind her.

Isabella shot first and missed a guard coming at them, gun drawn, as Jack put him down, one shot one kill, he said, "Why are you following me, it is too dangerous."

He moved quickly, this time he fanned out, to motion for them to go along the building side, and go into the parking garage, as Jack stood in the middle of a field, he would fire back at on coming guards and drop them, then from behind him, he felt something whiz his leg he turned around to see a fan of women all dressed in tank tops and shorts, he felt powerless, until they pulled up their guns, then a thud was heard, in replace of silence, the screams of agony as a long range shooter was taking them out, Jack retreats quickly to the forest line to see them all get waxed, while they peppered his position, he hid behind a tree, till the shooting was over, a calmness was there as

Jack moved, past the fallen beautiful girls, thinking what a shame, so beautiful yet so corrupt. The plane that Jack requested flew over head, its camouflage markings indicated its his plane, Jack made it to the garage, and out of visible danger, he pulls his phone out, and goes to his car, it says press to enable, so he did, and saw all sorts of data streaming down his monitor screen, he thought this can take forever, so he put the phone away to see, Isabella and Tatiana, behind a car, shooting it out with the guards that surround the car, for Jack to say, "Aim for the car, it will ricochet off of it and help us some."

In between shots and Isabella said she was out, and tossed her weapon to say, "What now?"

"Keep your heads down, I'll go get my car, said Jack in a full run, as it caught them off guard, open passenger side door, "Sara."

The car door opened and Jack dove in, as the door closed itself, Jack spun around, as the guards were hitting the car as Jack said "Employ protective measures."

A thick gas was emitted from the car, deadly to the smell, for Jack to say, "Start Sara, back up, now forward, stop, open the door, to let the two girls in, and the door closed as Jack took the wheel and powered the car out of the garage, only to see Miss Monica, standing at the curb, shaking her head, as Jack took off, he crossed over, the grass to the plane, where the ramp was down, and the girls were being helped in, by a tall lanky girl, Jack stopped the car, got out to see Mike, and Jim, to say, "Can you help me out here."

"Yes I can see that, your hands are full", as he takes the two girls off his hands then turns to say, "Was there something else?"

"Yeah I was just wondering, if you can coordinate my phone with the car?"

"Let's see it" and receives it from Jack, to say, "Yep, there it is, oh no, well, no, sorry, oh wait."

"Come on Jim for our techno guy to be stumped, I can't believe your having trouble."

"I'm not, I'm the one who sits around developing these gadgets for you to enjoy, Oh no it looks like you already did it" as Jim hands it back to Jack, and smiles.

"What is the range", asked Jack.

"Oh I'd say 5 miles or so, actually I really don't know, I guess that's between you and the car" said Jim.

"How can I find out?"

"It should all be on the phone?"

Jack looked down as Jim, Mike helped load the rest of the fragile girls, for Jim to say, "Where to?"

"Where ever you take yourself and can turn them over to the right authorities, and the one zip tied up." Jim just looked around for Jack to finish.

"Or to a good interrogation room" said Jack.

"Will do boss, be back tomorrow, any other orders?"

"Yes matter of fact, as Jack moved around to the trunk, to say "Open", it did to say, "Where is any gear, weapons there is nothing here?"

"Well actually, when we got the call, the back was in the middle of an inventory, and what kind of stuff do you want?"

"A backpack, one with a breathing apparatus, night vision goggles, smaller version, a clingy rope, a riggers harness, a first aid kit, how about a cooler, with stocked drinks?"

"Anything else", Jim said sarcastically.

"No, oh how about a belt full of C-4 and bag of blasting caps."

"Sorry I asked, listen Jack, were still kind of in the experimental stages of development, and yes we have all of that under advisement, but it takes time to make it spy ready, so in the meantime, make do with what I give you, oh Jack this is Simone, she too was in deep cover."

"Thanks for your help, can you escort them back and help out those girls" said Jack.

"What about afterwards, can I come back?"

"Sure, although it's not up to me to decide that, good luck." Mike makes his appearance in front of his boss, to say, "I failed you miserably."

"No you didn't you soften her up for me, you did as you were asked to do, no harm no foul, which one gave you that black eye and swollen mouth?"

"It was me" said Isabella, stepping down the ramp. Mike actually looked frighten by her presence, for Jack to say "Enough, go wait in the car or do you want to go with them?"

"No I'd rather stay here and help you" said Isabella, as Tatiana, joined her.

"Well I guess, I learned my lesson" said Mike to Jack.

"Which is?"

"That there can only be one spy, that has a reputation no other person can fill, I know my role now, and will stay within those perimeters, I do have a lot of respect for you, and will prove to erase this mistake from your memory."

The two shook hands, and as Jack said, "Alright go home, with Jim, get as much of the stuff I need, and bring it all back, and make sure those girls get home safely."

"Will do boss", said Mike.

Jack watched as the ramp was raised and the plane took off, he turned to put a arm around each girl to say, "Who's up for the afternoon on the beach?"

"Me, Me" they both said it together.

"You know that there is a great spa at Arus, on the other side of the island" said Tatiana.

"I did not know that, I'll punch in those co-ordinance and we'll be off, get in girls" said Jack as he slapped them on the butt, as they both went to the passenger side, as Jack slid in the car, the doors shut, Tatiana sat in the passenger seat as Isabella, was getting in the small back seat, usually empty, he looked back as he was having his hands between her legs to hear her say, "Hold on we will do plenty of that after we get out of here."

"Oh sorry, is there a bag back there?"

"No, if there were I don't think I would have fit" said Isabella.

"Brian", he was the one who saved me", thought Jack, then said drive on Sara, as he got back on the road to see the assembling of guards, he tapped the steering wheel, to see a electronic lights come up, he saw the alphabet, remembering that it use to go up to K, was now Z, as he drove right through the gate as it was raised up, the guy saluted him, Jack hit the horn, to give the sound of thundering horses.

The car picked up speed, as they left Ensenada and cruise the coastline, he was going pretty fast, then decide to drive, and took control of the wheel, his leg hurt a bit, so he said "Sara dial up Mitzi", moments later she answered, for Jack to say, "Meet me at Arus resort and spa, have several room available."

"Five minutes away, ?"

"She seemed nice who was that your girlfriend" asked Isabella.

"Nah, just like you, once part of spy club, now a dedicated team member."

"So what your saying is that, if you want you can elevate anyone to your team?"

"Sure I guess I could, I haven't thought about it, why are you interested?"

"Absolutely, when can you make that happen?" asked Isabella, as Tatiana watched but said nothing.

"All you need to do is talk with Mitzi at the hotel, she is the coordinator for the spy club."

"Really and that's it?"

"Well not really, I guess I'd have to like you myself, and I do, I think if you can knock out Mike then your alright with me." "He was too easy, he was a lamb among wolves" said Isabella, taking her hand and fingers and running through Jack's short hair.

"How so, what do you mean" asked Jack.

"Well simply put, his eyes gave it all away, like for instance, he was surrounded by all those beautiful women, he spun his wedding band oh half a dozen times, any girl there would have given herself to him, and he chose Allegra, a safe choice, did you see how ugly that one was, well then I knew something was up, so I volunteered myself, he acted like a little boy with me, so I knew, he needed to be corralled, so I threw him on the bed, and unbuttoned his shirt, I took my top and bra off, and looked down to see the name Mike on his belt buckle, come on."

"So just because he wore a name of someone else you punched him?"

"No its much more, it's all about tests, since I've been with spy club, I've screwed my share of wealthy, well commanded men, and realized it's all in the eyes, you know if any time he had a backbone, and told me what to do, I would have done it."

"That's good to know." Said Jack. To add, "And for me, will we have the same war?"

"Hold on, wait a minute, it's totally different for you, there is no book, you have a reputation, and I know you, you're in, there isn't anything you have to do, to either prove something to me or not, you're in, you have those eyes, their wild, I can't read you, and that's what makes me frighten of you, so you have me, anyway you like, let alone all those girls you herded up and saved their lives, oh no, you're the one, and those bad men better watch out, because trouble come with it."

"Interesting, how you can spot if their a spy or not, I think I could use that type of talent?"

"Well whatever you want me to do, you can count on my loyalty."

The car fought Jack almost the whole way in wanting to drive, they came upon the luxurious hotel, overlooking the ocean, all white, as the car came to a stop, and the girls got out, Jack spoke, "Valet mode" then to the guy, he said "Just need to park it."

Jack was greeted at the door, by Mitzi and Trixie, the two girls followed, as Mitzi said "I have you the ambassadors suite, as for the girls I have a room, here, Trixie will get your sizes."

Mitzi helped Jack as he leaned on her, he was tired from the earlier workout, she opened the room up, he went with her, to look around eventually to the bathroom where Mitzi asked, "Would you like me to run a bath for you?"

Jack unbuttoned his pants, they were blood soaked, for her to say "Oh my god, you have been nicked."

"It happens from time to time" said Jack.

She knelt down, with a towel, and dried it up to say, "You're so lucky, it was just a scratch, you'll be fine, she used a washcloth to clean out the residue, she had blood all over her white blouse, she took it off, to call Trixie, who answered, "Yes, clothes right away and a med bag."

"It's been a while, I'll be there soon, the girls are restless and want to see Jack" said Trixie.

"Just tell them that he is resting and when he is ready he will summons them."

She looked up at him, with a smile, finishing cleaning the residue with a warm wash cloth.

She said, "What do you like about me, am I doing my job well?"

He looks down at her, to say, "Your simply the best." "I was the best candidate for the job."

"No, it's because I can trust you."

"Really that's so nice, if you want I can take off my bra, it isn't like you haven't seen them or touched them, really I don't mind" said an eager Mitzi.

"It's up to you, said Jack as he eased into the bath, as he sat on the ledge, he turned down the water, when a knock on the door, he pulled off his holster, and windbreaker, and black t-shirt. The bath filled up quickly, he slid into the tub, as he had his eyes closed.

Mitzi turned off the water, she went to the door, to see Trixie, she took clothes and the med bag, to say, "Keep the girls busy, give us a couple of hours."

Mitzi, threw the clothes on the sofa, with the med bag in hand, she dropped it at step, as she slipped out of her bra, her big breasts, were flopping, as she sat on the edge of the tub, she broke out the soap, and began to wash Jack's privates first, she wanted to make sure they were hard and ready, for her as she unbuttoned her pants, and pulled them down, as Jack watched, she turned around bent over, then pulled her panties down, Jack reached up to feel between her legs, it was wet, she turned and smiled, as she lowered her nude body onto his, and guided him in, she did all the work, as she pulled off of him before he let loose, she cleaned him up, and then herself, got dressed, put on a new blouse, as the very nude Jack stood at the doorway, Mitzi had some swimming trunks laid out, to say, "There is a pool, right out on the balcony, so enjoy."

"Wait, I need to ask of something, what's the hurry?" She sat on the bed, while watching him get his swim trunks on, thinking, "That's a kind of man I need, a chiseled body and great looks".

"How can I add another to our team?" asked Jack.

"Just ask them, are they in the spy club?" "Yes, I don't know, what if there not?"

"It doesn't matter now?" "Why's that?"

"Because you're the boss, and our new overseer is Miss Meyers, so who do you have in mind?" "What about Jodie?"

"The girl you extracted from Cuba?" "Yeah, she is the one . . ."

"Funny that was what she said, that you inspired her, and that she would love to be one of us?"

"There you go, make it happen."

"Your wish is my command, I'll call Miss Meyers to allocate the grade and title."

"Whoa wait a minute" said Jack, "I'll I mean, is just for this one mission."

"Ah I got you now, you mean only for this job?" "Yeah, what did you think I meant?"

"Oh nothing, in that case, you can have as many as you like?"

"Alright I want Isabella too." "No problem."

"Fine make it happen, I need a rest, thanks for being who you are."

"Anytime that's what I'm here for, serving my master, in many ways than one" said a very smiling Mitzi.

She closed the door so he could rest, she continued down the hallway to the two girls room, she knocked, the door opened to see the two thick-haired brunettes, Mitzi made her way in to say

"Alright you too, let's get something straight here, you being his new partner, there is some ground rules, you need to be on your best behavior with him, unless he invites you in, consider you sleep here, next your job is to collect intelligence, report back to me through Jack and lastly don't crowd his space, now for you Miss Isabella, Jack tells me you want to be part of the team, is that true?"

"Yes Ma'am, it's exciting to be part of a famous Spies life."

"What special talents do you possess, for our team?" "What do you mean, like sex or what?"

"No silly, every girl can provide that to any boy, No, what I'm talking about, is like me, I handle everything like ground preparations and logistics for Jack, and the other girl Trixie handles all and everything in the air."

"Oh I see, how about the ocean, do you cover that, cause I am a certified diver, former super model."

"Now that's what I'm talking about, a certified diver, yes I think that would qualify you to join the team, coordinate with me, but tomorrow, go down to the harbor, and rent a boat, arrange scuba gear for him and the two others."

"Three of us will go out together" said Tatiana.

"Fine, the three of you will go out together, good day, girls, remember do not disturb Jack."

The two girls waved goodbye to her, as she left.

Isabella got up to say, "Are you gonna let her talk to us that way?" "I didn't know you're a certified scuba diver" said a surprised Tatiana.

"I'm not, but I had to think of something to say to her, like she knew everything, so a girl has to do what a girl has to do."

"You're so smart" said Tatiana.

"Yeah and I got a right hook to boot."

CH 5

A night at the casino

Jack got up from his rest, slipped on his flip flops, and a shirt, on went his holster, and reloaded his clip, he found his light grey windbreaker, then he found a large brimmed hat, he looked down at the butterfly bandage, he straighten up, he picked up a magazine, then picked up his card key, and went out, he strolled down to Isabella & Tatiana room knocked on the door, no answer, he went down, to the main reception area, to see the front desk clerk, the guy looked up to say, "Yes sir how may I help you?"

"Have you seen two stunning brunettes?" asked Jack.

"Well seeing that there are ten rooms and two suites and you are in one, the two brunettes are at the pool."

"Why didn't you say that in the first place?", Jack walks off shaking his head, towards the pool, he steps out onto the patio, to see two girls swimming in the pool, Jack finds a lounge chair, up under a huge umbrella, he takes a seat, reclines back, he relaxes and opens the magazine with pictures of travel what fun he thinks. He closes his eyes, that was until two girls begin to giggle and splash him with water, half wet, he leans up to get a face full of water. He looked at them through his sunglasses, see through or not, at this point it didn't matter, both girls wore little more than a wash cloth extra small, combined, every part of their bodies were exposed, it didn't help when they both came up to him and pulled him in the water, as Jack pulled both of their tops off, as the two of them clinged onto him, the three went on to frolic some more, that was until Mitzi showed up and the fun stopped, as she yelled at the top of her lungs, "Get out of the pool and put on your tops young ladies."

Jack followed the girls out, on a slow walk, Mitzi threw a towel on each girl, and handed one to Jack. To say, "You should be ashamed of yourself, playing around with these two young girls."

"It was really nothing, you sure have a way of ruining things" said Jack.

Jack went back to his room, defeated, he didn't know what was going on, she was acting weird, he slid the wet card key, in and the door opened, he took off his wet windbreaker, then his holster, he hung it up, he pulled out his cool gun, and set it in a box, that was set up for him while he was away, he pulled off his wet t-shirt, and went into the shower.

Mark was arranging gear, down by the rented house they had at the beach. He was thinking when was the last time he was doing Mike's job, as a car approached, parked, he looked out from the window slits in the garage, it was a gorgeous blonde, he bent down and lifted the door up to say, "Hi, may I help you?"

"Hey Hi, I was looking for Mark, is that you?" "Yes it is, who are you?" said Mark defensively.

"Don't fear for your life, I was sent by Brian, for Jack Cash, you know the one who rescued me in Cuba?"

"Yes I know, I was there, sorry I don't remember you." "That's alright, I'm just one of those blondes that get misplaced in the sea of all the women Jack attracts."

"That's for sure, can I help with . . ." he said as he looked her up and down, I mean can I get your bag?"

"Nah, what do I need to do?"

"Well let's get you in here first, let's hug or something" said Mark.

"Alright, I guess."

The two embraced warmly, as Mark whispered, "There may be people watching, and let's give it an appearance that your welcomed."

"I got you" the two broke the embrace for her to say, "That was nice."

"It was for me too, come on in," said Mark as he led her inside for her to say, "This is totally new for me."

"What do you mean?" asked Mark.

"Well the last job I was in deep cover with Carlos who is now his brothers-in law, so how will it work with Jack, do I visit him at night?"

"No, Jack is Jack, unlike any spy I have ever worked with either, I've learned, we give him space, if he needs something he calls, in the meantime, we are his eyes and ears on the outside, like a little later he is going to the Casino in Pounce, for dinner, and maybe some casino play, then there, we take on a secondary role of either observer, or in a support role, but never approach him, even if you see him, think of him like gold, you can stare at him, but you can't touch him."

"How do you know what he is going to do?"

"That's easy, we have two friends who help guide him in that direction, and also we have a tracker on him, here you will have one too, besides you're astute beauty what are your talents?"

"Oh you know, everything athletic, I was trained as a long range sniper, I'm a certified scuba diver, I've done some deep sea welding?"

"Enough I hear you, you have nothing to prove to me, let me show you to a room, you can use to sleep and in your down time."

"I didn't come here to sleep, I was asked to help out, what can I do, can I call Jack to let him know I'm here?"

"I'm sure he already knows, but come out in the garage, and help me out with the tanks."

"Are we setting the gas to oxygen levels."

Marks phone rings, it was Mitzi, it wasn't a business call, it was personal.

Mark says, "Hold on, wait a minute, calm down, wait," Mark leaves the garage, to stroll into the back yard to say, "What is it Mits?"

"I made a huge mistake", she said frantically.

"Calm down, it can't be that bad, explain it to me."

"It was with Jack, I was a little jealous of his two new playmates that I reprimanded him in the pool."

Mark was silent, to say, "That is serious."

"Come on you know how he acts like a kid from time to time."

"I don't care about that, that who he is, but my concern is that your jealous, of what, that's what he does, plays with young girls who want to be around him, it happens all the time, pull yourself together, it could be worse, he could have you and Trixie all tied up in his room, I'm not mentioning any men or anything, but you know where I come from, and to them to Jack is way totally different, Jack is just bizarre."

"Yeah your right, I over reacted, do you think I should apologize?"

"No, don't do that, it shows a sign of weakness, and let's leave it at that."

Behind him he heard a voice, say, "Is he asking about me?" "Hold on, a moment", he said to Mitzi, to turn to say, "No, I'll be back in a moment, Thanks."

"Who was that, do you have a girl with you?" "Yes I do, her name well I don't really know."

"Is she the blonde blue eyed, girl Jack sent for, her name is Jodie, Jack wants her to relive Brian at the outpost, and hold her position, give her a map of where he is at, and directions, and then a ear piece to communicate close in with us." "Will do."

Mark slid his phone closed, to see her, to say, "I liked our visit, but you have assignment."

"Yes what is it", she said eagerly.

Jack finished dressing, as Mother hen, Mitzi told him she had made reservations for him and his two playthings for dinner and then a night of gambling at the casino."

He thanked her even though it was awkward for her he went along just being Jack, he adjusted his tuxedo tie, and picked up his dry card key, and went out, in the hallway talking were Tatiana and Isabella, red was her favorite color, as she wore the stunning dress and jewelry well, Tatiana wore black, with heels to match the taller Isabella, Jack met them with a smile, he locked a arm around each of them, as they walked out in force, the valet had retrieved his Mercedes, it was running when he tipped the guy a twenty, Isabella got in back, as Tatiana commanded the front seat, Jack got in, and took control, and peeled out, of the semi circular drive, and down onto the road, traffic was light, that was till he came to the massive city, a hundred thousand people in a five square block city, where the Pounce casino and towering hotel broke the skyline, then it was bumper to bumper traffic, going easily five miles per hour, Tatiana, took that time, to place her hand on his sleeve in a show of affection, he looked over at her to see she was looking at him, he thought, "She is so fun, yet so young, but I'm in the moment so let's live it up."

Jack saw an opening, and went for it, from zero to seventy in a split second, and along the shoulder he went, to the exit, and off the gridlock, down to the extra long wide drive, the luxurious casino, is truly for only the rich and famous, cars like his million dollar car, are let in without stopping or restriction from the massive gate, and guard station, regardless of who was in that car, all was welcome, with that statement, and so does the tips, Jack parked it at the entrance to whisper, "Valet Mode."

And gets out, and gives the porter a large tip, who came up to assists both girls, as they exited the vehicle.

Jack stands to see the valet take the car away. Jack walked in with two girls on each arm., the entranced narrowed down to a huge metal detector, Jack allowed the girls to go through first as a line of bodyguards stood waiting, then Jack hesitated, then walked through, nothing happened, for him to hear, "Sir, please swipe your playing card, so that we may place a card to be assigned to you based on . . ."

Jack pulled out the card, that Erica gave to him to use, he swiped the card, the tally was well above the showing number that the count went way past one billion dollars, Jack looked at the guy who pulled out a gold card, to swipe it for Jack to say, "No, one for each girl, also."

"Yes sir", said the guy with a smile.

"Girls go have fun, mingle, tonight's on me", said Jack. Each girl smiled, then left him and went their separate ways.

One person was staring through the thick one way glass observing Jack, as Miss Monica made her presence, to say, "What are you looking at?"

"I don't know, maybe your accomplice, you're not in too much despair, seeing he is the one who took your whole operation down, who is he?"

"His name is Jack Cash, a international bounty hunter" said Miss Monica.

"What does that mean?"

"Well Ivan, unlike your father, you should be wary." Ivan looks down to see a familiar face, smiles to hear the door open and a out of breath, guy was at the door, saying, "Ivan, Ivan we got some trouble."

"Whoa wait a minute what's the problem?" "Your sister is here."

"Yes I can see that, as Miss Monica saw Tatiana, to look at Ivan her brother, to wait for a response, for Ivan to say, "So, we knew eventually she would come back."

"Yes, but this is hers, she must be playing a scheme with that guy."

"Well whomever he is let's get a couple of our guys over to him, and escort him to the holding room, let's see how this turns out" said Ivan watching with Miss Monica.

Jack looked around as he saw both girls at a blackjack table, he strolled to the bar, to say, "I'll have a rum and coke."

"Yes sir", said the bartender.

Jack noticed a sinister looking guy who spoke with two big guys, then disappear behind a door, then as Jack slides his wrist watch beside the drink, to confirm the contents are what they are, he drinks the drink down, places a twenty dollar bill down to say, "This is for you."

"Thank you, sir."

A big burly guy comes up to Jack to say, "Excuse me sir, my boss would like a word with you, could you come with me?"

"Have you noticed that were the only ones in here?"

"Well sir, the night is still young, besides where were going is where the real play is."

"Really, that sounds good lead the way" said Jack who followed the Oaf, to the door, a special knock, the door opened, he went in, then Jack followed in, where the door closed shut to a dark passageway, and a club, came down to strike Jack, who side stepped the strike, as he extended his right foot backwards, to come in contact with, the big guy's knee, a huge moan, then a cry of agony, Jack turned, rolled and kicked the other guy in the knee to drop him as Jack felt his head being used as a ball to the club, swing by swing, Jack slumped forward, then falls onto his back.

"Pick him up and take him to room two, one is filled." They lifted Jack by the arms and drug him to a open door room, pulled him in, to a chair, they tried to cuff Jack's wrists together but his sleeves wouldn't come together, so they realized it was something to do with Jack's jacket getting caught on, so one held Jack's sleeves as the other injured guy, unbuttoned Jack's sports jacket to see and say, "He has a gun?"

"So get it and use it on him already."

The guy reached in to hesitate, then grabbed at it, he short circuited, long enough, for Jack to get up, pull the gun, and drill the other in the head, he fell back dead, the noise of the gun echo'd only in the sound proof room, Jack was on the move, he quickly searched them both, collecting their wallets, and two rolls of thick money wads, he tried to move one, it was no use too heavy, and same for the others, when the door swung open, as Jack pulled his gun to aim at the guy to say, "State who are you, and what do you want with me?"

"Calm down, there is nothing to be afraid of, my name is the Professor, so that's what they call me, and I own this club, now we were a little apprehensive when someone who has more than the whole casino, value, wants to come here, that's all?" Jack hesitated, long enough, for the Professor to escape, and close the door without getting a shot off, the door was locked, Jack looked around, then an idea came to him, "Ah the belt."

Jack pulls off his belt, strips it apart, to see a small bead of plastic explosives, he took off a piece, then found a blasting cap, to say, "Lucky I have only one door to blow down", then saw at the end was a row of blasting caps as he finished stripping it apart, he rolled up the rest into little balls, and placed into one pocket and the blasting caps in the other, then taking one, he placed at where the hinge would be at, he did three, stood back, pulled out his phone, dialed it up and blew the door, it feel flat, crushing a guard, as Jack stepped out, through the hallway, he pushed the door open to see both girls at that same table, while both Ivan and Miss Monica look on, with the Professor still trying to catch his breath. When he said, "We got trouble, this guy blew out the door and put down our three men."

"Well it looks like he wants to play, then guide him to Ricki's table, and see if we can't take money from him" said Ivan

"She isn't on the floor, we have her in the back dealing a game" said the Professor.

Ivan scanned the floor, to see a tall blonde, with a very revealing outfit, to say, "Ah that one, what's her name?"

The Professor looks out to say, "She is one of Miss Monica's girls, before the big deportation occurred."

"She is one of our big producers of recruits", chimed in Miss Monica.

"Excellent have the boys guide our Mister Cash to her table" said Ivan.

Jack stood at the bar, with the bartender drinking another rum and a guy came by to say, "You to play at a table he selected specifically for you."

Jack finishes his drink, to say, "Hey Jimmy, I'll have one more please."

Jimmy made it up and gave him a wink, as he took it and followed, another burly guy, Jack looked around, to think to himself, "Our casino in Cuba, is far nicer than this one, this is so drab" that was till he saw, a very pretty blonde, her outfit alone, inspired Jack to say, "Hi."

"Please sit down", she said.

Jack sat across from her, her name badge read, "Corrine".

"What will you play?"

Jack tossed out the gold plastic card.

"What increments do you want, you know a fourth, half three quarters or all?"

Jack saw his two companions come up but were whisked away, as another table was opened by a Adonis looking guy.

"A Million at a time," said Jack.

"Wise choice sir."

"Changing out one million dollars, she pushed a considerable stack of chips to him, as Jack's eyes wandered around, Jack tosses out a chip.

"The game is casino choice, blackjack, I'll give you two cards, you can then Bet higher, and add a card, as needed" she to winked at him, as she lit up a cigarette, took a long drag and blew it out at Jack, Jack diverted his face, to miss her shot, he looked at his cards, then set out that same chip, she said, "Do you want another or are you done?"

"I'm good" said Jack.

"Then turn them over."

Jack showed twenty, she turned hers over and took another card and was bust to say, "You win."

Quickly Jack won more hands than he lost, as he was having fun, getting toasty and making lucky money. Upstairs, they were plotting, as Miss Monica sat back to see men come and men going, and then Ivan just flipped out as the Professor came up with a report, to say, "Were losing big with this guy, first he kills three of my best men, now he is cleaning up at the tables."

"How much are you down?" "Oh about four in half million."

"Alright listen up call everyone, I want to put this guy down."

Jack was self-absorbed in himself, as he figured out what the wink's meant, he was wining far greater than expected, as the two girls were losing just as much, also men by the dozen were filling in and around, but also the main room filled up with wealthy patrons, they then changed out Corrine with someone else, as Miss Monica strolled over and took a seat beside Jack to say, "Let's talk."

"Cash me out", said Jack, looking towards her, as she leaned in, to whisper, "I had nothing to do with what happen to you down there, I hope you can forgive me, it was a game right?"

"Yeah sure", said Jack, receiving the highest denominations possible.

"Are you mad?, because I overreacted?"

"That's a understatement, I do what I do for the adventure, like you, I too like to play games, so why are you running with this gang?"

"It wasn't always like this, I had a reputation as one of the best match making services in the world, and then Scopus Tyrell came along, and . . . ."

"Scopus, who is that?" asked Jack sincerely, to say, "Can you charge that to my card please."

Miss Monica looked at him, to think about what she really wanted to say, then said something else, "Why, only the most notorious criminal the islands have ever seen, some call him Master Mind."

"What's he like?"

"What do you mean, I'm not following you, you saw him he was carrying that silver suitcase."

"Ah he is Scopus, so what does he have on you?" "Well that was one of the reasons why I wanted you to come here, he has taken my children and my ex-husband, in exchange for five hundred girls."

"How many had you given him?"

"Over five hundred, Scopus had a new plan, he assured me that I will be allowed to live, in exchange for another five hundred, I'm no dummy, this could go on forever, so that's why I need you."

"Sounds like you're the victim now, but you don't look like a victim?" asked Jack.

"Come on, if I ever put up a fight, It would be in one of those rooms up there" she points up at the glass windows, "It is where all of his henchmen would take their turns with me."

"Really who is all involved and where do you think they are at?" spell." show." forth."

"Well take here for example, the Professor, is under their

"Who is doing all that?"

"The henchmen, those guys in black suits run the whole

"Yes, but who is the leader?"

"He is upstairs, he is looking at you right now." "Go on, why do they allow you to talk with me?" "There actually afraid of you, what you can do and so on.

"What do you mean" said Jack, looking to see more henchmen moving in, Jack was thinking a blood bath was coming, to hear, "You're a suppose super spy, meaning you work for the most powerful leader of the free country, in addition to all your support teams, you can command the Army, Navy, Air Force and Marines, your just as if you are the President, of the country to which you support."

"Really I have all that, your mistaken Miss Monica, I'm on my own, sure I have some people helping me, I have all that too?"

"Listen Jack, Ben, you know Ben right." "Who's that?" asked Jack.

"He is the west coast or called the California kid, is one of my clients, ten of his wives, report back to me, and what Ben is allowed to do, is virtually carte blanche."

"Maybe for him, but I do as I see fit."

"That's just it, on American soil, you're the supreme authority as your immediate boss is the President, there is no one above your head, you can kill whomever you want?"

"And the same goes for me, they can kill me, you're a crazy bitch, leave me alone" said Jack getting up, with two cards in hand, he went to the cash out window, as she joins him, to say "Are you going to help me or not?"

"Why don't you call this Ben guy?"

"I would have, Lisa Curtis of the CIA said, this was your territory, if Ben came in here he would have to turn it over to you, so will you help me out?"

"Cash or credit sir?" said the lady behind the counter. "One of those cases, do you know if they are bulletproof?"

"I don't know sir" said the clerk to add "The total comes to 4.5 million, will rounded up, to a even quarter number, as she put the cash in the briefcase, to say, do please come back again" said the clerk.

"I will", said Jack holding his briefcase, then says, "You better get out of here there looks like some trouble is brewing, take this briefcase, and if you want my help there is a card to where I will be at tonight, be there no later than 9 pm."

"Alright" she said happily.

"Now run off, I have some work to do", as Jack stepped out from under the half ceiling he stepped back, pulled his gun and took a shot, the round pierced the bullet proof glass, instantly, the whole sheet came down, Jack saw a young man with bright big eyes, a guy next to him, who sported dreadlocks, next to him was a very muscular tough guy."

That was it, as rounds were being directed towards Jack, he was on the move, a picture, of the three, were his new targets, Jack counted about fourty men, his gun was out, as he hid behind a huge table, his shots were true, but he kept backing up, as the shots kept coming his direction.

Jodie was getting use to her ear piece, and driving her mid-sized sedan, when she heard on the radio, that Jack needs help, her job as was told to her was to mirror Jack, at a half mile away, she parked on a hillside overlooking the Casino, and turned off her radio, she got out, to survey the grounds below, then decided to position herself, on a berm, in the trees, for cover, her earpiece was mumbled, she pulled out her tracker, she then, pulled out a mat, that attached to her she pulled out her weapon, affixed a silencer on the end, and then changed out her sights with an infrared, without laser pointer, next, she closed the trunk, with two full mags, in hand, she waddled, through the brush, under an old tree, to kneel, then lie down, she lay her rifle down, to pull a camouflage poncho, from her cargo pocket, she attached two ends to her boots, and pulled on the other two on her arms, then settled in as the rain started to fall, she eased the rifle in position, while looking through a pair of binoculars, then according to her tracker, Jack was on the other side of the wall, she set down the binoculars, to position the rifle butt in her arm, the rain, was flowing on both sides of her sturdy mat, she was dry and unaffected by the rain, she waited, a side door opened and two girls in high heels were being escorted out, she thought, "Are they friendly, do I have to take them out, is it a head shot", just then the door in front of her view opened, it was Jack, running, to a container, instantly four huge spotlights lit up the courtyard, she thought, "It was a trap,", it was so well lit, she pulled off her infred scope for a regular scope, then she loaded, her magazine, pulled the bolt back, aimed, released the safety. she spoke saying, "Do I have authorization to fire?"

Meanwhile on the ground Jack looked up at the three, who were all laughing at him, as thirty plus men were coming at Jack, when all of a sudden, those same men were dropping dead, from head shots, as there laughing soon turned to pain, as the clear leader was struck in the leg, instantly they helped him away, as Jack was on the move, he said, "Sara start, come to my position", Jack fired as Henchman fell all around him, then it stopped, instantly, as he dove, over a short fence, into a parking lot, Jack saw a black van, as he saw Tatiana's head, Jack was firing for good, as the one by the door, went down and the other guy was going for his gun, only to fall away. Jack met them as his car pulled up, the driver's door opened, as Jack led them in under the hail of gunfire, as bullets riddled his car, only to bounce off, Tatiana was in the back and Isabella was up front, hearing the rounds riddle off the bullet proof glass, Jack slid into the driver's seat he hit the steering wheel, a display panel showed A-Z choices, he chose H—for right side guns, he hit it once, and the right rear guns, shot off, on the men going up the bank, they fell away, as the car took off, the rear guns spun off, as they went half black, on the display, Jack scanned the remainder, to chose C—rear spikes, which released, near the entrance, eight point spikes, as the exit gate was open, his car sped off. The ride back to the spa, was quiet and no one was behind them, as the car slowed, in front of the spa, the car parked, Jack led them out, and he let the car park itself, Jack said, "Shut off", Jack checked his phone, to see he missed five calls, and equal messages, he listened to hear his team check in. especially that Jim and Mike are back waiting word, Jack looked at his watch, it was a little past 11 :00 o'clock, PM, Jack dialed up Jim, to say, "Sorry to disturb you."

"Never, were here for you, a little update, Mike has been cleared to return to service."

"That's nice, I used some items on the car." "We will update them tonight", said Jim.

"Make sure that the team has enough support ammo." "They do, who are you talking about?"

"I don't know, whoever was above the bluff overlooking the casino."

"I'll check on it, anything else you need?"

"Anything you can find out about, this Scopus Tyrell, or he is called Master Mind?"

"Will do" said Jim, as Jack hung up as he slid his phone shut. He got out, looked around the heavily lit parking garage, he took the elevator up, he got out on the main floor, he went past the girl's room, to reach his, he used his card key, he went in.

Jack looked around his room, saw no sign of anyone, that was until he went into the bathroom, there Miss Monica sat in a tub full of bubbles, she smiled, to say, "You're a popular man, you sure stirred up the hornet's nest, I just got talking to Ivan and he tells me that his Father and an army of men will be here tomorrow morning, are you afraid of that?"

"No why should I, why with all these games you play." "Listen Jack, there are worse people more cruel than myself, It's my job to prepare you for the future, especially Ivan and his henchmen."

"What's so special with them?"

"Well when they find you, there gonna be playing some games with you, if you know what I mean?"

"I doubt it, the very next time I see them will be their last." "What does that mean?" asked Miss Monica, motioning for Jack to join her.

"Just what I said, so what great honor do I have to have you in my presence?" he said as she stood, to say, "Can you hand me that towel?, she said as she turned on the shower head, as he watched her wash off, then as she finished he tossed her a towel, she stepped out of the tub, she turned to unplug it, while he watched, it was a pure turn on for him, she past by him, to climb on his bed, she laid out to watch as Jack stood by the bed.

"Why don't you undress, and come to bed with me" said Miss Monica.

"First tell me why you're here?"

"Well you invited me, and it seems where ever you go, you seem to destroy things, don't get me wrong, I rather appreciate a man, who can take charge and get things done, that's actually why I wanted you here in the first place." "How so", asked Jack.

"Well I have connections all over the islands and when I heard from the grapevine that you were up for a new partner, and it was to come pass that Tatiana, was the strongest candidate, so I asked her to whom I knew to recruit you to come here, and help me out."

"What is it, I could do for you?"

"Well I know I owe you for going through the gauntlet, and I'm sorry, I will make it up to you tonight, but first may I ask of you one favor?"

"Sure what is it?"

"Well to be honest with you, I'm being blackmailed, that guy you saw at the fort was Scopus Tyrell, he has my two children and my ex-husband."

Jack paused to say, "Where are they at?"

"I don't know, if I did I'd hire the best mercenaries in the world, but what would probably happen is that he probably would kill them, and all of us girls, you know I have a reputation to uphold and of all my girls."

"Speaking of girls, where do you get them all?"

"Well I could tell you but I imagine you probably won't like what I'm about to say."

"Go on tell about it, I'm listening" said Jack.

"Well it all started some fifteen years ago, when a friend I knew wanted to marry the prettiest girl I could find for him, and she must be young, he said, so I went to the local university, and recruited one girl, and with her came five more, all wanting a rich man to take care of them, so I made a deal with them, if they could pass it along to all their sister sororities the secret, then I would allow them to join, so over the years some things have changed, but ultimately one thing stays the same, I only allow the prettiest to come."

"What of those that decide to do it, then back out?" "Well those are dealt with."

"Meaning what exactly?"

"Well they are either shipped away or are killed" she said in a somber voice.

"You don't get it do you, maybe this Master Mind had someone you recruited, or killed, and for that he chose for you to send him girls."

"I hadn't even thought that, wow, why didn't I think of that" she said in a astonishing voice.

Tatiana said something to me, that her younger sister was somewhere deep inside, but what is more startling to me is that this was left on my phone this very night" Jack pulls out his phone, to hit his only saved message, he pushed play "Jack Cash this is Senator Webster from the state of Florida, today my daughter was kidnapped, in plain sight, in which two of her bodyguards were killed, the President has authorized me to tell you have all means necessary to find her and get her back, here is my number call me at," Jack slid the phone shut, to say, "Now you know, but let's see if your with me, who is handling the girl trade?"

"Well I do have handlers."

"How so, who are they and how do they work?"

"Well to be honest with you, they work off of sex, is there real payment, and how it works is they meet with the girls, if they think they are worthy, they sample themselves, if they pass . . ."

"Enough, I want all their names and where they work at and all your contacts, is it on a flash drive or something?" he looks at her, as she pulls the covers down to expose her lovely breasts and bats her eyes to show him what was hanging around her neck, for Jack to say, "Let me have that, but also I want you to write out how it all works, then I may consider helping you."

She looked at him to say "before I give you this flash drive I want you in this bed now."

"Nah, that's not how this is going down, you had your chance to play fairly, and you cheated", as Jack looks around, to say, "Where's the briefcase I gave to you to bring to me?"

She looked down, as Jack yanked the whole sheet away, to see that she had her phone in hand. For her to say, "I had to give it to them, to get out safely, how about I let you have my phone, All the contacts are in there" Jack held up his hand at her, to lift up his phone he stroke one letter, within moments the door opened, and the smiling Miss Monica, had a frown on her face, to see a brunette, appeared, to say as he made his way around the bed to say, "Slid off, hands behind your back" Miss Monica grabs her towel to place around her body, to say, "You could have had all this and much more", Jack zip tied her wrists, her towel was on firmly, as he pulled her up, and gave her a little push, to say,

"Take good care of her, and get as much information you can from her, and ask Mark to come in."

The door opened, as Mitzi escorted the very sad Miss Monica out of the room, only to see a handsome fit man go in, and shut the door.

Mark stood by the door to say, "You wanted to see me?"

"Yeah, assemble the dive gear, I want to go out and visit a few islands, oh and we have a new girl joining the team" said Jack undressing.

"I know about her, what shall I do for her?"

"She is staying in the room with Tatiana, on the end, coordinate with her, she is a certified diver, and see what scuba equipment we need?"

Mark looks at Jack to say, "Oh, another girl, got cha, will do."
"That will be all" said Jack to ad as he slid into his bed

"Can you turn off the light?"

Mark flipped the switch down, and went out, thinking to himself, "It will be nice to spend time with that blonde", when he came to the end door, he knocked, moments later, the door answered, it was Isabella, wearing only a bra and panties to say, "Yes, what is it were trying to sleep?"

"Jack asked me, my name is Mark, to speak with a new girl, is that you?"

"Yes, maybe, my name is Isabella."

Mark looks up and down to see how magnificent she looked, in her revealing outfit, to say, "Well Isabella, Jack wants you to coordinate with me tomorrow morning on the dive were all taking, can you be ready with all your gear at say 0430 AM, that we will go off about 5 AM, I'll have a boat ready, so make sure your ready", she closed the door, she thought "Oh shit, it has worked, but I need to get this all going."

Tatiana called out to her, "Are you coming back to bed?"

"Sorry Hun, I can't, as she frantically looked through the phone book under the small kitchen dome light, to see two shops in this cove, one Ricky and the other Scotty's, she thought then said" I'll go with Scotty, so she dialed him up, it rang, and rang, and rang, she closed her phone, to dial up Ricky, two rings and he answered, to say, "Ricky's divers, how may I help you?"

She began to speak when she heard, "After the beep please leave a message, beep . . . .

She slid her phone shut, and turned out the light and then crawled back into bed with Tatiana who was fast asleep.

CH 6

A dive to remember

It was 4 AM, the team was on the move, Jack was dressed, and ready to go, a fully dressed Miss Monica, was being escorted by Mark, Mitzi and Trixie, came out front to see a car driven by Mike, the four of them got in with Miss Monica in the middle, for Mark to say, "To the docks", that was the only thing said as they knew they had the enemy with them, behind them was Jack in his McLaren, Mercedes, he read a Intel report on his newest enemy, Mister Master Mind, or triple M, as his closest friends call him, has a outpost on the island of Santa Isabel, and thirty other smaller islands, they neared the docks, where a moderate sized fishing vessel, sat two deck hands sat on the second deck, one female one Male, Brian slid down, and Jodie followed suit, to meet with the team, to hear "Brian, take her to the captain's quarters, see that she is taken care of and watched every minute that there is air that you breathe," the four stood in a circle to hear Mark say, "Before he gets here, what was the story last night?"

"As far as I know he survived alright" said Mitzi.

"Know that's not what I meant, usually, the girl would sleep with him, why did he call us in?"

"I don't know, I was up all night getting cooperative information from Miss Monica, if our Boss wants me to do that I will", said Mitzi.

"Maybe she isn't his type, you know he likes our blondes better" said Trixie.

"True, true, I know what that girl is capable of" said Mike

"You were never suppose to be on that boat in the first place, I hope you realize your place now?" said Mitzi.

"I do, and it will never happen again" said Mike, so what's up with the new girl, is that one of his?"

"Hush" said Trixie, as they all looked at Jack, who's car disappeared, as he walked up on the dock, two brunette's dressed in yellow, with some surfer guy, met him on the dock, it was Tatiana and Isabella, who said "Jack this is Scotty, he is a local diver who knows the waters in and around here, he looked them up and down, then, let them get aboard, on deck was four wet suits laid out, with tanks and a small machine, which the crane was attached too, they got on board as the group broke up, as Mark, went to the wheel house, but noticed that girl he talked to last night, as Jack shook his head, to go down below, his team was doing what they do best, while Jodie, Tatiana, Isabella and Scotty, were all on deck together, then Trixie came out, to say, "We all have a job to do on this boat, can any one of you cook?"

"I can" said Isabella, "Alright follow me, the rest of you can stow gear, we have a small three mile trip" said Trixie.

Mitzi stood by Mike to say, "You'd better be on better behavior, or I will have you replaced, don't forget this is the Jack Cash show."
"Believe me it will never happen again, I'm sorry."

"Your forgiven, now, we got another problem, I need you to keep an eye on our new recruits?"

"What the two girls in a wet suit, who are they to us?"

"Well the short brunette her name is Tatiana, and she is his partner?"

"I know, I saw her at the boathouse" said Mike looking at her itsy bity body suit.

"Yeah it's a game to him, hands off her and the other one, who says she is a certified scuba diver."

"Don't believe it", countered Mike.

"She put you down didn't she?"

"Yeah, but I was a little outnumbered."

"We can go through this all day, leave her alone, she may be competing for your job."

"Is that what Jack said", said Mike.

"It doesn't matter, I'm the one in charge, so says Erica." said Mitzi leaving him behind.

Mike watched Isabella, who looked up to see him, she went to him to say, "So your part of the team, sorry" she said factitiously.

"What's up with the yellow suits?" "I like to stand out" said Isabella.

"Come on who are you trying to impress, surely not Jack" said Mike.

"Your right, he doesn't even see me, let alone hang out with me, say, if you play along, I'll reward you."

"Forget it, you're on your own, I work alone."

"That's what got you into trouble before, suit yourself, you may be sorry" she said, as she used her hand across his face. Jack opened the door, to the captain's cabin, with a sandwich in hand, he waved Brian out, to stop him to say, "Thanks for the support at the casino."

"Your welcome, but it wasn't me, it was Jodie." "Fine, let her know to be well stocked next time." "Will do, do you want me to wait outside."

"Nah, send Mike down here, and have him guard the door, I want everyone else in the wheel house in five minutes."

"Yes sir" said Brian as he shut the door.

Jack looked at Miss Monica, to say as he finished his sandwich; "I decided to help you as I checked out your story, and your right he has your children, so if you want you can chose, to stay here, accompany me or I can send you back."

"What about the fortress?, that is my home?"

"Perhaps, if that's what you want to do, then go ahead, but if it were me, I'd like you to shut down your operation, for now, after all this blows over, start back up, but only if it's on the up in up, besides we have another problem, I just got word, Senator's Webster is fuming and wants answers, do you have any idea where I can find her?"

"Yes, start with Ted Jacobs, he runs the Florida chapter, he could be at the fortress in a couple of days."

"Fine, I'll send you back with a support team, to free her and "Don't worry, I believe you now, and will do everything I can to help you out", as he went around and clipped off her zip tie.

She massaged her wrists to reach up to hug Jack to say, "I meant what I said, you can have me, now if you like."

"Nah maybe a rain check, you're out of here." "But were in the middle of the ocean."

Jack was at the door, then opened it to see Mike, to say, "Guard the door, keep her here till were ready."

Jack pulled out his phone to dial up Jim, Jim answered to hear Jack say, "Air, pick up and drop off on island, in ten mikes."

Mark steered the boat to say, "What's that?" "Where's the weather balloon?"

"In that bag, over there under passenger seat." Jack pulls the bag out, to unzip it and pull out the harness, passing Mark down to see Mike he say, "Ready the weather balloon", as sees him leave his post, Jack opens the door, to see Miss Monica on the bed waiting, for Jack to say, "Stand up."

Jack has her step into the harness, as she is saying, "What's this for?"

"Your going for a ride."

"What like a para-ski behind the boat?"

"Nah something more like a game, you know how I like to play games, and you will love this game, trust me."

"Well if you insist, but let me make it up to you."

"There you go, your all cinched up and ready to go, follow me" said Jack as he led her out onto the deck, as Mike held the guide line, as Jack takes the clip to the rear ring, to say, "Bye Bye, as a plane overhead, snapped her up and instantly she was up to the plane, as they all watched, for Mike to say, "That sure looks fun, some fifty stories in less than 30 seconds."

Mitzi pats him on the chest to say, "You'll never get that chance, it's a fifty thousand dollar ride."

Jack just looks at her to say, "Really."

"Well for you, its free, for him well it will cost."

Jack watches Mitzi, to give her a strange look, then over to Mike, who he is not too sure about, on the deck was Tatiana, Isabella and Scotty, with Jodie in a side seat watching the two girls struggle with the equipment.

"You know she isn't what she says she is" said Jodie leaning into Jack.

"How so, well for starters, look at how the tank sits in their carriage, besides, I'll let you in on a secret, we all are going to free dive, for at least one minute, to get to the cavern."

"How do you know that?"

"Its world famous dive caves, I thought that's what we were going, to do?"

"Well I haven't thought about that" said Jack. Jack leaves, to go down to the room, he opened the door to see Mitzi who just plopped down on the bed, for her to say, "Can you let me know when Jodie knows when we get there?"

Jack turned at the door, to say, "What, the hell" she turned into a she demon, as Mitzi sat up on the bed, for Jack, to see her nose was flaring, just before she moved Jack grabbed her arm, as she had some sort of a panic attack, she dropped, and was out, to look at him, he said, "Calm down, it's no big deal", as Jack pull his phone out and dialed 9-1-1 as he saw Mitzi breakdown as she was out, and not breathing.

Meanwhile up on deck all was quiet and calm as Mark piloted the boat as Jodie was reading off some coordinates, when two F-18 Super Hornets scrapped their position, enough for Mark and Mike, and Trixie, checked their phones, to see the 9-1-1 distress call. Mark slowed the boat as he saw the helicopters, with the strike team above floating down to them. He froze, as he stopped the engines, Mike had come up to Mark as the strike team were landing, into the water, Mike slowly opened the door, to see Jack was sitting on top of Mitzi, as he yelled, "Get me a defibrillator now, she has gone into cardiac arrest" as Jack continued the heart strokes, Jack was helped off of her as a team member worked on her, as a ship came out from nowhere, to board their vessel, Jack was helped up onto the ship, as all the equipment was carried aboard, Jack was led into the Captain's quarters, he took a seat that he was offered, Jack sat, to see the Captain, he wasn't happy, for Jack to hear, "I want to tell you a story, our job is to specifically follow you around, were you aware of this?"

"No" said Jack.

"Let me tell you how important you really are, as it was explained to me, you're like the President of our United States, Jack, you have extreme power but at times your reckless, for you to dial 9-1-1 on your phone, dials directly to the President Himself, so what do you think he said to me?"

"I have no idea."

"Try if you're not there in five minutes or less, I'd be going to a place, I'd never see the day of life again", there was a knock on the door, "Yes what is it?"

"Sir the diagnosis on Mitzi is that she suffered a stroke, and from all accounts, need surgery, she has a stuck heart valve."

Jack stood up to say, "May I see her?"

"Absolutely, but wait a moment please, close the door", Jack swung it shut, to hear, "Please, please from now on call us, or call me directly, were part of your support group."

"Really what does that entail?" "Well it's a whole battle group." "Consisting of what?"

"You mean ships."

"Yeah how many ships do I have ?"

"Well it depends on the group, but I'd say twenty eight, give or take."

"So let me get this straight, there are twenty eight or so ships at my disposal, and that is from the Navy,"

"I know what you're thinking, but really it's not my place to tell you all this, actually, it has been that way since November of last year."

"So what your saying is if I want Intel, for some coordinates, you can do that?"

"Yes, but not us, were the rescue and welfare ship the Santa Monica, and I'm Captain Ron Daniels, I think on your phone should have everything you need", he said looking up to see Jack was gone.

Jack entered the sick bay, to see Mitzi was awake and in better spirits, as Jack held her hand to say, "How do you feel?"

"Like a two ton truck ran me over." "What do you think caused it?"

"It was stress" spoke a voice behind him, to say, "Jack I'm Doctor Jacobs, as you can see we have the state of the art equipment on board this ship, and all thanks to you, you saved her life, her heart stopped, you massaged it, we restarted it, to bump open a valve, we found with that body imaginer, that was designed exclusively for you, and the fact that you dialed 9-1-1 simply meant you saved her life."

Mitzi smiled at Jack, to hear, "As you say the word she will be flown to D.C. ASAP."

"Well make it happen, don't let me stand in your way." "Yes sir."

"Jack, I Love You" said Mitzi, to add "Thank you for saving my life, so what are your plans now?"

"I don't know, I've lost the only women I can really trust, to run my ground operation, without annoying me" as they all heard a helio land.

"Cheer up honey, you'll be fine, I'll have Trixie fill in", said Mitzi.

"Between you and me, I think she would be happier if Mark and her had some babies, I don't feel like she is in the game anymore."

"Wait, no that's not right, I hand selected her at the academy, and she pledged that she would obey and support only you."

A knock on the door, "Its open", said Jack, in walked Trixie to say

"A helio just landed, we can go now."

"See what I mean?" said Jack as several handlers came in, to her bed, as one of them pushed Jack away, only to hear a woman's voice yell, "Stop that man, all of you handlers out of this room immediately", Jack saw it was Erica, in her command voice, flanking her was Claire and Debby, who went to Jack to help him up, as Mitzi spoke, "It was all my fault."

"Yes it was, but your alive all that is all that matters, what is the current mission?"

"Well Jack has uncovered the sale and disbursion of women to the world."

"Is it shut down?" "Yes, for now."

"So mission accomplished, so what is happening now?" asked Erica, as Jack was watching all this unfold, it was Mitzi running the show, for her to say "Well he is going after the Master Mind, behind all of this chaos?"

"Alright, that's all I needed to hear, so what do we have on him?"

"Well" said Jack entering into the conversation, "Were going onto the island through a cave system, and surprise them." "Nah, you don't need to do that, your Jack Cash, you could, park this vessel on that dock, get off, and walk up to his front door and arrest him."

"Me, Myself and what army?"

"That's just it, you have close to ten thousand men at your disposal, look around you, you have the support of the Navy, you work on a Marine Corps base, and the Special Ops Group from the Army is on standby, you can have Intel flown by the AWAC plane anytime you like."

"Well let's just do that, let's take this huge vessel in and see what happens, as Jack looks at Mitzi who was getting excited. Jack says, "Lets at least wait till she is on a plane back to DC."

"Jack needs my replacement" said Mitzi.

"That's easy, it will be Claire, and you Debby will be Jack's new partner."

"What about Tatiana" asked Jack.

"What about a girl, who is a spy, who is a bit of a ditz and is sexy?" said Erica.

"Exactly, listen being a spy doesn't mean she has to look like Mitzi or Trixie, or Jodie, it is more on how they look, and then react in a situation, will either make or break a spy, besides that was the whole point was that she was a spy, and she is the daughter of the Master Mind, don't you understand it's really all about the games, like when you and I met." Said Jack.

"Enough, I get it, and your right, have it your way, besides I may have a new assignment for you anyway."

Jack watched as the men came in, roll her past them only to stop them to say to the man who pushed Jack out of the way "If I ever get wind of you pushing Jack around again, I'll prosecute you myself."

The Captain stood at the door, to say, "Relieve this man, and take him to my quarters, do you need anything else?"

"Were fine, some privacy please" said Erica, like a viper. She looked around the room, to say "Alright you two, get on deck and assemble I need a word with Jack alone."

Jack stood to his back to the wall, as Erica locked the door, she came over to him to whisper, "Were all alone, isn't there something you wanted to put inside of me?"

"Seems like your pretty bossy, is that the boss ordering me to do that or the wife I hoped to have?"

"The same in one, listen, I need to exert my authority so that they get it the first time, it's like carrying around a big stick, which I get to use from time to time, and this is one of those times, I'll bend over and all you have to do is stick it in."

Jack saw that she positioned herself holding onto a lamp fixture, as he moved behind her, he lifted up her loose skirt, to see her nylons, and white thong panties, taking his two fingers, he pulled them down past her big butt, the wetness in her panties showed her excitement, which got Jack going, he undid his pants, and released it, he grabbed her hips and it went in easy, he was much larger than expected or she was tighter, as Jack plunged deeper, till he struck gold, and she erupted, not before, Jack grabbed a towel to block the gush of fluids, he pressed her for a good half of an hour, till at last, she let go, as did Jack, she collapsed and he followed her to the floor. Jack was sweated. He knelt up, to see that her panties were soaked, so he ripped them off, and stood up, and zipped up, he then helped her up, as she adjusted her skirt, she turned to say, "Alright have it your way, but you really should check out that phone, you won't believe how many resources you have."

She watched as he was gone, as the door was swinging, Jack made it to the control room, to say, “Where can I see the ship’s video room?”

The Captain, pointed to the room, Jack knocked then entered, to say, “Do you have footage of the sickbay, can you pull it up for the last two hours, let me see the remote”, Jack gets it then scans it to see it was only focused on Mitzi, he says, “Erase from the moment when she arrived until now.”

Jack left that room, to see the Captain, he says, “What course are you on?”

“Why to Santa Isabel and the great caves.” “Who told you that’s where I want to go?”

“I did” said a red head, who smiled as she exited another room, to add “Jack were all here to help you capture this Master Mind and restore order down here.”

“Where do I know you from?”

“Remember back on the base, I was sent by the President.”

“Yeah, yeah, I know all about that, but who put you in charge?”

“Well, I just assumed, you needed some guidance, the longer we wait, the less the chances of capturing that guy.” Jack just left the wheel house, down some stairs, out onto the deck, to see the boat they had was being towed, he sees Mark to say, “Pull that boat alongside were getting off this ride, where’s the girls?”

“I think they went looking for something to eat.”

Jack dials up Mike to say as he answers, “Find the three girls and get back to the deck were leaving.”

Jack spun the phone’s wheel to see resources, he clicked on that, as he scrolled, Air Force, Army, and so forth the got down to the Navy and clicked on it, to see anything and everything, then, he saw SEALS, he clicked on that, and dialed to hear a voice answer

“This is Commander Scott Mackenzie, how may I assist you Mister Jack Cash?”

“What resources do I have available to me?”

“Why, we have two teams, on the ready and up to five more in four hours, then.”

"I get it Commander, how would you like a mission?" "Absolutely, name it."

"Currently I'm headed to an island, Santa Isabel, to the swim caves, can you have your teams dive and have transport devices, armed, for an assault?"

"Yes but will you be there?"

"No, matter of fact I'll be at the front door, I want you to report any contact, do not fire until I give the order, do you understand this commander?"

"Yes sir, but you have to be there, for our action to occur." "I'll be there, what is you ETA?"

"Five Mikes."

"Carry on," said Jack as he moved the Commanders name to the top of his favorites, then he backed out of that file, to scroll down even further, before stopping on women, he clicked on that, to see a 1 of 2500, and as he scroll the number increased in tens, woman from all over, it showed their face, measurements and profile, he saw a girl, he was familiar with, it was Dylan, her whole profile appeared, literally ten screens worth of info, to see the classification was a 2nd level spy, he knew he hit the gold mine, as it became apparent, that everyone he has ever come in contact with is, in their, as some of the names he was familiar with, he stopped at Isabella, he opened her file, as he read, it became apparent Jodie was right, she has no classification as a diver, yet, she is an expert marksman, and won several awards while serving in the 82nd airborne, "Impressive" thinks Jack, as he back out of her profile to type in Tatiana, her profile was disturbing as she was an abused woman, who was in fact the daughter of the Master Mind, and at the bottom of her profile double agent, and extremely dangerous, handle with care.

Jack backed out of that file to type in Jodie, three popped up, to type Thomas, and her profile was impressive, she was impressive, but a wild card, as he looked up to see that the girls had returned, Jack exited the program and slid the phone shut, thinking, "I need Brian?"

Mark and several crewmembers helped everyone back over as the ship had slowed its speed, Jack saw Brian come running to them, as he jumped aboard, with a bag in hand.

"I gather you got my text?"

"Absolutely, I just didn't know how much time I had, but I did as you asked."

"Well give it to them, did you get any holsters for them?" "Yes of course."

Jack stood by Mark as he instructed him to slow, to an idle, to say "Hold this position, I want to let Jodie off, Mike make sure Jodie is ready, as Jack went forward, through the door, to see Brian, showing Tatiana her weapon, as he handed her four clips loaded, he also saw Isabella, with hers on her hip, on a cartridge belt, he sees Jodie to say, "I've decided I want you to lead up the invasion under the water, Mike is on deck waiting to help you get suited up." For? Jack."

"I'm not comfortable with him."

"I've been hearing that a lot lately, so who do you work

"Why of course you . . ."

"Precisely, get going, that's an order."

"No, no, I got it, and you'll never ever have to tell me again, Jack stirs up some coffee and lemon, to take a sip, as Tatiana has her gun in her hand pointing right at him, he shrugs his shoulder, to walk up and onto the bridge, to close up close to Mike to say,

"I want no funny business here, this is a mission."

"I'm always professional" said Mike with a smile, which Jack caught, as Jack saw the two girls come up from the galley, to say, "Alright I want you two to go with me to the entrance and hit the house."

"It's just going to be the three of us?" "Why do you ask, Isabella?"

"Well that place is a fortress like, Miss Monica's place, he has hundreds of guards, with hundreds of weapons."

"Funny I had no problem at Miss Monica's" said Jack.

"That's because, she only had twenty at the most."

"A hundred, two hundred, five hundred, I don't care, if you like you can stay here, that goes for both of you" as he thought of Blythe, he thought he would have to look her up."

No, I'm your partner, for the good and the bad of situations" said Tatiana.

"I'm in too, I realize it's now or never, I'd probably have ended up behind some desk" said Isabella.

Jack turned to hear Mike say, "She is ready."

Jack approached Jodie to say, "You have your ear piece in?" "Yes."

"You'll have two teams of SEALS behind you, on your wrist should be a tracker to me, follow it in, and suppress the enemy at my command only, you got that?"

"Actually can you check my equipment please?"

"I trust Mike with my life, your safe, focus on this mission, and I'll see you at the mansion."

"One more thing" she said innocently.

"Yeah, what is it", said Jack.

"Will you give me a kiss?"

Jack looked her up and down, to say, "If I give you a kiss, I get to touch your breasts?"

"Sure, their yours it isn't like Mike hasn't had his hands all over my body without asking", said Jodie.

Jack leaned in and gave her a mouth to mouth kiss, it lingered, as he felt something his hand was poised to touch, but held back out of respect, they broke apart, as Jack's phone rang, he said,

"Yeah, your under us, good, I'm sending my partner down to lead you in."

"Really, you mean that."

"Yeah, you have all the qualifications, now go and be safe."

"Thanks", she said as she jumped off the boat.

CH 7

Attack on Scopus Tyrell

Mark sped the boat around the far side of the island, as a traffic of ships were parked at the huge entrance of the caves. The boat approached the furthest south part, sat a huge mansion, on the only hill, and with it was a huge helio-copter out front, for Jack to say, "Brian can you and Mark blow that thing up, wait, it has a Magnetic impulse device, can you Mike go with them and pull it out, that will be your guy's mission, while I go to the front door, with my two girls."

Mark brought the boat up to the long dock, and Mike roped it down, Jack and the girls were on the move, as Jack thought about the strike team, he dialed up Jim, to text him, "Strike team, here and now, both teams" he waited to see, "Confirmed in ten minutes."

"Alright lets go, fan out, Tatiana you go to the left, Isabella on the right, you see anyone shoot to injure not to kill!"

They both shake their heads, in agreement. Jack had made it to the door, he was at the door, he tried it, it was unlocked, he went in, to see a magnificent grand piano, a crystal chandelier, and a huge flowing stairwell, he went through a door, to hear a television was on, a handsome man was lounged back as Jack stood in front of him, to say, "State your name?"

The guy was laughing at him, as Jack pulled his weapon, pointed it at him to say, "State you name."

The guy went for something and Jack shot him, the agony of pain seared through his leg as Jack grabbed him to pull him to the floor, he pulled out a zip tie, and did up his hands, interlocking his fingers, and then his ankles, then he knelt down at his ear to say, "This your last chance, or you die."

"Then kill me."

Jack struck him with his gun, and got up, and was on the move, through the window he saw Isabella walking casually, with her gun drawn, he began to think, "This place is deserted, maybe someone tipped them off, and the game is all about me?" Jack stopped at a short hallway, but knew it was a good place for the basement, he used his phone to locate the secret latch, he undid it, to see a passageway down, voices were heard and screams of young girls, Jack turned the corner, to use his phone as a mirror, to see a group of men, surrounding what looked like a girl on her knees, as his phone was vibrating, he pulled it back to hear, "We have encountered heavy troops, their guarding the entrance, to what appears to be a submarine, old class obsolete."

"Go ahead and capture, maim do not kill, and zip tie them up."

Jack used his phone again, as a mirror this time some guy was coming straight for him, as he stepped down and caught the guy by surprise, Jack kicked him in the inside of his knee and the guy fell, in pain, Jack held his gun out as the others opened up their circle, just as another pushed the panic button, the door behind him slid shut, and another door opened up and men with wet suits were coming up weapon armed, Jack was in a corner, his though for preserving life quickly changed to survival even at the two nude girls a blonde and brunette pulled a gun, and with no where to hide, Jack began to fire, shooting to kill, with a blur, he connected head shots, quickly through one magazine, he let fly, Jack just charged, through the door way, to a bigger sub-terrain basement where metal bared cells showed rooms with women, children and some men, he looked around at all the screaming, crying, and name calling, as he went to the west side where windows allowed some light in, to the door, which was vacant, and down to a huge underground cavern, where the SEALS and Jodie were engaged in an all, out battle, mostly it was a one on one knife duel, probably because their ammo was spent, among the huge sub at the dock was a pristine cigarette boat, that had absorbed most of the rounds, it sat nearly all the way in the water. Jack was on the move, till he stopped and switch his phone to speaker, to say "Listen up stop what you are doing and drop your weapons, my name is Jack Cash, International Bounty Hunter, allow my men to take you into custody, or I will kill each and every one of you".

As everyone complied, a single shot rang out, everyone looked around, but it was the blonde in the yellow wet suit, that stumbled, then fell down, as two SEAL members went to her, while Jack went back up, the stairs to the cages to hear "She is hiding over there", Jack approached her as she shot at him, point blank, as the bullets bounced off his heart, she said, "What are you superman?"

"As he whacks her with his gun, she falls to her side, as he zip ties her up, as Jack calls the Captain Daniels to say, "Yeah I need a transport for one hundred people ASAP at my location."

"Let us go mister" said one guy.

"Hold on, there is still danger, just give me ten minutes", said Jack on the move, up the stairs, to hear a huge explosion, he raced up to see, the helicopter was destroyed, as helio parts were all over the front grounds, as he raced out, he heard a shot, and moved as it caught his arm, and he deflected it off, as he went to the ground, he turned to get up to see, Tatiana got it even worse, shrapnel, littered her body, she lay in wait, as Jack approached her, to assist her. She shot at him at close range as all the bullets stuck to his heart, as he kicked the gun out of her hand to say, "So you want me dead, why?"

"You killed my friend?"

Behind them several helio's came in, and just as the strike team's Casey reported "Jack its Casey, west side is all clear, as a group was about to leave, we intercepted them."

"Good come to the front."

Jack bent down to see all her cuts to say, "Who is your friend?"

"Her name Alysia, she was a red head?"

As Jack spins through his phone to hear, "You killed her in . . . ."

"Brussels Belgium, she is right here, alive and well, in the US", said Jack.

"What the reports said that all women were killed, by commandos."

"Here she is video of her just yesterday, she actually sent to me for rescuing her", Jack placed the phone on open, to allow her to view the video, with time and date stamp.

"Ah", she said as she laid back.

"So this is what this was all about, you wanting to kill me because I took the life of your friend, here I will dialed her up" she tried to reach for the phone, when Jack said "No, No, No, only I handle this phone, to hear, "Jack Cash is that really you," "Alysia it's me Tat, are you doing Okay?"

"Yeah, sorry I couldn't call you, you know with your dad's connections and all that, I was asked to keep quiet, I'm fine, so how are you?"

Jack pulls the phone up, to say, "This is Jack Cash, she should be fine, but she got hit with some collateral damage, I'll have her call you."

Behind him he heard Casey out of breath, loaded down, to say "Were bringing the last of the prisoners."

"Good do you have the weather balloon?" "Yeah, right here, showing Jack the backpack."

The helio's all landed and quickly the place was full of relief personnel, even Debby and Claire were there to say, "Nice job Jack" as Debby rubbed Jack's back, to say "Wow, it looks bad what happen?"

"The helio exploded." "Oh too bad for her."

"Yeah, it's ironic how she lured me here on putting fake scars all over her body, now she will have real ones, for the rest of her life."

"They will probably find a way to hide them, say what are your plans now, that this is over with?"

"I don't know go back to Mobile." "Yeah, about that", said Debby.

Just as a young girl came and gave Jack a big hug and a kiss on the cheek to say, "Thank, you, thank you, thank you for rescuing me, and especially my boyfriend, he tried to come down here to rescue me just yesterday, and they locked him up, you're a savior, thank you again."

"Your welcome", he watched her get on a helio as another person said "Thanks, we weren't really in danger, it was a ploy to get my estranged wife to knock her down a bit."

"Lock this one up" said Jack.

"Wait what did I do, you can't, I'm an American citizen." "Come on mister, as Mark applies the zip ties to his wrists, he was being led out by a Navy man, who said, "He has not a reason to lock you up, he is an International Bounty hunter."

"As I was saying, I think Miss Meyers needs for you to make some decisions on spending needs" said Debby.

"Sure I'll fly up there, for a couple of days, I'd like to get back."

"I'll let her know you're on your way."

Jack watched as they continued to extract the shrapnel from Tatiana's body as Casey stood behind him with the harness ready, for Claire to say, "Put that away, its only design was for you Jack, not every women you see fit to rescue, besides it costs us fifty thousand dollars, to do that."

Jack looked at her then at Casey, to say, "Your right, I was out of line, as he was about to walk off towards the blown up helio when two children ran out to wrap up both of Jack's legs and held on tight to say, "Thank you Mister, I'm Jesse, and this is my brother Skylar, our mom name is Monica Knight can you take us home?"

"Sure", said Jack as he turned around to see Claire, "Oh right, I can't use the weather balloon, Mark, lets load up the boat, looks like there is some kids that need their mother."

Jack and Mark and the two kids hit the dock, and was lifted into the boat, as the SEAL team Commander, said "Wait Jack we found treasures."

Jack phone rang, he picked it up to say "Yes, Commander how may I help you?"

"During the search of the submarine, we discovered some gold and riches, what do you want me to do with it?"

"Have your men tow it out, catalog the entire find, then I'll have Claire check around and if it comes back that no one claims it, it will be yours and your teams wealth, take care."

Jack closed up his phone to see Brian say, "All guns accounted for, as the strike team picked them up to deliver to him, were getting kind of a rhythm down now."

"Good for you, can you go down and relieve Mike, with the children."

"Our destination is still the dock?" asked Mark.

"Yep, I hope you were able to extract the MIR"

"Absolutely, it was all Mike's doing, he is a wiz with all that stuff."

"Where's it at,?"

"In that crate, ready for pickup." "Then let's get it out of here."

"But what about what Claire says?"

"Who cares Mark, it's my operation, and they gave the money to me to use as I see fit."

"That's true" said Mike, to add "That's why I didn't go on the island."

"Why is that, Mike, sit down, we need to talk, Mark can you set it up for pickup, and contact Jim, Jack takes over for Mark, behind the wheel, to add "I've gotten several complaint's that you're not very nice to the women who work with me, now I could chalk it up as you are jealous of them and want to be my partner, or"

"Let me."

"Please don't interrupt me" said Jack looking at Mike with his head down, to add "Mike you're a wonderful and loyal helper, but that is all you'll ever be to me."

"I understand", he said in a apologetic manner.

"I wasn't finished, look at me."

"Cheer up, this is by no means a chew out, I wanted you to feel like you accomplished something, I need you more than I need a partner, you're a specialist at what you do, and I accept that, do you?"

"Yes, thank you", said Mike.

"I wasn't finished, your such a valuable asset, that everyone associated to me are scarred of you, because you're in the spy data bank, as one of my assistant's, so for that fact you are protected, but I need for you to take some down time, a vacation with your wife and family, for a month or so, I want you to go see my wife Sara and she will have a bag of untraceable cash for you, when you get back, come to Quantico and I will have a new assignment for you, until then, I appreciate your service, are we good?"

"Yes, I want to apologize for my behavior, for so long I was this guy who wanted to be like you, so when the chance came up well it was my shot, your right I am somewhat jealous of Mitzi and Trixie, and the slew of new girls all the time."

"But that is me."

"I wasn't finished", they both laughed, for him to say "I realize after the encounter at Miss Monica's house, I was overwhelmed with all the distractions, and all those beautiful women, I don't know how you do it?"

"It's simple really, find a girl who you have compatibility with and is very nice to look at, instantly you'll know if she is into you, then the sex is easy part."

"Did you say sex or next?"

"Either way it doesn't matter, take Jodie for example, all she wanted was a kiss, yes she wanted more, but I gave her hope, and for that she performed her greatest."

"Sorry to hear about her" said Mike.

"So am I, what a shame, I guess I need to keep those I care about back behind me, and allow those the opportunity to shine next to me."

"That makes sense now, what about all the sex?"

"You mean next" said Jack, "Look dude, it's all part of the game, yeah I know your married, so am I but the world is big and mighty, there will be a time when moral belief's will be tested, like at Miss Monica's, if you happen to be someone other than not connected to me, they would have thrown you down the shit chute." for."

"Wait, what's that?"

"It was a trap door, down to a quick sand lake."

"Wow, I guess you do have to be careful on what you ask."

"No, not really you know, take for instance, when I asked Brian to get the two girls guns, I'd rather they had live bullets than dummies, to show them I trust them, but when they were cornered, they showed their true merit, and I took them out."

"Interesting."

"Go back and help Mark, as a plane was seen, Jack slowed down, long enough to see the package lift off, and away they went.

"Miss Meyers this is Debby, Jack has agreed to come up for a visit, but we may have another problem, that worries me?"

"What's that?"

"Well it was something Claire said to him." "Be specific, what did she say?"

"She told Jack that the weather balloon thing, he uses for extraction, is only for his use only."

"So what is the problem then, of course it's just for his use only."

"I know that too, but she implied it was for Jack's use only, no one else, because it costs 50,000 a lift off" Said Debby.

"How does she know that number?, I have it here, it is roughly 2500 dollars a pickup, maybe she was talking about when another service is used, then it's about that number, maybe a little less, but it may be different now that were an official entity, listen thanks for the heads up, is she around there?"

"Yes, but Lisa's group just landed."

"Then you need to get out of there, and make sure Claire is with you."

Lisa's team helicopters landed, in the field, as men in blue suits emerged, she led them to Debby to say, "How is Jack?"

"Not good" she said honestly.

"How so?"

"Well with you, you backed off, till Jack was through, it was Claire's call to jump the gun, and rain on his parade."

"Thanks for the info, I'll deal with it, I know I can count on you" said Lisa.

"Well don't get use to it, this maybe my last interaction." "Why's that?" asked Lisa.

"It's all about the academy and getting more field agents." "Good luck on that."

"Why do you say that" asked Debby.

"Well the German's spent billions of dollars training multitude of agents and not one is alive today, except for Jack, Jack was my find, and he is an enigma, there won't be another like him, we have over a thousand male agents in the field, and not one of them is close to being selected for a license to kill status."

"Why, what about the guys that surround Jack."

"They make huge mistakes, take Mike for instance, he had a choice to sleep with fifty willing women and he chooses one of his own, no Jack will take on thousands whereas most men coward away from that much action, no I see I need to get back involved, and help you out."

"There she is."

"Who?" Lisa turned to see the one barking out orders.

"The one who thinks she is in charge, Claire."

"No she isn't, I'll see you, load up," said Lisa as she met Claire halfway, to say, "Do you have a moment?"

"Yeah, I just finished the last of the details, the SEAL team discovered a huge submarine filled with gold coins."

"Wait what are you doing, I don't even know who you are?" "The President, appointed me to run the base operations, for the new spy academy", said Claire confidently.

"Does this look like your base, if I were you I would hop on that helio and fly yourself out of here before the UN inspectors come in."

"What are you saying, I'm in charge here."

"In charge, you're lucky you're not in jail for obstruction of justice, I'd suggest you get on that helio, Oops here they come."

"Well I'm waiting to see what take we have from the submarine."

"What, who are you, well I guess will wait together" said Lisa.

The UN helio landed, and shut off, as two individuals stepped out, both dressed in white shirts and blue pants, as the guy said, "Nice to see you Lisa, will we ever see Jack, looks like his handy work, who's that?"

"She says she is in charge, her name is Claire" she extends her hand.

"Really" said Gene Garp.

"Oh one more thing, down below is a submarine, loaded, and she may be carrying . . . ." Said Lisa.

"Who does she think she is Mrs Jack Cash?"

The Gene called over to his companion to say, “Looks like we have a goddess complex going on, how do you want to handle it?” “She looks like your type” said Roberta Myers.

“Well we have a submarine down below, that the SEAL’s have secured the vessel, which is loaded.”

“I’ll get the paperwork” said Roberta.

“You know it’s his”, said Gene leaning into Lisa.

“Yes I know the routine” said Lisa.

Gene casually walks over to Claire to say, “What are you doing here?”

“Overseeing the extraction of the gold on the submarine.” “Well its down below, underground, but listen, let me tell you how this all works, there is actually only one person eligible to be here, and that person is a man, and that man is Jack Cash, do you see him around here?”

“Well I work for Jack.”

“Really dial him up, let’s see if he approves you being here.”

She tried, with no use to say, “I guess he is out of range.”

As the UN inspector, just looked at her, to punch in one number, moments later he said “Jack Cash its UN inspector Gene Garp, I have a woman here who says she works for you, really, she said that, no we will account for all of it, thank you for having the SEAL’s present, will do, I’ll tell her”.

“What did he say?” said Claire.

“Your under arrest, as he pulled his gun out to say, “Under the international treaty you’re in violation of three articles of treason and insubordination, which carries a twenty year prison term.”

“Wait” yelled his partner, who didn’t look happy, Lisa watched as the two UN inspectors converged on her, for the woman to say, “Strip, take it all off.”

“What the hell I work for . . .”

In that moment the guy pummeled her with fists and she went down, as he cuffed her, only to see a ground force land, in a weird looking boat, as he jerked her by her cuffs, she began to cry, until she saw the troops, dressed similar to the UN inspectors, as they took her out to the ship, Lisa, saw Gene who held his hand up, as she was allowed onto the boat, and down stairs, to see a guard, who yelled VIP on deck, open up."

Lisa stepped in, to see Claire was nude, stripped of her clothes, her hands still bounded, as she sat weeping, the door closed as she looked up, Lisa began to speak, "Let me tell you how all this goes, currently your charged with violation of the treaty, in most cases, even Jack Cash couldn't save you, you would have been shot to death, and that would be it, the way you talk is so disrespectful, especially to Jack Cash, do you not realize he has the same power and authority as the President of the United States, and for you to send Jack away, like you did, has for one caused a major incident, not national, until tomorrow when it won't be the ruling of our President, it will be a council of the 175 countries within this treaty, especially these two UN inspectors are handpicked by the council to follow Jack's work, also Jack has at his command every branch of the service, and now there is you, I will try to help you but I will tell you this, you're in deep trouble."

"Guard" said Lisa.

"Wait, I'll I wanted to do is help out."

"Help out, who, the Treaty states, only Jack Cash is allowed on US and foreign soil, if he likes he may have any size force with him, when he is through, usually it's the UN inspectors that comes next, when it's clear my team comes in, or vice versa, there is at no time do you fit in, and for you to say you're in charge, you may think it's all about you, but really it's all about Jack, and there are people who worship him, so from now on, if I were you I'd keep my mouth shut, and maybe we will see you in Geneva at the end of the month."

"What's going on there?"

"As I said you have no idea what is going on, it will be the meeting of the Super powers."

Lisa left, as the door slammed shut.

The boat docked as Jack stepped off, with the two children in hand, Mark and Mike and Brian worked diligently, doing their job, as Jack walked the children to the invisible car.

Jesse asked, "How will we get there?"

"By the car, show yourself", it removed its cloak of invisibility, for the kids to "Ooh and Aah, for Jack to say, "Get in", as he holds the passenger door the two kids get in. To say,

"Sleep." Jack goes around, and gets in, to place his phone into the dash, as the knock out gas took care of the kids, as he punched in the coordinates to Miss Monica's fortress, also he dialed her up as she said, "I heard from my ex, that un-grate-full chump."

"That's alright, I have your children and they are safe, should be there in a half hour, or so."

"I'll have the gate open for you, come into the garage and park."

Jack drove the car, as the car sensed a little special care, so the drive was a little longer, at her exit according to his GPS, he drove in to see the gate was up, as he slowed to wave past the guard, and off to the right, around as the two children awoke, to see their mother, the door opened, and they jumped out to be in her arms, Jack parked his car, to see the very happy Miss Monica, weeping as she held onto her children, for Jack to say, "Any word from this Scopus, guy?"

"Not yet, but when I do, I'll call you now." "Absolutely, well I should go."

Jack jumped in, to back out and sped past her to dial up Jim, only to see a plane fly right over him, it landed on the strip, Jack caught up with him, the ramp lowered, and Jack drove on and the ramp went back up as Jack parked it in the grooves. He got out as it shut down, the plane continued on."

Jack got out, past, Brian, who took out and laid out tie downs and Him and Jack secured the car down, then Jack went past his room to see Trixie, who said, "Hi Jack nice to see you, I'll have dinner ready for you."

"That will be fine, as Jack went into the flight cabin to see Jim, and another guy flying the plane, for Jim to say, "Where too boss?"

"To Quantico, I'm interested in testing the car for pickup, and doing some weapons shopping."

"Well about that, it's on hold, Claire put the kabosh on that."

"Well you won't have to worry about her for awhile, listen I'm going to get some sleep, can we slow the airspeed, to give me another hour of rest, before we get there?"

"You got it" said Jim as he follows Jack out for Jack to see a table set up, a hot steaming plate of roast beef, Jack went to the sink to wash his hands, and mouth, he used a towel to wipe off, and took a seat at the table, he drank the milk, and ate the sliced roast beef, with whipped mashed potatoes and fresh gravy, the roasted corn chowder, was superb, as he finished it all with his two chocolate milks, to get up, to see Jim to say, "Thanks, but you didn't need to do that."

"Sorry, It won't happen again."

"Don't worry about it, Jack turned the latch to step into his room, it was semi dark, with candles lit, a smiling Trixie, who said "Allow me to take care of you, follow me."

Jack stopped at his white box, to pull out his weapon, and remove the magazine, he set down and placed the gun in its place, and closed the lid., to turn to see Trixie was nude, as she helped him undress, as he took his time, with Trixie's help even he was weak, yet, as she helped him into the shower, she washed and cleaned up, she dried him off, and led him to his bed, she crawled in next to him to say, "Do as you please with me, I'm all yours."

Jack fell fast asleep.

Trixie laid awhile, only to get up, and get dressed, to slip out, to the galley, to begin the cleanup, to put on the coffee, she sliced up a lemon, into slices, she went forward to the cabin, to hand the pilots a thermos of coffee, and two coffee cups, and the other pot, she went back into Jack's room.

Trixie, set the pot in a warmer, as she undressed a second time, taking everything off, this time slid in on the other side, with her back to him, she slowly eased, in to pick up his hand, and slid it over her firm body, to rest his right hand on her firm breast, and her head was on his other arm, she closed her eyes, but only for a brief moment as he adjusted his position, he was awakening, as she smiled, he was moving his free hand all over her chest, she spread her legs to allow him easy entry.

CH 8

Fun in DC being Enzo Bonn

Jack awoke to silence, he felt something firm and soft, the skin was pure, he felt refreshed, he pulled his arm from under her as she moved away from him, to face him, he saw the time it was 2:35 PM, "Wow" he thinks to add, "I must have been tired", he tried to calculate the sixteen hours of sleep, he looked at her, thinking was that Sara, "Nah, she was a little rougher, to touch, his mind went back to Marci, Terri, and Cassandra, or also known as the three girls on the hill."

He opened his eyes, to see it was Trixie, "What a nice surprise." She smile back at him, to say "I thought you needed some company last night."

"Indeed I did, but the last I saw you was flying off with Mitzi."

"She and I had a long talk, and she made it simple to me, be there for you or find a new place to work, and here I am, here for your pleasure."

"What about Mark?"

"Mark and I, well were really not even an issue, it was he who came on to me and it was him, who wanted this, sure it was nice attention, but we never did anything, you're the only one, who has ever had me."

"You make me feel like I should marry you" said Jack, now smiling.

"Nah, my job right now, is to fulfill all your dreams, for as long as you will have me, and coordinate, the two aircraft we have for you and your teams."

"You do that?"

"Yes, my specialty is logistics, and deboardatation, anything in the air, and everything that surrounds it is my job."

"Really so I say, I want to go to, say the Netherlands for vacation." Said Jack.

"I believe I call Jim, to tell him, what your plans are, is that right."

"That sounds good to me" said Jack.

"Well the way it goes is," she adjusted the sheet, to fully cover her breasts, as Jack tugged on it, she just pulled it down, to say, "Just ask, if you want to see it all or go for another round, this is a mere fringe benefit, you have no idea how many female agents want to be where I am now, as I was saying, the protocol, is that Jim, will call me, saying he talked with you, as to what you want to do, but most times its Mark and Mike, and Mitzi who tell me what they think you want, and now Casey, who's main job is to have the weather balloon, for your disposal, and when we pick up whoever is in that harness, it will be me, organizing where they go and what were your needs."

Jack pulled the sheet down further, to see it all as he was rising for the occasion again.

"Sure, why not, as she jumped on him, the two of them went at it several times more, as next to them, a loud jet could be heard, as it parked, then it got quiet again, then the hatch door, began to turn, as Trixie, stopped what she was doing, to look back, it stopped to hear a loud voice of Jim's who said, "Did you knock?"

Outside of the partly opened door, Jim added, "The last I knew he was in there asleep, look above you."

"Ah shit, sorry" said Brian, as he quickly closed the door. Jack pulled her off to say "I think it's over for now, say another time and a another place?"

He dressed quickly, adding all his stuff back on his body, he took a deep yawn, to see Trixie get up as well, her nearly perfect body in full view, thinking "Yeah, she is sure sexy, for her age, and she sure likes to work out, it shows, he poured out some day old hot coffee, with a couple of slices of lemon, to watch her get dressed, she past him to say, "Next time I'll go slower" she smiled, to undo the door, and steps out to see it was empty, expecting to see the team working, the empty cargo bay it seemed deserted, she went out down the cargo ramp to see darkness, the huge hanger door was closed, she tried the side door, to see the next hanger was all a buzz, everyone was all over that jet, Jack felt her back as he pushed her forward, she turned to say, "No, let's go out the back." Jack let her go, as they exited to the rear, down the stairs, to an awaiting golf cart, which she drove, and Jack was the passenger, time was suggesting it was getting later, as they drove down main street, to see on the right was the assembling of his new obstacle course, building he remembered that were there, were gone, as a field lay to the hill, to show the fresh new clean up, only to see his administration building having a huge makeover, in the south of the building rose a three level parking structure, for her to say, "That's where were going now, it's great, now we all can park our cars under cover, as they turned right at the crossing, Jack said "Slow down, let me see, as he had his hand on her chest."

"Not here, in public please." "Oh, right sorry."

"Don't be, I'm still a little shy about all this."

"Wow" thought Jack, as Trixie moved it along, to take another left, then one more for Jack to say, "Hold on, let's see what all that is."

So she, continued to go to the east as a guard at a shack came out, as they slowed to a stop, he stepped out and saluted, for Jack to say, "At ease Solider, what is all this?"

"Sir, this is the loading and off loading area, for your base supply."

"May we go inside?" asks Jack.

"Absolutely sir", said the guard as Trixie said "This is the first area that was completed, as you can see there is a big turn out for incoming trucks, as supplies from all agencies, are sending us the state of the art in equipment just for you."

The huge newly concreted surface, showed the lineup of trucks waiting to back into the thirteen bay, and off to the very right showed it was the armory, they parked to see that the parking garage hid the commercial truck operation, she parked and they got out, as he held the door open for her, she went in, then himself to see the air conditioned, huge counter top, and a young man behind the counter to say, "Welcome Mister Cash, are you here to see all of your weapons?"

"Sure" said Jack, as the guy buzzed, the door open, the glass door, was unlocked, as Jack past him, the guy's smirk on his face was disturbing Jack a bit, to see eight racks deep of assault rifles, then along the back wall was the large equipment, for Jack to say, "Let me see that one."

The guy was all frigidity, as he fumbled with his keys, to unlock, the grate, it opened, and he reached in there and pulled out the rocket launcher, he admired it, for Jack, to say, "I'll take this one."

"Right now" he stammered.

"Sure why not, are you saying I can't have this weapon?" "No, no sir," said the guy, now very anxious."

As Jack adjusted the sling, to pull it over his shoulder, to sling it onto his back, to say, "Where are all the rockets for it?"

"Over there", said the visiting armorer.

"Good can you load them up on my cart please."

As the guy moved, Jack said, "He sure isn't very cooperative."

"I get that too" said Trixie, to add "I'll carry something for you."

"In a minute, ah, he has the keys, can you go get them?" "Yes, be back soon . . . ." Said Trixie.

Jack went to the next door, he touched it, it opened, to see the long rifle sniper weapon, then the next case, then all the way down which ended that row, Jack turned to see Trixie, as she gives way to Brian and the keys clanking as he meets up with them, his armorer, who said, "They are all open for you, Jack, to add, "Whatever you like."

"How come we don't have this on the plane?"

"We do now, everything in here is in that armory you had built."

"Really." Said Jack admiring them with Trixie on his arm.

"Yeah, did you want to go fire off some rounds?" "What do you think?"

"I'll make the call, and have the rocket range available for a night assault."

"Yeah, hey I want to test all these?"

"I'd say yes, but, the logistics will take some time." "Why's that?" asked Jack.

"Well for one were sharing this base with the Marines, and all shooting are governed under a strict protocol, if we were in the field, I'd say when and where, but here on base everything is watched, but before I say something that might get me in trouble, let me call."

"Go ahead", as Jack reaches in to, to see the gold rifle, he pulled it out, he admired the beauty.

"That piece is magnificent" said Brian, who adds, "The Base Commander, lent it to me personally, all the ranges are yours, just let him know the times?"

"I don't know from now till tomorrow morning?" "Over night?" said Brian, caught off guard.

"Yeah, do you think I can shoot everything, by then?" "Perhaps, I'll need all the teams together for that."

"Well make it happen, hey where is, that other guy?"

"Oh he went back to his unit, you see every time I'm off, armorer's from this base fill in, till I get back, and he was a bit over welmed in your presence, and asking to get all the weapons out, well, frankly he was scared."

"So staff, whom you need", said Jack.

"Well about that, our Base Ops person is in jail in Geneva Switzerland, awaiting obstruction charges, so were fluttering until she gets back" said Brian.

"If she does" said Jack.

"Can I ask why did that happen to her?"

"Well let me put it to you this way, she told me that she was in charge, and that I couldn't use the weather balloon on anyone but myself, so I let her feel the wrath of the UN inspectors, while she waited to extract all that gold we found, or shall I say the SEALs uncovered, so I gather this is one of those pieces?"

"Yes, I actually had it flown back here by a supersonic jet." "Thanks, did they discover who's gold it is?" said Jack,. seeing Brian was visibly upset.

"It's yours, all of it, and the SEALs involved, are part of the Navy that has no right to it at all, but I've said way too much." "I know you sound bitter, sorry about Claire, honestly I didn't care for the bitch, now or ever will."

"Not really, I was hoping to see my girlfriend tonight?"

Jack puts the rifle away, to turn to say, "Your right, you guys need some down time too, call off the range fire, here is your rocket launcher, as he hands it to him, a disappointed look on Trixie's face to Brian, suggests trouble was brewing, as he took a deep breath as Jack said, "That must be your private room, come on Trixie lets go, can we go out there, this way?"

"Sure" said Brian.

Jack pushed open the door that was buzzing, to let her go first, to see the huge warehouse filled with wrapped pallets, he began to think, "Respect, ask before doing", as a familiar face, came to him with a hug and a kiss on the mouth, to say, "Looks like you got the sleep you needed."

"That's what I love about you, you know how to cheer me up, Debby, so a little later you and I."

"Sure, just let me know, is it tonight?"

"Hey what about me" said Trixie, they all laughed, for Jack to say, "So it looks like progress, what was so important for me to being here?"

"Well before Claire's incarceration, we were ready for you to sign off on some operating budgets."

"And now, the whole operation, is in standstill" asked Jack.

"No, on the contrary, we actually have pressed forward, we thought of it as her job, as coordinator, can be replaced, as Erica has assumed that role, but our staff, is set, and is working, there all here to meet you" said a happier Debby.

"Why is it quitting time?"

"Well it was for them, twenty minutes ago, but I can call them back?"

"What hours do they work?"

"Nine to five" said a surprised Debby.

"Oh, then send them home."

"It doesn't work like that here, were all coming in, and they are helping the off load, and securing of weapons, rounds and cleanup, to be ready tomorrow morning for another mission", said Debby.

"So let them go, and we will assemble tomorrow morning at 0900 for a base meeting, do we have a auditorium?", actually you know what, how bout we meet in here" said Jack looking at the glass room, as they stepped through the doors, it was still warm, to hear, "Were ninety percent completed, it is surely remarkable how quickly it went", said Debby, showing him around. Jack marveled at the different food group signs, the breakfast shop, the grocery store."

"That is tied into me, it's a small convenience store, to buy toiletries, and along the south wall is the kitchen, open for five meals a day and a daytime deli, the convenience store will be twenty four /seven, manned by our staff, we were thinking, of using a card to track all purchases?"

"Sounds good, what about a gift store?, T-shirt hats, ect, ect" said Jack, being comical.

"Sure, and we have new offices along the west wall there to house a gift shop, if that is what you want?"

"Good lets go see the rest, using that same card method, you would swipe a card, to get in the north east doors, to the heart of our operations", she holds the door open for the two, down the large hallway, to the right, where a huge control room, of screens filled the east wall, the double doors were open to show the room.

"Looks like mission control" said Jack.

"It is said a familiar voice, Jack turns to see it was Erica, who says, "This is our war room, from this point forward, a camera will be on your jacket's heart in the form of a diamond, with your crest on the left side, were trying to research your background, any idea?"

"There was this woman, her name was, ... hold on, let me check my phone" said Jack as a call came through.

"Also we need to talk", said Erica, bothering him.

"Sure, I really like to meet the staff" said Jack.

"There all over the place, they will be working late, then we will have a meeting tomorrow morning at 0900 to discuss your expectations" said Erica.

"Sounds good here she is, her name is Natasha Rogers, sorry I don't have her number, as his phone went dead.

"We will find her for you and find out about your past, so come with me, girls go rest, see you tomorrow", Jack waves good bye to them, as he walks through a door, that said, "Top Secret Clearance Only", to a secret only door, then to a secretarial pool, Jack notices the worn desks, to say, "Second hand desks, same for the computers?" asks Jack.

"No, there all leaving after the construction, they are makeshift till everything is done, but what is done, is your office, this door has a hand print for entrance if you're not here, a voice command room, similar to your car, recognizes danger, and that person will receive a great shock, as you can see the door is last to be put on, just minor details, on the right is a half bath with a shower, toilet, and sink, it will have everything you can imagine, from hair coloring kits to hair dryers, towels that will be changed out, daily, while you're here, a single person will have a card key, with a tracer, to monitor, where they go in here and how long, there is a leather couch, to see your oversized clear topped desk, here will be a fire proof file cabinet, book shelf, huge wall for displays or gifts received, over there a closet, in side drawers, the visible floor safe, a rug will hide it, a random code be given daily, or just your hand print, were still working out the details, a mirror, and a reading sofa, anything else you would care to have?"

"What about a sitting ottoman, I think that's what they call it, and a small refrigerator" said Jack.

"Whoa, I'm only making a suggestion, you can have it anyway you like" said Erica smiling. She was showing him how he could take her from behind, as she had her hands on the wall, and looking back at him.

Jack follows her, to out across from his room is a long counter, for Erica to say, "This is where Tami your assistant will be at." "Doesn't she get an office of her own?" asked Jack. "Yes, but she choose this place" said Erica.

"Sure seems smaller than I imagined."

"Well that's because all the walls were reinforced, but I know what you mean."

"How many people work in there?"

"Six right now."

Jack shakes his head, to see Erica shows him the first room on the far west side to say, "This will be the orientation room, windows, blinds, and chairs, leads right into my office, as I will be administering the details, as we past the secretary, and Tami's station, this is my office, then or now is Tami's new office, up the stairs there are the remodeled rooms, come let me show you." She led Jack around the corner, and up the stairs, to show him, the new rooms.

"These are done", said Erica, as they walked, they turned to see an elevator shaft, and across from it was number one, for her to say, "This is your room, as she use her key card to get in, to see as the lights went on, a kitchen to his left, with a bar, as he opened the cabinets he saw it was well stocked, then to the refrigerator, which was stocked.

As Erica said, "Mitzi stocked it with what she thought you might like, but I have a survey for you to fill out of what you like or don't and all the changes will be made, a table small was on the end on the linoleum, then south was a newly carpeted, rug, to a huge table."

"You can either push that up against the wall, or leave it," Jack saw the huge bed, and all the pillows, then on the other side was a pool table and another sofa, for him to say, "This is sure cozy, everything A guy could want."

"That was just it, a place you could come to that was yours, to be by yourself, then a full walk-in closet, as you can see its empty, and over here is the bathroom."

Jack looked in to see a huge wash sink, to hear, "No that isn't a raised tub, for you to get into, well I guess you could if you wanted, its design, is a place to wash up, and over there is a discard hamper, all show you mine to see what the women's looks like."

Jack saw two toilets, and a long double sink, with mirror and lights, a huge four person shower, over to a huge tub, that resembled a hot tub."

"That's for the long soaks or the overnight guests" said Erica with a smile.

She pointed to the his and hers toilets, to say, "I could show you how that one works."

"Nah, I think I could figure that one out" said Jack.

"Come on let me show you my room", she said with enthusiasm, they did a left turn to number 7, for her to say, "There are 16 suites up here, all like yours, here is mine."

Jack walked in to see it was fully decorated, for her to say, "I just moved in, but first I met with Lisa, today, while I guess you were asleep, and we had a very long talk about you, your direction, that is as a spy, and most importantly the events that will take place at the end of this month?"

Jack continued to snoop around, as she continued, "Also this and all rooms are soundproof, and camera free, except for your jacket, take it off."

"This one?" said Jack, ready to discard it.

"Yeah, Trixie switched it on the plane, as I was saying, I want Lisa to be with us rather than against us." "That's fine, I like Lisa."

"Good, the next concern is with Claire, what is with you?" "What do you mean?"

"Well when Mitzi went down, I thought she would step in and assume her role?"

"That's fine with me."

"Then why is she incarcerated?"

"I think you were meaning why was she obstructing UN investigators, if she wasn't suppose to be there and they ask you to leave and refuse, whose fault is that, mine, your or hers?"

"Your right, Lisa did ask her to go, and she said she was just doing her job, did you know she had your gold coins in her pockets."

"It's not my gold, it was someone's at one time, but not mine."

"Under the International treaty, that gold has no home, and researching it is taking some time, so as we know all of it is coming up here, to be housed, after a year if no country claims it, then it is all yours, some one hundred million dollars worth, and some of that stuff is sheer priceless."

Jack looked around to see her motion for him to sit, he takes a seat, at her big table, she pulls out a huge manuscript, to plop on the table next to him, to say "Begin reading this, please."

"Before or after we do our business?"

The title said "International Treaty, Super Spy information, read it, sign the last page and mail it back, then burn this copy."

Jack went on and started reading the manuscript, when Erica placed on some music, so Jack picked up the pamphlet, and went for the door, to hear "Wait, I thought we could spend the night together."

"Did you want me to read this or not?"

"Yes, but there is actually, something else I want to talk with you about."

Jack comes back and takes a seat, and holds the document, steady, to listen, as Erica, begins to strip, undoing her blouse, she took it off, next was her skirt, and allowed it to fall, she motioned for him to come to her, as she undid her bra, to allow her breasts to be exposed, for the first time, Jack's eyes grew, to say, "Now those look spectacular."

"That's right you have never seen them before?" Jack continued to admire them, as all she had left was her panties, for her to say, "Come over here and mount me", she reached for him, as he allowed her to take his hand, and he got up, and followed her to her sofa, whereas he sat her down, legs spread, and went down between them and began to lick, and use his fingers in her box, only to hear, 'What I want to ask of you . . . ." "Not now, I'm in the middle of something", said Jack concentrating on pleasuring her as she continued, "What I was going to say was, "I'm getting a divorce from my husband, so that I will allow you to marry me, and I'll have as many children as you want, I do however want to keep my job, and continue to be your boss?"

He responded, "Fine, whatever . . ." continued doing what he does best.

"Are you hearing anything I just said?" said Erica.

She grabs at his ears, to pull up his face, to say, "I have a special request?"

"I know you want it from behind?" said Jack, as he was at the ready, he dropped his drawers and just like that he sticks it in, he mounted her, for the very first time taking his huge thing, he did all the work, as she laid back to take it all, some time had past'd, and several position changes later, Jack rode her out till she collapsed and he followed her down, as he let loose, and rode it out to the finish. He stayed where he was at for some time, till, she turned to say, "As I was saying, earlier" . . . as Jack pulled out, and away from her, he was still swaying back and forth, for her to turn to say, "This is where I should have called for reinforcements."

"I don't know, I'm sure I can find some help?"

She thinks about that to say, "Well maybe, but come here and put it back in, I'm ready to go again, I guess."

Jack obliges, and mounts her once again, as she went an let loose, as it was becoming a mess as he was wrecking her sofa, as she caught her breath, to say, "Just continue what you're doing, I don't mind." Jack was a trooper, but soon realized he may wreck her, and let go a second time. It was as if she was out, and the panting was intense as she was in a position of being in a euphoric state, mumbling her words. Jack pulled out and away, he got dressed, still looking at her, she was wrecked, her legs were spread wide, and she was sweated, she showed she had no care in the world, as Jack went back to the table and began to read the treaty, in places he took pictures with his phone, and finished, he took a handy pen and signed it, on the back side was a pamphlet, he saw all the choices, and went for it, he checked off, chocolate milk, his favorite foods, and what girl he preferred, he looked over at Erica, her legs still spread, thinking about another girl he wrecked on his honeymoon, with Sam, he just needs to hold back. Thinks Jack, as he was through, with the questionnaire, as he went to her, to say, "Go another round?"

"No, no, but I want you or would like you to help a young lady out?" as she closed up her legs, and smiled at him.

"Are you asking me or telling me, and what is she to you?" "Nothing really, although she will pay your fee?"

"What fee is that?" he said kneeling down ready to part her legs again, all the while his hands were playing with her breasts.

"All other agencies are required to pay for your services, then if you capture someone, you get a million on top of that, and lastly if there is unclaimed property left over like cash or coins, well that is yours too."

"What is my current fee?"

"I have you priced out at 100k, So, on to my earlier question, a young woman, has asked Lisa if we could help her, and I told her we would, will you?"

"Sure why not, where does she live?"

"In DC, I have her address here", she was reaching over, as Jack got up, to allow her room, she hands him the paper, to see him going to the door. For her to say, "Don't you wanna know what it's all about?"

"Nah, I trust you, I'm sure the young lady will fill me in." "What about me?"

"How about you rest up and we will go another round" said Jack as he was out the door, out and down the steps, and through the front door, to awaiting golf cart, he stepped on the pedal, and did a u-turn, only thinking, maybe, I ought to go back upstairs and stay with his next wife, but he was halfway to the hanger, to see a flurry of activity, as he parked it, he went over to see Jim, to say,

"Can I use the car?"

"Absolutely, when do you want it?" "Now, I got a mission?"

"Where are you going?", asked Jim.

"To DC, like over by the Georgetown area."

"Alright hold on, I'll have Brian help me out, oh by the way, did you hear about the Police Officers, who were killed, and they were massacred."

"Nah, not really, was it bad,?" "Over 100 were wiped out."

They pulled the car out of the plane, with the door open, Jack slid in, set his phone in the dash, and allowed the car to back up, and go forward, and down the street, to the gate guard, as he was waved on, turned right, and outside the gate, past the hospital, onto the freeway, and up to top speed, and just like that, into DC, he took the freeway to Georgetown, got off, and allowed the car to drive to the young woman's house, he parked to see her lights were on, so he got out, and went to the door.

He rang the door bell, instantly the door opened, for her to say,

"Enzo is that you?"

"Nah, my name is Jack Cash, you asked for my services?" "Oh yes, will you please come in,"

She let him in, he went into the living room, as she offered him to sit, and asked, "Would you care for something to drink?"

"Well now that you asked, Dark coffee with fresh squeezed lemon juice."

She looks at him to say, "You seem so much smaller than what Miss Curtis described you as?"

"How so", asked Jack thinking he should of finished what he started with Erica before coming here, as she called out to him, that the coffee was ready, and came back in, to say, "Do you need sugar or cream?"

"Nah, this will be fine," as he took a sip, to say, "Now that is a good cup of coffee."

"Well the trick is to freshly grind the roasted coffee beans, and then I place a vanilla bean in my bag."

"So what is it I can do for you?" asked Jack looking at her. She looked him over to say, "How does this all work, I give you the money you seek now or after I get my revenge and retribution."

"Now or later, depends, what is your revenge and retribution involve."

"Didn't Miss Curtis tell you what happen?"

"Nah, I was asked by my boss to help you out, so that is why I'm here", said Jack looking at the girl, she wasn't really that attractive nor ugly to look at, he just sat there listening as she went through it again, to say, "The revenge I seek is what was done to my husband, he was killed in the line of duty, beaten and mutilated."

"How did that happen?" "They cut off his testicles."

"Oh, that is pretty bad, and I imagine they tortured him as well", adds Jack.

"Yes, they beat him up and . . ."

"What is the precinct doing about this?", I know the Police Chief, and . . . ."

"Nothing, they can't."

"They can investigate the crime and come to some conclusion on who did this?" asked Jack.

"Well we know that?"

"Who is it?" asked Jack pulling out his phone ready to type it in, for her to say, "His name is King Huffa, and suppose to be from South Africa, where he has Diplomatic Immunity."

Jack looked over his phone, to see he needed UN approval to go after that one, so he texted a request, he waited, a message came up, that said, "Wait till a response is sent over." Jack then looked at her to say, "Alright, that's done, as he begins to get up for her to say, "Wait, I have more?"

"What do you mean? Asked Jack sitting back, to hear, "I know your fee is one million dollars, but I want retribution from all those involved, and for that, I could give you a million two,"

"Really", said Jack looking very interested.

"Yes but, you need to go collect it, that is if you can?" "What do you have?"

"Well my husband I guess liked to bet a lot, well his total from this book is 1.2, but when I went to the bookie, he was only going to give me 200k, and keep the million."

Jack motions for the book, she carefully hands it to him, he looks at it, and takes pictures with his phone, page by page, for all of six years, for Jack to say, "From what I see here, he has 4.5 million due."

She leapt up and practically in his arms, as she was trying to see his phone, only for him to say, "Sorry it doesn't work like that, you can get off of me now."

"Sorry," as she got a good whiff of him, to smile, she said getting off of him, to look back at him to say, "You know you could be a splitting image of my former Husband?"

"And who was that?" asked Jack, ready to type it in.

"His name was Enzo Bonn."

Jack looked him up, and his credentials, to see that there was some resemblances but that was it, to say, "Anything else?"

"Well I want proof, I got retribution?"

"Like how?" said Jack, now getting annoyed with this one.

"I want to be there when you do this?"

Jack looked at her, and then to his phone, and thought about it, to hear her say, "Something wrong with that?"

"Nah, I've never had that request before, it's usually my helpers, but what the heck, like what will you do?"

"I wanna watch you exact revenge on this King Huffa." "How much time do you have?"

"What do you mean?" she asks earnestly.

"Just that, wait in line, things of this nature take time, not to mention the clearances, and then when I do catch him, then I'll have you come and face him, and watch him be deported."

"Wait, I'm paying you for the revenge."

"You have to be more descript than that, revenge is so vague, be more specific and I'll tell you what I can do?" said Jack getting seriously annoyed with this one.

"Exact revenge on the one who killed my husband, what part of this do you not get, are you stupid or something, if I had a gun, I'd do it?"

Jack gets up, and was going to the door, when she grabbed his arm, to pull him back to say, "Listen I'm sorry for what I said, come back in here", as she wheeled him around for them to embrace a bit, for her to say, "I'm just upset over this whole situation?"

Jack sat back down, as she sat by him, her perfume was a bit intoxicating, for him to notice, she pulled away from him, to say, "Are you trying to look down my blouse, you are a weirdo, yes maybe you do get out, reaching for him, she fell into his arms, and she was struggling to get up, all the while he held onto her, until he finally let her go, and she fell back to the floor, she got up and she was mad, she went to the nearest thing, a plate was on display, and threw it at Jack, he deflected it off, and was on the move, to the front door, as the barrage continued, as he was out the door, and quickly he ran to the street, and got into the car, thinking, "Yes, I need to go back to Erica, on his laptop was her book, he opened it up, to see the name of Keith, and at Barney's pizza, so he asked the car to start, he looked back up at the door, she stood yelling, and crying, as he fired up the car and sped off.

The car took several turns, and to a deserted pizza place, at 7pm, not a soul, he got out and said, "Secure, armed." He went into the pizza place, not a soul, till a young guy came out to say, "How may we help you?"

"Looking for Keith, I have a bet to settle", said Jack. The young guy, motioned for him to Hush, and said, I can take you down", with that, he says, "Care for a piece of pizza?"

"Nah, it looks heavy" said Jack. As he followed the guy down the stairs to see a full blown games in action, behind the counter, was a huge guy, wide as he was big, a caller said, "Place your bets, the next race is on, for Jack to think, "Its legal in Cuba", so anyway, he takes a picture of the guy, and it spits out his name, it said "Keith Nicoletti, for Jack to say, "Authenticate yourself?"

"What did you say, Mister?"

"Confirmed", to add, as Jack spoke up, to say, "Alright Keith, I'm here to collect Enzo Bonn's reserves, and winnings", said a confident Jack.

"Did that bitch say what we owed her?"

"Nope this book did, and according to what was owed and what was paid off, he gave you a million to start . . . ."

"It was dirty money" countered Keith.

"That doesn't matter, your stalling, for what, behind him, came down the stairs several men, as Jack pulled his weapon, and shot after shot, till all three were down, all the play stopped, for Jack to announce, "Alright, all the games are over, Line up along that wall, hands in the air, anyone, tries to go for it I will put a bullet in your head, as I was saying, Keith, I don't mess around." "Do you know who you're dealing with?" responded Keith, with his hands up.

"No and I don't care, so I want you to write down this number, as Jack read off, the account number, then said, "Now transfer the 4.5 million as I will count to ten, either slowly or fast . . ."

With his pearled handled gun in his hand, the guy, frigidity to say,

"You got a whole lot of trouble coming your way, you are robbing the Nicoletti family, and that of my brother Daniel?"

"What did you say, are they pretty big around here?" As the guys with their hands up began to laugh, till it was complete, for the guy to say, "Who are you?"

"Enzo Bonn's immediate brother, why do you ask?" "That's where the family will come and visit you later."

Meanwhile back at the Bonn house Kristy called her sister to come and stay with the children. She arrived to run up to her and the two hugged as Kristy was crying, for Jaime to say, "What's wrong dear?" consoling her, to say, in between sobs, I had a guy visit me, and it was awful, he was all over me and he took my husband's book."

"Calm down, what book?" "His gambling book." "What, he did what," "Yeah, he was a gambler."

"Oh, dear, I'm sorry, I guess we really don't know anyone, what was this creep like that assaulted you, let's call Ron, he'll go get him."

She thought about it, to say, "I think he said his name was Jack, Jack Cash."

Her sister looked at her, and then placed her hands on her sister's arms, to say, "Listen are you sure it was him?"

"What are you saying do you know him?"

"Know him, who doesn't he is in all the papers?"

"What do you mean" said Kristy, as Jaime broke away, and went to the local paper, and pulls it up and say, "There is some reporter who calls him the new caped crusader, here he is, as she wipes her tears away, and begins to read, "For all of those rich folk who were expecting a holiday in the PR, withdrawl of those young pretty girls, you can forget it, our man Jack Cash, has just put the famed Miss Monica, the matchmaker out of business, as it was reported to me, his real target is that of the Master Mind, who had better watch out, Jack Cash is on your case, and soon, you'll either be caught, captured or killed, he can do all of that, he does have a license to kill whomever he wants."

Kristy let the paper go, to say, "Oh my god, he is going to kill me isn't he."

"Hush up sis, what could be worse, now what did you say, and do to him?"

Jack was cruising in his car, as the Intel came back, that Daniel had a prominent Attorney firm, worth over 450 million of dollars, so he went to the address, and parked out front, and waited, he had several hours to kill, so he went to sleep, to say, "Secure, weapons ready."

CH 9

Daniel Nicoletti where are you ?

It was 0900 and the 42nd floor was a buzz, as paralegals were loud as they were going over the case load, and in the big conference room, sat Daniel and the rest of the partners to discuss the day's events, and as they discussed the day, he received a call, he got up and exited to take the call, to hear, "Its pretty bad, the feds are here and they have shut down us, and their . . . . the line went dead. He saw it was from his brother Keith, as it was a text that Enzo Bonn, was alive and wanted out and his money, he took 4.5 million, we need help."

Meanwhile Jack exited the car, and took the elevator to the 42nd floor, to see the receptionist for Jack to say, "Here to see Daniel Nicoletti is he available?"

"He is in a meeting, with the partners . . ."

"This way", points Jack, as he did a semi circle loop, to the big conference room, as the receptionist, was pulling his arm, he pushed her back, into a desk, went over it and she was out. Jack tried the door, as everyone stopped talking to say, "Can we help you with something?" said a senior partner.

"Yeah, shut up and will the real Daniel Nicoletti please stand up?"

A guy raised his hand, to say, "He is out, showing the chair was empty, as Jack swung it around and took a seat, to say, "All of you place your hands on the table, any quick move and I'll drain you were your at."

Moments later Daniel appeared, to say, "What are you doing in my chair?"

Jack gets up, to say, "Have a seat, we need to talk?"

Daniel takes the chair to say, "What is all of this?"

"It has come to my attention, that this firm is engaged in some illegal activity, not to mention Defense, Trade secrets and the government and thus is benefiting from these ventures, with a show of your hands how many know that this is true?"

Slowly one by one hands were raised as Daniel pleaded, with them, "You don't need to tell him."

As the senior partner said, "Obviously he is a regulator?"

"No, Mister Christman, said Jack after a picture, showed confirmation on who he was, to add, "I'm just an average guy, who gets fed up when, I found a piece of paper, with your firm's heading on it, in a known terrorist possession, do you know what that means, Mister Christman?"

He spoke freely to say, "Associate."

"Precisely, so Mister Daniel Nicoletti, pullout your phone, and transfer 450million dollars to this account, as Jack read it off, Daniel placed it in, for Jack to say, "All of you that raised your hand, rise up and come to me one at a time, as one by one, they got up and came to him, he pulled out a zip tie, and cinched up their wrists behind their back all eleven of them, leaving four clueless women, shaking their heads, for Jack to say, "Ignorance isn't tolerated either, for you four women, I want you to get up and come over to me, that leaves you Mister Christman, get up."

"I'm not a fraid of you, trying to look for something to pull out, only for Jack to say, "You pull that out and I'll canoe your head, do you want to scar, these four innocent women's life forever."

One guy said, "Ha, innocent."

Mister Christman watched as Jack unzipped his wind breaker, and pulled his weapon, aimed at the guys head, and fired, it hit him, he shook and expired, the guy went down, he was dead before he hit the floor.

Instantly Mister Christman got up, with his hands out as Daniel also was in high gear, till the noticed came to Jack, for Jack to say, "Thank you, oh before I go", Jack went to Mister Christman, took his hands behind his back, and cinched him up, then turned to the girls who were either crying, or cowarding their eyes, to one who had a just right smile on her face, to say, "Alright, stand up Daniel which of these women did you steal from Miss Monica?"

He looked at him, not knowing what he was saying, for Jack to, recognize a girl from the raid on Miss Monica's, to say, "Simone, please step forward, as Jack held his gun out, in the ready."

Un-be-know'st to him, he said, "Are you a spy?"

She stood out to say, "CIA, undercover", we have been investigating this firm."

Jack eggs her on, to divelge more info, for her to say, "Yes, I know about all of his illegal operations, and money laundrying."

Just then Mister Christman collapsed to the floor, as the blonde went to him, and said, "I think he is having a heart attack."

Jack motions for her to get up, and back, as he turns him over, to see snot running out of his nose, to say, "Nope I think he has expired, now whose next, he turns to see the door open, and Daniel has fled. Jack thinks to himself a minute, Daniel where did you go?"

Daniel was on the move, with his phone in hand, he called in some reinforcements, as he went into the bathroom, then into a stall to hid. As Jack motioned for Simone to go after him. Meanwhile Jack observed three remaining girls who stood in a line, with their backs to the glass, in which one says, "What's your plans now?"

"I don't know yet, but I'm liking the whole professional look, and it would be nice to know what is under your clothes."

The older blonde looks at him, to say, "So your thinking of playing a game with us, what will that accomplish?"

"I'll see you naked, that's something I didn't expect."

"So you're asking us to strip?, and for what, who are you anyway, we all have rights, well except for Henry who is dead now?"

"For my pleasure, rights, you don't have any rights, once you have ties to a known terrorist, all of your rights vanish."

Jack moves around, to sit back against the table, to say, "Alright which one of you was Daniel's mistress?"

None moved or acknowledged that question, as they faced him, a dark brunette with cute dimples, in the middle was the reddish to brown hair, and a long blonde, all had a smile on their faces, for Jack to motion, and say, "So what are your names?"

The oldest spoke first, to say, "My name is Burke West, I'm the senior paralegal, as she stopped, next to her on the right, spoke,

"And my name is Renee, Ellison, I'm a Junior Partner, and lastly the blonde spoke, "My name is Sunny Ecyles, so what are you going to do with us?"

"Watch you strip."

"Strip, said the blonde, to add," What for?" "Because I want you to?"

"Everything?" asked the blonde a bit more willing then the other two, as she undid her blouse, and pulled it over her head, as the other two watched, as Jack was amused by the blonde, who smiled the whole time, as she wiggled out of her skirt, to reveal a garter belt, as one whispered,

"I never knew?"

"Hush up you too" said Jack, enjoying the show. She popped her big bra, and allowed her assets to be viewed by him, and them, while the men were still face down, trying to get a view.

She slowly slid down her panties, to show him a thick blonde bush, to say, "What do you think?"

Jack cleared his throat, to say, "Nice, your next", pointed to the middle lady, who wore a three piece suit, slowly one button at a time, till the blazer was undone, she pulled it off, to reveal a blouse, next was her skirt, she unbuttoned it, and it fell away, her near perfect body, reminded Jack of Alex, and when she had only her bra and panties, it was as if she stopped, but Jack motioned for the rest, with that she popped her bra, to reveal a nice set of small breasts, and a frown on her face, as she slid down her panties, to say,

"Did you want them?"

"Nah, you keep them, as he waited for Renee who was stalling, to say, "Are you going to have sex with us?" Jack looked at her, to motion her along, then a huge smile on her face appeared, as she went really fast, by pulling off her dress, to show him she had no bra or panties on, to say, "Now what?"

Jack was growing tired, so he said, "Alright get dressed?" Much to Sunny's and Renee's disappointment, Burke was nearly complete, as Jack said, "Turn around, as she did he got up on her and pinned her to the glass, as she closed her eyes, smiled and said, "Take me from behind."

He cinched up her wrists with a ziptie, and whispered, "Lie down, she wheeled around and went down, to see her boss, had a smile on, for her to say, "What are you looking at? Said Jack.

"Ron, I'm suing this company." Jack placed his foot on her back, to say, "Hush, I may change my mind and take you with me" As he cinches up the other two, much to both of their desires. Jack placed them down on the floor to say, "In a minute or two, federal agents will be here to take you all in custody, now, where are you Daniel Nicoletti?"

Jack was on the move knowing Daniel escaped, so he was heading down the elevator, as it opened in the lobby, as federal agents swarmed, by.

Jack went out, to see his car, got in and off he went.

Some time had past, as he made it back to the Bonn residence, he pulled up in the driveway, got out, and thought to himself,

"I better get ready for tonight."

He went into his trunk, and pulled out a wireless portable camera, and went up to a garage door, tried it, it was locked, he pulled his pick set, and unlocked it, then, went in and saw a ladder, he hit the garage door button, the door went up to see the she devil, who was biting her lower lip, and hands on her hips, to say, "What do you think you are doing?"

"Just borrowing your ladder." "What are you even doing here?" "Finishing a job you hired me to do?" "I didn't agree to it."

"You don't have to, once I was asked, I was on the case, besides, I'm near complete."

"How so, you get King Huffa?"

"No, not that, he has Diplomatic Immunity, but I did make a call to the Prime Minister for South Africa, so I'm still awaiting a response, so what about you . . ." he stopped when a real doll appeared, she too smiled back at him, to say, "Jack Cash, is that really you, you do resemble Enzo, I never knew?"

He stared at her great beauty, who wore a huge smile, she was cute thought Jack as he went past the two of them for Kristy to say, "Sis stop drooling, he is only a man."

"Yes, but a man, I'd like to get to know."

Jack positioned the ladder at the front door, extended it out, laid it against the second floor, and climbed up the ladder, taking off, the sticky back he affixitated the camera on the siding, turned it on, and adjusted it out ward, he went down the ladder, and pulled his phone, to survey and line up the frequencies, to see what the camera saw, he was happy, he put the phone away, and went back for the ladder to hear, "So what are you doing", asked Jaime.

"Oh not much, what about you, your Jaime?" "Yes, how did you know?"

"Oh, your sister told me, how you are the nanny, and she relies on you."

"She said that, you must be mistaken, she would never acknowledge that I can help her, as she watched him, put the ladder away, and close the door, turned the knob, and closed the door, checking the knob to see it was locked, to see Jaime was in front of him and Kristy was gone.

She said, "Now what, what are you going to do?" as she holds his arms.

"What do you have in mind?" asked Jack.

'Why don't you let me make it up to you on how rude my sister was, and make you some dinner, and then later you and I can go a round or two?"

"Perhaps, what do you have in mind?"

"You come in, I'll run you a hot bath, then I'll come join you and wash your back, then you can wash mine, and so forth and so on, she said with a smile.

She didn't wait his answer, she already was taking his arm, and leading him to the back door, he followed.

Later that night, after the bath and a spectacular dinner, Kristy was warming up to Jack, as her sister was smitten by the spy, as six turned into seven, and Jack was relaxed, wearing shorts and Enzo's tank top, Jaime led Jack to her room, and they both went in, he took up a place on the bed, and she was at his arm pit down, half hugging him, in some sleep wear, comfortable, while he was on his phone, coordinating tonight's events. Jack communicated via texts, and listened to Jaime talk, "Jack, you know my sister was confused earlier can you forgive her?"

"Sure, she is off the hook" he continued the details, for her to say, "Will this be our last night together, I kinda like you, especially how large you are, I" . . . .

He covered her mouth, to say, "It's show time."

Outside nine sleek black limousines pulled up, the doors all opened, and over thirty eight men got out, as Jack Id, Keith, and then said, "Daniel where are you at?"

Instantly they pulled out fully automatic weapons, and took a stance facing the Bonn residence, where as one guy had a bull horn, who spoke up, "Enzo Bonn we know you're in there, come out and your wife, your two sons and the sister will be spared."

Just like that a pair of fully loaded black hawk helio-copters, swooped down, one on the north side, and one on the south, streets, to hear, "This is Special ops, put down your weapons, or we will unleash our 20mm machine guns."

Instantly there was a silence, then out from the bushes, the strike team pounced on the men, three to one, and subdued them. Jack got up, only to hear, "Jack please come back to bed, let's make love again" asked Jaime. Jack slipped on a pair of flip flops, and went down stairs, he opened the door, and saw the teams had taken the men down, zip tied them, and were sitting on them, essentially, as Jack strolled up to them, across the grass, to say, "Daniel Nicoletti where are you at?"

A guy was wrestling up to see Jack peering over at him, and then motions for them to get him up, to say, "There you are, it's not nice for you to run away from a federal agent, now you and your family will suffer the most from this."

"I'm getting an attorney, he voice was drowned out by the big black helicopters taking off, with a wave off to Jack Cash, they flew off, and Jack went back up the grass to the door, the strike team and the cars were all leaving, with men inside, till they were gone and the street was cleared.

Jack went inside, closed the door, and into the kitchen, to the refrigerator, he finds a apple, and washes it, then takes a swipe with his watch, it was clear, so he took a bite out of it, only to turn to see Kristy, only in a see through lingerie, to say, "Can I make it up to you, I had no idea who you were or what your capable of, as she was pulling down her top, to show him her beautiful breasts, and till it was down to her ankles, to reveal her thick bush, for her to motion to him, to come to her, she said, "I've grown complacent, I've allowed my husband to wander, will you Enzo, make love to me, like you did my sister?"

Jack looks her over, and then went to her, embraced her, as she led him to the master bedroom, he came in, and she closed the door, and locked it, then turned to see Jack was at the ready, naked himself, still wearing the flip flops, she was awe of the sight of his manhood, and went to her knees, and easily took it fully, and began to work him over, he kept strong and solid, all the while he stroked her hair. After some time had passed, he lifted her up as she went up freely, and over to the bed, and laid her down, he mounted her, and put on protection, then slipped it in, as she held her legs wide out, he did all the work, from time to time, he changed up the postion, as she was growing tired, and wearing out, but he just kept drilling her, orgasm after orgasm, till she could go no longer, and collapsed, forward, while he drilled her from behind, she was out, as she maintained the turtle position, Jack realized she was out, so he pulled out, and watched as her inners ran out, as he allowed her to fall to the bed, he got up and covered her over. He unlocked the door, opened it, and left.

Jack opened Jaime's door, and went in.

The next morning was weird, it was as if he was married to the two of them, a breakfast was made, for him and the children, the five of them ate, as the talk was, "What shall we do today?" asked a smiling Kristy, who for some reason was walking bull legged, while wearing a huge smile.

Jack was enjoying the meal, as his phone was constantly ringing, he saw it was familiar, so he read the text.

"Your quite a hero, but now you have put his widow in jeopardy, what is your plan?" asked Lisa."

"Marry her, and her sister."

"Alright that solves that, now onto a more pressing matter, since your taking down of the Nicoletti family and enterprises, I've gotten several requests for your assistance, from every major city in your territory, not to mention New Orleans, they would love to have you come, in addition the South Pacifica has been spotted there, interested?"

"Perhaps, do I stay under cover or go as Jack Cash?"

"While under cover, you'll haunt this King Huffa, and it will give you time till the UN decides what you can do with him."

Jack pondered his next option, to say, out loud, "How does a trip to NOLA sound?" he looked over at Jaime, then to Kristy, they both agreed, but Jack said, "Alright, I need to visit one more person, I'll have you taken to the airport, and you four will be off tomorrow."

Jack went back to texting to say, "Alright, I'll go to NOLA, undercover, and help out that city, as for my future brides, I need trans . . ." he stopped and texted her, "Will do, see you there."

Then he texted Jim, who, responded, "Were here waiting, room for your girls."

Jack, took his plate to the sink, he washed it up, and put it in the dishwasher, then cleared the rest of the table, then went upstairs.

Jack talked with the girls, and they agreed to follow Jack to the airport, in Kristy's car, Jack went outside, through the front door, looked up at the camera, used his watch, spun the dial, aimed, the ring, swung around and retrieved his portable camera, then, put it in the trunk, shut it, then over to the front of his car, got in, it fired up, and off he went, Sara drove while, he was answering E-mails, different states, wanted his form of law, each city had unsolved case files, whereas the defendants got off, and they were guilty, and Jack was in a bind, because he couldn't send in another agent, it had to be him, exclusively. Jack reached Andrews Air force base, as he was directed to a secure site, by a gate guard, on a motorcycle, to a huge hanger, a smaller door opened, he drove in and around, and parked, behind him was their car.

They got out, Jaime helping young Kenny, and Kristy with Clarance, they hoisted them up, and saw the strike team, a fully armed man, going for their luggage, up the ramp, whereas they saw all the military, and the grimness, and then saw an older gentleman, say, "Ladies, in through this door, is your quarters, my name is Bill Bilson, I'll be your pilot today. Both girls stepped over and into the fully equipped room, instantly their eyes grew big, on the stark difference, especially when the door closed, it was quiet. Jack was in the cockpit, going over the where's and when's, and finally, Jack saw the car come up and said to Brian, what about their car?"

Brian looks down the ramp, and seeing the difference, to say, "I'll check with Jim, possibly?"

Jack went into his room, and closed the door, while Jim, listened to Brian, and lifted up the cots, on the starboard side, with the strike team's help, and the small car was loaded, secured, as for the car, a tarp, was set over it, as for the strike team, they all sat up front in fixed chairs, and waited the flight out.

Lisa had coordinated with Jim, where to fly, and it was onto Lakeshore airport, a small commuter airport with one big hanger, that appeared overnight, and ready for Jack when the plane landed, taxied, the huge door opened, and closed, Bill turned the plane to face outward, and shut it down. Jack was first to emerge, as the humidity was pretty bad, everyone wore sweat at their armpit, as for Jack, well the warm weather, made him break out.

Jim was rushed as he got their car out first, as Jack kissed them goodbye, and gave them the coordinates of their new house in the garden district, whereas Jack had a new assignment, directly from Lisa, report to NOLA police headquarters, a new assignment awaits you.

He walked down the ramp to see his car was ready and waiting, as Jim was talking a mile a minute, Jack said, "Yeah, alright, I gotcha" as Jim says, "Hold on, and hands him a stack of cash, to add,

"Ten thousand as usual, try to spend as much as you can this time, and good luck. Jack got into his comfortable cooled Mercedes, and placed his phone in the dash, and said, "Off to police headquarters." Sara sped the car off of the obscure airport and to the heart of NOLA. The heartbeat of the city, blocks off of Bourbon street, to a sign that read, police HQ NOLA, right next to the old mint building, he drove, and parked that read visitor. He pulled his phone, and got out, and said, "Secure, with recognizable intentions." Jack went inside to immediate hustle and bustle, police in light blue uniforms, of all shapes and sizes, Jack went to the front desk, who was barking out orders, "Cam get me my coffee, and someone answer that damn phone, to see Jack and say, "Who are you and state your business?" "Names Enzo Bonn, I'm here to help out."

Instantly the guy gets up, and following him was a round of claps, which grew louder as the entire floor joined in as the guy said,

"Were all a huge fan, you took down the Nicolette family, as he was trying to shake his hand, while he was being whisked away, by the arm. A tough looking harden cop, said, "Don't linger too long with them, were up on the second floor, my name is Lou, or just call me the Mizer, that was something pretty special to get old Tompkins up and cheering for something, now were in here."

The doors opened for Enzo, as people looked up at him from desks, that went around the windows, as in the middle was a conference, as the Captain stopped what he was saying, to announce, "Listen up folks, we have a new addition to our family, from Washington DC, one Enzo Bonn."

Everyone turned to see Jack, some smiled some were disinterested, and others simply were whispering, especially to harden brunettes, both girls had smiles on their faces, only to hear, "Enzo, will pair up with James, now all of you go back to work." He had his hand out and shook Jack's to say, "Were always happy to have some assistance, especially a man of your caliber and reputation."

"Thank you" said Jack, as the Captain said, "Come into my office I have a few forms to fill out." Jack followed him in, only to briefly hear, from one of the girls, say, "I bet you that is Jack Cash, the International Bounty Hunter."

The Captain closed the door, to motion for Jack to sit, he took a seat at a makeshift table, and the Captain slid a form in front of him to say, "I don't know who you are, and after a finger prints, and for you to take this test, I'll be satisfied, you have two hours to complete. As the Captain left his office. Jack reviews the test, as it read, "Detectives test NOLA, Jack promptly pulled out his phone, and punched it in, and just like the test, the phone had all the answers, he wrote as quickly, as he could scroll down the confidentially answers, twenty minutes later, he was done. He turned over the form, and began to look at his phone, and all the messages, as the Captain, noticed Jack was on his phone and came back in, to say, "Mister Bonn you have time to be on your phone?"

"All finished Captain" said Jack proudly. Handing it up to him, the Captain looked around, to say, get up empty out your pockets, Jack pulled them out, to show him nothing, for the Captain to say, "Let me see your phone?"

Jack showed the Captain, who saw a normal looking phone, to say, "Either you cheated or your who you say you are, twenty minutes, I hope it above 99 percent."

"Try 100, I'd not settle for anything less." Said a cocky Jack, as a police woman came in, and took Jack's prints, and swabbed his cheek, to say, "This should tell us who you really are?"

The Captain motions for Jack to follow him, to say, "Let's get you a weapon."

"I already have one?"

"Really how did you get in here, we have the state of the art in metal detection."

Jack realized he better be quiet, to say, "Mine's not metal?" "What is it then?"

"porcelain."

"You mean ceramics?" "Yeah, I guess."

"Well you're going to have to turn it in, and we'll give you a gun while you're here."

"I'd love to but mine was a present from the President from our United States, and he told me, I should carry this on me at all times, now I know Mister White personally, shall I call him?"

"Nah, as they got to the armory cage, as a familiar face appeared, to say, "Mister Enzo Bonn, weapons please."

Jack pulled his weapon, and handed to Brian, who held onto it with white gloves, to say, "Now, as Brian turned his back, and then did an about face, and handed Jack's gun back to him, and Jack quickly put it away, to hear, "Please sign in here Mister Bonn."

Said Brian with a wink. The captain spoke up to say, "Now there that wasn't so bad, what did you get?"

"Whatever the armorer issued me."

"Excellent, now were all on the same page, have a seat, I have sheet of those that NOLA is about to release from prison, I guess the Feds, had enough of them, scan through the list and see if anyone jumps out at you, then head over to the prison and testify against them, or speak on their behalf."

Jack picked up the paper, scanned the list and saw no one, till the last name was on the list Miss Carly Curtis, Jack punches her up on his phone, and she was one in the same, from operations criminal catch, as Jack read it he remembers her as CC, and gets up to see his new partner, James, who said, "Not so fast, were waiting your test results, then if you like we can do some patrolling, so Jack sat, as two of the more prettier girls comes up to him and say, "We have a bet you're the famous bounty hunter, Jack Cash.

Jack shrugs his shoulder, as she bends over to show him her assets she is working with to say, "It really doesn't matter who you are, If you like you can take my number down and give me a call."

"Call us", interrupted her partner, to say, "My name is Abigail Smith", she extended her hand out for him to see it, only to get it slapped away by her partner, who said her name is, "Roxy, Roxy Carr, you know my undercover name, but you can call me whatever . . ." she said as the two were talking about the sheet, as the Captain, held onto the results to say, "Listen up, our man is who he says he is, he is Enzo Bonn, and he scored a perfect 100, his official title, Lieutenant Detective Enzo Bonn, now go off and get me some criminals, and those going to the prison, keep them in".

CH 10

Carly meets Jack again

Jack caught up with the two girls, as he put his arm around the pair, to say, "Where you off to?"

"The prison, we got a few getting ready to walk." "Really, who's that on our list?"

Roxy spoke up, to say, "Oh this guy named Greg Rice, a serial rapist, we can't seem to keep him in long, he has a way of getting rid of our victims."

"And I have this sleaze bag, counterfeiter who worked with some woman, who he says she was the one, but he is the brains behind, over ten million dollars worth of bills here in NOLA, than anyone else, what about you Enzo, what do you have?"

"I don't know yet, maybe I'll play it by ear, can I tag along?" "Sure, I imagine we can get ourselves into some trouble" said Roxy, holding down on Jack's right hand for Jack to say, "See you later partner."

Jack was ready to led the girls to his car, but was pulled into a police minivan, to hear, "This is the only way over there, no personal cars, were going underground" said Roxy, hooked into him. Jack sat back next to Roxy, as the ride was secretive, and partly underground, to a stop, they got out to see a sea of police, attorneys, families, all waiting a turn, Jack used his phone to take pictures, thinking, "When does all this end?"

They were all led to a huge room, similar to the Supreme Courts room, everyone was segregated, as it was the same old story, the prisoner was humbled by the experience, the family pleaded, the police state their circumstances, and the board would rule, then, if a prisoner had no one, they were free to go, the hot topic was Greg Rice a kid, who liked to rape coed's, basically, kidnap them, rape them repeatedly, and hold them, till he is through with them, then dumps the starved body, either off some sort of tall place like the bridge over the Mississippi, and then if they do survive, he has them killed, or so it seems. He was next he said, "How he was not guilty of this crime or any, he was merely a student in the wrong place at the wrong time, he even said he dated the last victim", Roxy was outraged, as Jack held her back, and calmed her down, as the Mom, and sister, painted a whole different picture, and asked that the nightmare be over, then it was Roxy's turn, it was as if she was trying to convict him of multiple crimes, but in the end it fell on deft ears and he was released. A dejected Roxy was ready to leave, as Abigail was next, and Jack said, "You go ahead, I'll see how this next one pans out".

"Suit yourself" she said in a huff.

Abigail basically lost as well, it became apparent all was getting out either way, the prison was over crowded, and no place for them to go, Abigail lingered a bit, next to Jack, but left, as the criminals became a less of a threat. Last was CC, she appeared, a bit harden, her partner, Carter Grimes was released, now it was a matter of a formality, as she said she was sorry, as asked to say by her attorney, her auburn hair, was out of place, from the blonde he had remembered, most of all the room was clear, as the board manager, said, "Now for the family who's there to speak?" it was silent, till the attorney, said, "She has none."

"And then for the police department?"

Jack stood for some reason, and said, "I'd like to say something?" "Alright I will allow it, state your name?"

"Name is Enzo Bonn, Lieutenant detective, NOLA." "Go ahead Mister Bonn, proceed."

"I'd like her to state her relationship to this Carter Grimes?" She sat in silence, not even looking up, nor caring what was going on, for the manager, to say, "Miss Curtis answer the question, or we shall send you back into isolation?"

She looked up to get a focus on the person asking the question, to say, "What, who is that?"

"His name is Enzo Bonn detective, his question was what is your relationship with Carter Grimes?"

"Oh, were just business associates, why?"

Jack was ready for the next question, only to hear, "This isn't a place of get together, state your business and be done?"

The Jack spit it out, "She will come work for me?"

"Excellent", so say the board, Miss Curtis is now in the custody of Mister Enzo Bonn, a bailiff, escorted Enzo to a holding cell, moments later appeared CC, with her clothes in hand, she wore the orange jumpsuit, to say, "You again, what do you want?" Jack watched as she had her back to him, as she undressed, to say, "Do you mind, I'd like a little privacy."

Jack continued to watch her, as she pulled down the suit, to expose a tank top and panties, which she pulled off her top, still with her back to him, to say, "What do you want of me?"

Jack could kind of see something, that was till she pulled down her panties, and stepped out of them, and saw one breast, and partially in the front, for her to say, "Do you mind?"

"No not at all, you sure not the girl I remembered?" "Remember, who you are, I don't know some guy named Enzo Bonn, sounds like some German smuck."

"Precisely," said Jack, as she pulled up her blue panties, and turned to show Jack her breasts, as she put on a matching bra, then a top, and a pair of pants, then slipped on some shoes, for Jack to motion for her to sit, she took a chair, to say, "Now what do I need to do, blow you to get out of here?" "Nah, I got another job for you?"

"All you are is a patrol officer, I'm free to do what I want." With that Jack jumped up, and lifted her up and rammed her against the wall, he held her arm behind her back, as his leg spread hers as he pinned her up against the wall, and whispered, "Now, I'm not playing around here with you, I got this job for you, and after wards, your free to go."

He held her tight, as she said, "Your hurting me Mister, alright, what is it?"

Jack held her tight to whisper, "I will give you a thousand dollars cash, go get a place to stay, once settled, meet me at Café Bonnet, at 8am tomorrow, you got that, and one more thing, no communication with anyone?" he waited a response, till he dug his leg deeper between hers, at her butt, till she said, "Alright, stop, it's like were making out, and then Jack turned her around, to face him, her eyes met his, and instantly she knew who he was, and instantly, lowered her eyes to say, "Yes sir." Jack pulled some cash from his jacket, and gave her thousand in twenty's.

Jack left her, as she slumped down to the floor, some time had passed, she got up and went out, to a holding room, silent, she made it to the bus, where a short ride, to downtown, she got off, and hurried, to the nearest hotel, and to the front desk clerk, as CC presented her ID, and paid cash, and used a counterfeit Credit card, as a deposit, up to her room, inside, she went to the window, then, went in to draw a bath.

Meanwhile Jack made it back to the HQ, only to get ribbed, for the video of him forcing a girl up against the wall, as Roxy came by, and whispered, "Maybe next time it is you and I."

Same for Abigail, who said, "That was hot and sexy." Several other women, and then James was back, who said, "There you are, no wonder you were gone so long, did you get your fill of that known thief, counterfeiter and bomb expert."

"You don't say?, Nah, I was showing her my point?" "That's what they call that?"

The Captain came out to say, "Who's working the evening shift?" James raises his hand, to hear, "Alright you two, over to the docks, there has been a murder, it seems someone didn't agree with someone who was just released." Spoke the Captain, as Jack followed James down the stairs, at the base seemed like a familiar person, as Jack took a quick picture, it came up as Gene Garp, UN investigator.

As he walked on past, to see Jared, who waved at Jack as he went out, to hear James say, "I'll drive, my cars over here."

Jack followed and took the passenger seat, as James fired up his powerful muscle car, as it roared out the parking lot, he said,

"Your sure getting chummy with Roxy and Abigail, I'll tell you she's off limits, she has a boyfriend."

Jack just sat listening, as James continued on, as the docks, were vast, it was following a road, that showed each a place, to dock, till they came upon, the yellow tape, and a swarm of police. They stopped and parked, Jack was trying to catch up with his partner, who led them into the crime scene, and over to what appeared to be a fatal shooting, the body was uncovered, to see the victim took one to the head, for James to say, "So what do you think partner?"

Looking up to see Jack was elsewhere, over to the building, a small trailer, he tried the door, it was locked, he thought about picking it, but only turned to say, "Can someone, open this door?" James came over to say, "I thought we were looking at the body?"

"Its dead" said Jack.

"Well there are angles, to estimate", said James.

"Or other bodies, as Jack was looking at his heat signature on his phone, as firefighter used a bar to pop the door, James had his weapon drawn, and stepped in front of Jack, to go inside, sweeping the area, on the floor, James cried out, "We got a live one."

Jack came in with paramedics, for James to say, "I found her, can you believe it, but she is pretty bad, one in the gut."

"So what is that telling you?" asked Jack as he took a picture of her, to do a quick scan, it came up with her name, Vanessa, as Jack said, "Take good care of Vanessa . . ." that was the last thing she heard, as the extra oxygen put her to sleep.

"So partner, this was quite a find, how did you think to look in the building?"

"Oh just a hunch, boyfriend over there, a blood trail, up the stair, she probably, locked the door, and fell back."

"Yeah, I could see that", said James, having an idea of his own, but saw that Jack had already left. Now James was following Jack over to the dead guy, as he took a picture of him, as he was zipped up into a body bag, as the coroner, said, “Do you need any more time Mister Bonn?”

“Nope, he is all yours” said Jack seeing James who was answering his phone, as it is constantly ringing, for Jack to say, “Now what?”

“How about we get some dinner at my sister’s house?” Jack nodded in agreement, they got into his car, and he spun out his tires as he turned sharply, Jack was wondering if he could do that in his car.

The ride was short, as everything was less than five miles away, as they were up by the lake, and over to a nice ranch style house and parked out front. They both got out, at the door stood a beautiful blonde who said, “It’s about time, you came over, my sink won’t stop running.”, then turns to Jack to say, “Who is this?”

“Oh he is my new partner, his name is Enzo, Enzo Bonn meet my very demanding sister Susan, the two just looked at each other for her to say, “Don’t I know you from somewhere?”

Jack shrugs his shoulder, for James to say, “Leave him alone Sis, he has just come from DC.

“Alright, you boys I have plenty to eat, I made a lasagna, fresh baked bread and a tiramisu, perfect for a late night of prowling around.”

Jack went and washed up, as James fixed her faucet, Jack snooped around, to see either she just moved in, or liked things in boxes, inside the Master bedroom, showed a whole different situation, the bed was made up, into the bath was bra’s seemingly there to dry, as he felt that they were damp, and matching panties, he went to the sink, turned on the water, lathered up his hands, till he heard a commotion, looked over and saw Susan, was stripping, off went her top, and in that instant popped off her bra, undid her pants, and was pulling them down, in one motion off went the panties, she turned to see Jack was at the door drying his hands froze her, not covering up, she bit her lower lip, to say, “There you are?”, enjoying the view?”

“Yep”, said Jack as he went back, put the towel away, and came out to see she sported a matching bra and panties, to say, “How does this suit you now?”

"I liked you better without anything on." Said Jack, as he exited her room, went down the hall, and to the dining room, where he waited till James was through, he washed up and sat, moments later, Susan appeared dressed differently, with a smile on her face, to say, "Dig in boys, the food is getting cold." As she looked over at Jack and smiled.

Back at the posh hotel, Carly had just finished her bath, and now she was putting in numbers to her disposable phone, especially that of her current boyfriend Carter, as she thought of Jack, and her decision, she had to make, to be with Jack or go back to the life of crime, this business proposal, sounds interesting, as she pulled out the covers, and slipped her naked body between the sheets, turned out the lights and went to sleep.

Meanwhile James and Jack was able to leave Susan, under good terms, and for the rest of the night cruised the streets, as dawn broke, both tired, James dropped Jack off at his car, to say, "Boy, you got yourself a nice ride, when you get that?"

"Oh, it was from the President, you know after taking down the Nicoletti family."

"Cool, how fast she go?"

"Don't know, I'm on for the ride, it practically drives itself." "Well cool man, I think my sister likes you."

"She is sure a good cook" says Jack.

"Indeed she is, she'll make some lucky guy a excellent housewife." Said her proud brother.

Jack waved off, James, and got into the Mercedes, the climate control, he could lie back and get some sleep, only Sara was looking out for him, as the car started, and she drove him home, she came to the drive way, and in the long drive back to a garage, the door opened, they went in, it dropped them down a level, where technicians helped the sleeping Jack out, and to his house, he went in, and found his bed, empty as the girls were both gone. Jack slept past his suppose appointment, however, CC had some company, as Carter, took a seat opposite her to say, "Up to the same old tricks, sit at the busy café, waiting for unsuspecting people you can pounce on, so what are you up to?"

"Get out of here?"

"What are you talking about?"

"I'm being watched" said CC quietly.

"How about you and I go up into that posh hotel and go a few rounds, hell it's been a year?"

"Sorry I can't." "Why not love."

"I got a guy watching me, so get out of here, he should be here anytime, and if he sees you, he'll kill us both."

"Come on love it's me your talking to, what guy are you talking about?"

"He is an assassin."

"Now, your joking, what does he want with you?"

"He has a grudge against me and my husband Jaime." "Really, this is the first I've heard of this."

"So run along, get out of here."

"Alright I'm going, but I'll be watching." He gets up and leaves as she looked around in hopes Jack would be coming soon.

She knew it wasn't today, but thought about, the police station, so she picked up her bag, and paid for her meal, she thought, "Its sure nice to have money to pay for things, and got into a cab, to say, "On to Police Headquarters."

A short drive later, she told the cab to wait, and she went in, her beauty turned everyone's head, especially that of Desk Sergeant Tompkins, who said, "How may I help you miss, he said with a smile. She smile back at him, to say, "I was looking for a detective?"

"Do you have a name?"

She thought about Jack, but said, "I think he is new?" "Oh you mean Enzo Bonn?"

"Yes, that's him, is he here or . . . ."

"Currently he is out till two, but if you want to leave a message, or your phone number?"

She thought about it, and knew it was the wrong decision to come there, until a arm was around her as she wheeled around, only to hear, "This one is sure feisty as she tried to knee him.

"Leave her alone Miz, she is Enzo Bonn's CI." Instantly he backed away from her, with his hands up, as she came forward to the desk, and took a pen and wrote down her number, and said, "Have him call me", she said with a smile.

Jared looked at the piece of paper that had three letters on it, 5, 7, 9. He placed it for Enzo in his new slot.

Jack woke around two, rolled out of bed, the house was quiet, he went into the shower, then dried off, got dressed, thinking about Brian, and realizing he missed the meeting with Carly, and finished getting dressed, went down stairs to the new basement, over to his car, only Jim was there, to wave him off, to say, "This car is so out of place here, come over here and choose something else, a curtain opens, and ten vehicles to choose from, for Jim to say, "Choose one or two, or all of them, Jack looked at all of them, from a truck to a car, and in the middle was Brian's GTO, for Jack to say, "How about this one, but can it be modified?"

"How so, Brian basically said It's yours to do what you want." As several mechanics stood by as Jack was saying he wanted to do a powerful burnout, and something about a supercharger, with NOS system, the mechanics were Ohh, and Ahhing, and all were smiling as Jim said, "That's what they all wish they could do, build a powerful street car, anything else Jack?"

"Nah, I'll take the truck on the end."

"Hey that's mine" said Jim jokingly, as Jack went to it, while the GTO was swarmed over, as Jack drove into the elevator, up, then the garage door, went up, he drove out. The ride was smooth, brand new smell, dual cab med box, sporty rims, and a souped up high performance engine under the hood, but stock. Jack got to the HQ in no time, and parked, now he had a set of keys, he had, he put them in his pocket, instantly that was uncomfortable, then on a belt loop, that was annoying, as he walked in, he saw the police sergeant say, "Mister Bonn, I have a message for you, directing Jack over to his box, to say, "Here you go, a young lady dropped it by." He said with a smile, as Jack said, "So is this my spot,?"

Jared, nodded "Yes."

Jack placed his keys in there, as Jared said, "No, don't set your keys, in there, they'll get stolen, allow me, I'll take them and log them in, and when you need them ask me or one of us, but they we be safe.

Jack walked off, reading the three numbers, 5,7,9, so he punched in the secret code in his phone, and deciphered the code as the most probable, as 5 =212, 7=241, and 9=1305 using one of his ten secure lines, he had his phone call, instantly a voice said, "What took you so long?"

Jack said, "Sorry, I was busy."

"Busy enough to stand me up, I got another issue I need your help?"

"What is that?"

"I got my former boyfriend, harassing me, I want to see you, can you come to my room?"

"Perhaps, I got roll call, then I'll try to get away, should I call you on this line?"

"Yeah, I hope I can get a better phone?"

"I'll see what I can do?" said Jack, as he closed her out, and dialed Jim, to hear, "Yes, the car will be ready tomorrow."

"Actually I was wondering, if I can get a secondary phone?" "Absolutely, we have all kinds, what is your application?"

"I have a CI and she needs a phone, private and secure." "Will do, it will be in your glove box in less than the hour."

Said Jim.

"Fine." Said Jack, stopping to see a new frosted glass door, was installed that read, International Terrorist Group HQ-UN, and went up stairs to see the whole gang, as the Captain was holding court, to say, "We have identified the victim, his name is Wes Thomas, his girlfriend is in the hospital, her name is Vanessa Kinds, she went through surgery, and will be fine, James and Enzo, check it out."

Jack followed James down the stairs, as Jack pondered what was behind that door, for James to say, "Some new task force, on terrorism, anything can help", Jack agreed, and followed him out, to say, "Hold on, I need to get something from my truck."

Jack made it over to the sleek truck, then realizing, he had not the key, he thought about it, and said, "Unlock, and passed his hand over the door handle, and the knob went up, he reached into the glove box, to see a phone, he put it in his pocket, pushed down on the knob and closed the door, to say, "Secure."

Jack ran over to the awaiting car, got in and the tires screeched as James did a burnout, on the wet surface, for James to go back at it, by saying, "My sister is sure smitten by you, and wants to know when you can come over to see her, can I give your number to her and have her call you for a date?"

Jack just looks at him, to say, "Sure, and spits out one of his most popular number, as James was scribbling it on a piece of paper on his dash, to say, "You're in for one good ride hang on . . ."

The hospital was somewhat busy, as James did all the work, getting her name, her room, and allowed him to led, Jack was getting use to this whole hospital thing, up three floors, and down the hall, to a semi-private room, he knocked, as family was in there, they entered as they filed out.

James was beside the girl, to say, "My name is James, Lancaster, and that is my partner, Enzo Bonn, can you tell me what happen to you?"

Her eyes were fluttering, as she spoke softly, James moved in to hear her, say, "A French man shot me?" she said in distaste. James looked back at Enzo to say, "Do you have anything for her?"

"Yeah, what were you doing there in the first place?" "Good question, why were you there?" asked James seeing her pass out. James got up, to say, "Were through here." Jack goes around the other side, and squeezes the tube, looks over her, as a gasp of breathe of air, as she rose up fully awake now, as Jack said, "Now I have you full and undivided attention, I'll ask my question again, "Why were you there in the first place.?" Slowly, she said, "We were there to steal some plans?"

"There finally the truth, as her breathing tube was released, Jack got in her face, to say, "So who paid you, to do this?" "I don't know some guy?"

"How much did he pay you?"

"Ten thousand up front and ten when we had the documents?"

"So where are they at?"

"That just it, we couldn't find them."

Jack looked at her, to say, “Do you know what you’re looking for?”

“Yeah, the guy said it would be in a yellow tube?”

Jack just looked at her, to think back at the desk, where a building was laid out on, to say, “Do you think, that they might have discarded that tube, and was looking at the plans on the table?”

“No, I don’t know”, she began to cry, as Jack unzipped his windbreaker, and pulled his gun, and pointed at her to say, “Are those real or are you just faking it?”

She stopped the act, and said “Fake, alright you got me.”

Jack holstered, and took a picture of her, with his phone, it came back career criminal, so Jack said, “One last thing, where were those that were in the trailer, and can you recognize them if I gave you a few pictures to look at, or?”

“Or over there is my purse, I took pictures of them, in case I was caught.”

Instantly James was all over it, as he dumped the contents, all over, to see her phone, for Jack to say, “Hold on, let me see it, as James hands it to Jack, who swipes it in front of his phone, instantly accessing all of her data, and sending a virus, in to destroy the memory, as he tossed it in the trash, to say, “Were done now, as Jack was on the phone, to say, “Pick up a one Vanessa Kinds.”

“Wait I have . . . .”

Jack led James out the door, knowing what he needed to do now Jack turns to James and says, “What are your plans the next few hours?”

“Oh, I don’t know, work out, visit my sis, you want come along?”

“Nah, I need to check with a CI, over some Intel, where do you want to meet up?” said Jack, walking faster, out of James range, he dialed up CC, she answered and said the room number and the place. Jack was out front, into a cab, and off to the hotel. Jack arrived at the posh hotel, went in, he saw some shady guy, standing by a pillar, reading a newspaper, it was down, as if he was watching someone, his stare was apparent, it was Jack, as he stepped in the elevator, he pulled his phone and snapped a photo, that, took a moment for face recognition, to come back as a one Carter Grimes, up to her floor, he got out of the elevator, down to her room, he knocked three times, then once more, to see she wore a robe, to say, "Come in, showing him her blonde hair, she just dyed, he looked at her to say, "Ah, the Carly I know so well, ready for your assignment?" asked Jack.

"Sure, but I have but one request?" "What that?"

"For you to fuck me", as she dropped her robe, for Jack to see her nude body, he was trying to remember, what it looked like, but remembers it wasn't like that as he said, "So as I was saying . . ."

"Wait, I'm here and in the now, no husband or boyfriend, I'm all yours, do what with me as you see fit?"

"Really, see as I see fit?"

"Yes", as she moved closer, to his zipper, to add, "Allow me this one pleasure, and I'll do whatever you want", as she went to her knees. Jack pulls her up to say, "Listen I don't have time for this, I have a job for you to do."

"It doesn't work like that, I'm the one who has all the power, besides you asked me to do something for you, so I want you to do something for me?" she went back to her knees, unzipped him, and reached in and got a hold of it, to say, "Whoa, your large", and paused to say, "And thick, and its growing, as he laid back spread his legs wide to say, "Now suck me."

Jack looked down at her willingness, almost too eager, but he was ready, he was weighing the two out, and decided to oblige her, as she was getting him harder, for Jack to think, she does have a relativity firm body, her blonde patch showed she cared about matching the rug with the drapes, as he grabbed her arm and wheeled her around on all fours, as he put on protection, and slid it in with ease, her excitement was well worth the effort, as she increased the pleasure, by her enthusiasm, and egging him on to go deeper. She showed him it was well worth it, as she came, over and over again, she kept rigid while he did all the work, he kept this up for the first hour, as now she said, "Come on drop that load already?"

Jack just kept on going, feeling how it was for her to wrap around his member, as the convulsions continued, till finally she couldn't hold up any longer and collapsed, on to the floor, her hole was still throbbing, while he continued on, thinking he could do this all night, his phone kept ringing, till finally, he dropped his load.

He pulled out, and watched her fall over, and lay on her side, she was out and he was calming down as he cleaned up, put it back away, and answered his phone to say, "Yep, what is it James?"

"My sis wants to know it you could come by tonight?" "Sure, I'm just about finished up here."

Jack closed up his phone, to see she was out, he knelt down and shook her, she was out, so he picked her up, and carried her to the bed, went around to the other side, and pulled down the sheets, he went back around, and set her in, and covered back up, to say, to himself, 'I'll have to come back later."

CH 11

Jack, (Enzo Bonn) visit's King Huffa.

Jack left her room, only to see that same guy was out in the hallway, on her same floor loitering around, as soon as Jack saw him, he saw Jack, Jack started to run towards him, and the guy, took the stairs down.

Jack slowed down, composed himself and got into the elevator, thinking, "Her and I have something, maybe another round or two."

The elevator stopped at the lobby, and Jack got out, and outside to an awaiting cab, got in and said, "Police HQ".

Back in the stairwell Carter waited, to realize that guy wasn't after him, doubled back up, and onto CC floor, and at her room, tried it, it was locked, he used a maid's key he swiped earlier, and it allowed him access, and inside smelled of sex, he looked around to see the bed, and went to her, to see she was red, her face was flushed, he pulled the covers back, to admired her body, her legs were wet, she was sweating, so Carter hoisted her up, and carried her to the shower, turned it on with one hand, and as he cooled the temperature, he set her in there, while he stripped himself, and went in and held her.

Jack arrived at the precinct, went in, waved at Jared, and actually saw Gene Garp, to say, "Got any criminals yet?"

"Nope, just waiting for you to catch some?"

Jack thought that was odd, what he said, and went up stairs, to see everyone was working, as Roxy approached Jack, took a whiff of him, smiled and said, "When are you going to give me some of that", she said with a smile on her face, as she drug her hand across his chest. Unaware of his smell, he see his partner, who said, "I've secured the warrant to search that trailer, wanna go, and then we will visit my Sis?"

"Sure, led the way." Said Jack getting a glimpse of Abigail, talking with some colleagues, but saw Jack staring at her, as she made her way over to him, she got a whiff of him, to say, "You have been a naughty boy."

"How so?"

"You got sex all over you, I have to admit, it's kind of turning me on, do you have a moment, as she leads Jack into the women's bathroom, and waits till he is in there and closes and locks it to say, "I have but a moment, can I see it?"

He motions for her to turn around and says, "You first, drop em". With her eagerness, she undid her pants, and pulled them down to show off her butt, and panties, as Jack pulled them down himself, he was ready to go, slipped on some protection, and tried for entry, it stopped for her to say, "I'm ready stick it in, already." Jack tried again, with no avail, as he turned her around, she saw it and said, "Oh my god, your huge", as she went to her knees, as she tried to put her two small hands around it, her eyes grew, as she tried to insert it in her mouth, finally she gave up, as she scrambled to her feet, and pull up her pants, and still trying to hold on to him, she leaned in to say, "This is gonna take some time, allow me a chance, I know I can take that thing of yours, if it's the last thing I ever do . . ." she stopped in mid sentence, as someone was complaining on trying to get in, she let him, go, as he tried to put it away, zipped up, and went into a stall, closed the door, as Abigail, unlocked the door, and saw the older police woman, quickly go into a stall, closed the door, as a loud sound was made, as Jack sneaked his way out with Abigail's help. Jack caught up with James, who was at admin, saying, "They screwed up my pay again, they shorted me 1200 dollars, I was suppose to get this and that, to pay for this and that."

Jack pulls out some money and hands James 1200 dollars to say, "Here take it."

"Really No I can't, but seriously, how much do you have there?"

"Oh I don't know, roughly 7800, give or take."

James pulls him over to the wall, to say, "Why do you carry that much cash on you?"

"Why not, sometimes a credit card can't be used." "True, I didn't think about that, I do know your buying dinner."

"I thought you said were visiting your sister?"

"That was before I knew you had all that cash on you?" "What does it matter if I have cash on me or not?" "Because it's all about the principle."

In the back ground a clerk yelled, I found out the error, Mister Lancaster, you'll see the difference on your next check."

James waved him off, and walked with Jack out the front to his awaiting car, saying, "Now where to the Commander's or the gumbo shop, Henri's on the esplanade, you choose the place, I'm ready to eat."

"What about your sister's?" said Jack seeing a new call came in, it was from CC, saying, "Sorry, I was out, that has never happened to me, what is your job you want me to do?"

Jack decided what better way than just text so Jack wrote a code of his own, ETGNOHETTHOUSCCIFIAP, and added, ASAP, not following the code, and send.

CC was up and dressed, and sat beside her phone as she received the message, saying, "finally someone who likes to play games as much as I do, as she wrote out, GET ON THE SOUTH PACIFICA, for her to say, "That was way easy, and then thought, what does he really want me to do?" then she noticed a pattern, take the three letter, TTUPFA, means the target is King Huffa. And said "Carter who is this King Huffa?"

He comes out of the bathroom, still nude swinging, to say, "Come on help me out, I saved your life."

"You did not, I was in a euphoric state of pleasure, besides I told you I'm not touching that thing ever again, now get dressed I have a mission, who is this King Huffa, and had you ever heard of the South Pacifica?, Do you know what it is?"

"No, but there had been some rumblings of a vast sea carrier in dock, that doubles as a party ship, you thinking about crashing it?"

"Perhaps why?"

"Well honey if you in, and so am I".

James drove out to the dock of the crime scene, it was empty, the trailer was gone, platform everything, as they came to a stop, got out and surveyed the missing trailer, for Jack to say, "It was taken by ship?"

"How can you tell?"

There would be some sort of weight marks on this soft asphalt."

Said Jack, as James says "Now what?"

"How about some of that good home cooking?" "Fine, but you owe me a dinner?"

"Fine lets go get some Chicago dogs." said Jack

"Or a muffalete sandwich" said James.

The ride over to his sis's house was short. They got out and saw the door was open for James as he embraced his sister, next up was for Jack, as she got a whiff of him, to say, "Oh boy, you smell of . . ." and bit her lip and smiled, and let Jack in, to see a serious spread, of crawfish, a platter of both, crawfish and catfish nuggets, melted butter, and the fixings, collards greens, corn on the cob, Jack took a plate and loaded up, he took a seat, and saw he had a text, it was from Sara, she announced, "She was accepted to the New Orleans cooking school, and starts next week, can you come and get me?, or do I need to drive?"

Jack wrote, "Don't worry I'll pick you up, darling."

"Thanks." She texted, as he put his phone away, as Susan sat across from Jack, she kept smiling at him, like he was infected or something.

Jack ate, as it was so good, and continued till James received a call, to say, "I gotta go, but I'll be back soon." Before Jack can get up James was out the door, Susan sat quietly, only to speak up and say, "Do you want more, or anything else that interested you?"

Jack just continued to eat, ignoring her as she now began to talk." "Funny", thought Jack two people, doing the same thing always talking."

For her to say, "I know your secret?"

"What's that?' said Jack in between bites.

"It's called high sexual tension, or HST for short, it's when your pheromone levels exceed all other scents on your body, and spill over onto others, so when you get close to other females, your attraction levels go way up and women are powerless to you, some like myself would love for you to come over here and fuck me, what do you say, Jack, I mean Enzo, so what do you say?"

"Well I say, I could be down with that, under one circumstance?"

"What's that you name it?"

"You need at least three more participants?"

"Three, I want you for myself, right here, right now" she pleaded with him.

"I'd love to accommodate you, but see I'm into what they call sport fucking, ever hear of it?"

She shook her head "No", and said, "But what about just plain fucking, I'm ready and here now."

"Well that's just it, I'm into long endurance fucking." "How so, do you take a purple pill or something?"

"No, just into the moment, but I like it to last for hours not minutes."

"How many hours are we talking about?" "Four hour blocks" said Jack.

"Four hours of you being inside of me? Your right, I may consider this, really, four hours of you inside of me, what like, you from behind?"

"Behind, in front, on the side, from the top and especially from the bottom." Jack continued to eat as she said, "So I do need reinforcements, but who", she said under her breath as she got up, and went to her phone, and made a call, she talked a bit to her best friend, who refused her, then a sister coed, who was intrigued, but said No, and finally a party girl, named Stephanie, who said she would try it, but for an hour well that was out of the question, she turned back to Jack to say, "This is harder than you might think, it has to be four hours, how many times have you done such a thing?"

Jack looks up to say, "Oh several, it's actually my new favorite hobby."

"I'd say it is, you smell of sex." "that's because I already had." "Had what today?"

"Yeah, earlier today."

"God you are a stud, and you're ready to go now?"

"Sure, I'm ready all the time, so call your girlfriends over, and we will all go at it, some will participate, while others will watch, ultimately, all have them will, some more than others, so are you still game?"

"Yeah, but why can't I just take you?" said Susan, to add,

"I'm a strong Italian girl, I think I could go around or two?" "Then let's go" said Jack growing and getting ready, he stood only to see James back through the door, to say, "I got a lead on a ship its suppose to be a party tonight?"

Jack left as he waved good bye, and saying, "Call me when you can get it together."

Susan cleaned up the table, when her best friend came by, and blew into the house, the tall black haired Greek woman, held her friend to say, "Alright where is he?"

"So what you're in now, seriously Sarah, what will your husband say?"

"He has already given me a free pass, for that Adonis I was with last summer in Greece."

"That was all summer long, this is going to be a long session."

"How long are we talking?"

"Well I'm good for at least an hour" said Susan.

"How long does he want to go?" helping Susan with the dishes, and the washing, and putting them into the dishwasher.

"His requirement is four hours, and wants to make sure he has something to put it in."

"What, No way, I could give him maybe twenty minutes top."

"That's just it, he is really into giving pleasure" said Susan.

"And he can go that long, Oh my how big is he, strike that how wide?"

"I don't know, but I do know of what he smelled like, and it like an infectious odor."

"Then if you have never seen him, what makes you think it's going to be all that great?"

"Oh trust me, the way he smells, instantly you'll know what I mean?"

"Fine count me in, oh by the way do you have what he might look like?"

Susan shows her phone and the picture of Jack Cash, for Sarah to say, "I think I know that guy?"

"How so?"

"He has been in all the newspapers, they classify him as the new spy, see it use to be that they were secret, but now with all the treaties, each country has designated a envoy to do its dirty work, and that guy is it, his name is Jack Cash, international bounty hunter, he can surely take me anyway he would like."

Meanwhile CC got the invite from a drug dealer she knew, and was going to the party, as for Jack he and James were going to the boat, the Police Captain, wasn't taking any chances, and called up his own reinforcements, to include Roxy and Abigail, Jack was on the phone of his own, as he called out to the strike team.

"Kilo one five Charlie, this is 1 over."

Jack acknowledged and said, "Take the ship and wound to detain. James slowed the car at the harbor, as cars were waiting the valet, a huge ship or transport carrier, was shutting on cargo, down below, a cargo hold door was open, standing at the door was a sharply dressed man, milling about were very good looking women, Jack got out long before James could get to the valet, he walked up in with others, in a mad dash to the buffet line, huge room, from one side to the other, gorgeous women all around, at center stage stood a proud a distinctive man, big head, bald, a huge tuxedo, with a black cape on the back, on his arm was a gorgeous woman, in a see through dress, as she spoke with a Russian accent, she had attitude, as Jack took a glass of champagne, as the host took the microphone to say, "Eat party and be merry, below a floor is gambling, and a floor above is pleasure, my wife, Pacifica will be holding court, I'll be down stairs enjoy?"

Jack felt a hand on his lower back, he turned to see it was CC, radiant as ever, she smiled to say, "When are we going to go another round?"

"Don't know, I may have a party tonight?"

"Count me in, as she passed him a note, he read it, to say,

"I Got it?"

Jack also saw a fast talker of a woman, one Jess Thomas, as Jack took a picture of her and of this gargantuan of a person, his hands were that of the size of a basketball and just like that, Tim Nelson and the strike team, enters incognito, it was if it was a pair down, King Huffa's girls versus Jack's strike team, led by Paul Clark and Casey, he saw Art, the sniper, probably looking for high ground, and the rest of the teams. Jack found the star struck James, who himself had a reputation, being flanked by two extremely beautiful women, who said, "Hi my name is Lyric, said the blonde, and the brunette, said, "Neci, and you are?"

"Enzo Bonn . . ."

They both looked him over up and down, then instantly left.

"There you go stealing the only girls I might have a chance with." "Doubtful", said Jack as he instantly saw three of his own agents, Audris, Esmeralda and Kosta. Eye contact let him know he wasn't on his own.

""What did I miss?" asked James.

"Pleasure up a floor and business down a floor, choose one."

"Where are you going?" asked James.

"Down stairs, I'll see what I'm looking for", said Jack as he sees CC and goes to her to say, "I need you to find a place and put a hole." He stopped realizing he had the answer all along, his watch, take it off, but as far down as he could go, he took the stairs down, a level to see it was a gamblers paradise, then to another floor, which was locked, also someone was now behind him, he thought about blowing the door, as he turned to see a guy with a gun out to say, "Mister, this is off limits, you need to go up a floor, if not I'll throw you over board." Jack rushed him, knocking him off balance, as Jack kicked his knee cap, to a pop, and pulled his weapon, and used it as a club, struck him down., the guy was out, thinking quickly, he pulled out a piece of explosive set it on the handle, set in the blasting cap, tuned to the right frequency, it blew off the knob, which in turn hit the wall, and down the middle of the stairs, till it clunk at the bottom, with his foot he kicked the door, which opened from the outside, and drug the guy in, and zip tied him up. Instantly he was on the move, as he flipped on light switches, to see it was holding cages, inside was not just women naked, but men, and some wild animals, he stopped to see the torture and the smell of waste, just like a fresh kill. This gross injustice had to come to a stop, as he searched his phone, for confirmation from the Prime minister, but there was still no answer, he thought about what the World Court Justice said, so he dialed her up, to hear, "Go ahead you have reached Meredith Holstein, how may I help you Jack Cash?"

"I have a situation here in Louisiana, whereas a South African national is claiming Diplomatic Immunity, what can I do?" "What ever you like?"

"No restrictions?"

"That's correct, South Africa is a non dissent country and extradite has been waved, with only a few exceptions, the President and the Prime Minister, then and only then you need my permission, so who do you have?"

"A guy named King Huffa?"

"Don't know him, but as of this moment his Diplomatic Immunity, oh here it is expired a year ago, just as his Visa, as far as I know, he is classified as a terrorist, and your free to shoot to kill, anyone else?"

"No not at the moment but thanks, so for the future I should just call you?"

"Precisely, so go have some fun."

"I was going by the protocol and calling their country." "That is what your suppose to do, according to the US playbook, but here at the UN, we have all those waivers and were the ones who issue Diplomatic Immunity, just like you have Diplomatic immunity for whatever you do, good luck Jack, have some fun for me."

Jack closed up his phone, and pulled his weapon, he was on the move, up the stairs a flight where the party was in full swing, Jack holstered the weapon, he saw King Huffa, walking around, Jack moved in, instantly a hot Cuban girl, wearing a see through dress, pulls Jack away to say, "You don't want to go after him Mister Bonn, allow me to as she pushed him into a side room, as the door closed shut, inside a group of women, guns out, and aimed at Jack to say, "Your suppose to be dead, I'm Captain Vick, and your gonna die, as all nine girls rushed him, he barely had time to pull his wallet, and drop it, and pull off the caps, before the wallet hit the floor, he was swarmed, first by a semi nude blonde. He heard, "Get em Maggie, Jack sliced her throat, as she went down, as another came at him, and he stroke her, and so forth and so on, till he made it through six girls, as the Captain held her gun out and fired, every round went down ward to the floor, as she realized what was coming next, Jack did a pirouette, and sliced her throat., Captain Vick went down, holding her juggler vein, which was spraying blood. Behind him lay eight and then he went back picked up his wallet, scraping off the bullets, and reinserting it back, in his pocket. He tried the door it was locked, he went to the other side of the ship, and tried that door, it too was locked, so he pulled out some more explosive, on the door handle, and set the blasting cap, set the frequency, and it blew back, nothing he tried the door it was stuck, he kicked it, then behind him he heard stirring, and went back over to the girls, one pleaded for her life, to say, "You're not Enzo Bonn, he was a coward to you, who are you, I got to know."

"Jack Cash." Instantly all was quiet, in the room, the camera on the wall, focused in on him, as Jack looked at it, to say, "King Huffa, I'm coming for you." Jack reached down and picked up the key card from the late captain Vick, went to the door swiped it, it opened, he stepped out to see everyone was out the party was over, as bodies littered the floor, on one side was the strike team on the other was a set of three girls surrounding the big King Huffa, who was yelling, "Diplomatic Immunity, I have Diplomatic Immunity. Jack waved his crew back, as he took to the center of the room, one by one, King sent a girl, first up was a wildcat, he said, "Go kill em, Meg, Jack did a pirouette, and sliced her throat, she went down, with her throat in her hand, Jack cut too deeply, next was a bigger breasted girl, who used them to get at Jack, trying to use her claws, Jack pulled his gun and canoed her head, as the bullet went around as she went off balanced and died before she hit the ground, lastly a blonde held onto him tightly, as he sent her in closer to Jack, he shot her in the knee cap, her right knee exploded, and nearly parting it from her body, as she fell in a heap. Jack stood two feet from the famous King, who had his hands up to say, "I have Diplomatic Immunity?"

"Turn around, as he did so, Jack zip ties, his wrists tight, to hear, "What no cuffs?"

"Nah, we don't use cuffs, now lie down, as others watched as Jack took his longest zip tie, and zip tied his large melon shut, next he used his credit cards, to strip King's sleeves, nicking his arm he tried to speak."

In walked past the strike team the attorney, who said, "Leave that man alone he is my client, "Jack looked up at her to say, "Who are you?"

"My name is Jess Thomas, I represent King Huffa and all of this property."

Jack stood up and motioned for her wrist, to say, "I'm Jack Cash, International Bounty Hunter, and you're in my custody", he zip tied one wrist then the other behind her back, and whispered, "I guess you didn't get the memo, your under my custody."

"I want my attorney" she screamed, as he motioned for his team to come forward, for Jack to say, "Attorney, hadn't you heard, I'm the judge, jury and the executioner, welcome to my world lady."

CH 12

A long ride to torture a well kept man

Peace was restored as those slaved were released, James was way up to no good, as all came to a crashing halt, civilian looking men, escorted the girls out of the pleasure floor, James was scrambling to get dressed, even Roxy got in the act, as she noticed James, as he cowered behind a curtain, for her to say,

"I can see you James, and I thought you were a decorated detective, you might want to zip up."

As she applied some cuffs, and led a girl out, Lisa Curtis team waited the word from Jack as he led the tall guy over to her suburban, for her to say, "What are you doing with that one, you even zip tied his mouth."

"Yeah, all he says is Diplomatic Immunity, he listened as Lisa said, "I guess he doesn't know it expired a year ago?"

King Huffa's eyes went big, as Jack with the help of Ramon, put him in the back seat. Lisa stood by Jack to say, as the door closed, "I know what you going to do here, revenge for Enzo is over we have him?"

"I'm just doing what was asked, I'll serve him up to Kristy and let her have her way with him, oh by the way, did you do something with her, or my kids, her sister?"

"Actually we had, they went under some investigation and inquiry, there back safely at your house."

"Great I'll be taking you vehicle."

"Wait I know A guy, who does this all the time, an interrogator."

"Don't need it, I see you have a winch on the front, that's all I need." Said Jack getting in, he buckled up and drove off. James was out and now inquiring, "Where is Enzo Bonn?"

No one said a word, as he made it out to see all the arrests, and the captured released, swarms of police, and even the Police Captain, was escorting prisoners out. James just put his hands in the air in frustration.

Meanwhile Jack drove and the King sat up straight as Jack made sure to have him fastened in, he drove to his house in the garden district, parked out front, went to the front door, opened it to see Kristy and her infectious smile, as she lit up, as she went to him, and hugged him to say, "Home for the night?"

"Nah, I actually need for you to come with me, so if you're ready, come on."

He sees Jaime who smiles and gets the two boys off to bed.

Kristy appears, changed, and Jack leads her out to the SUV, opens the door for her, she gets in, to look at the back seat, then puts on her seat belt as Jack gets in, for Kristy to say, "Is that him?"

"Yep."

"Wow, he is a massive guy, bout takes up the whole back seat, what are you going to do with him?"

"It's not me, it's what you want to do with him?"

She thought about it, as Jack drove, for her to say, "Where are we going?"

"Oh, I'm taking you both to a secluded abandoned warehouse, so you can have your fun with him", as the King's eyes got big.

"What do you mean?"

"What happen to all that revenge and retribution you wanted" asked Jack.

"Well that is all changed, I met you and my whole life is different, I'll be married to a real man and not some pretend guy." She said that as she looked around to see King Huffa, as Jack drove to the warehouse district, as he was following his phone, to a place, and inside, and then stopped, as a door went down automatically, as Jack did it with his phone, got out, went to the front, unlocked the winch, and turned on the release, he pulled out the cable and threw it over a metal cross bar, then went to the back door, opened it up, and pulled out the King, as he fell down, as he was able to slid off his mouth guard and he began to talk a mile to a minute, "My team is going to kill you, I still have Diplomatic Immunity, my prime minister will get me home?"

Jack looked at him, as he clipped in the snap hook, and instantly he was retracted upwards, he was somewhat top heavy, and leaning over with his weight, buckled the cable several times, till he was two feet off the floor, he caught his breath, to say, "You're going to be killed."

"Enough" screamed Jack, at the top of his lungs, to add, "Don't you get it, you caused that woman heartache, when you killed and mutilated her husband, now she wants retribution, I say send you along your way."

"I agree with you, send me along . . ."

"Well you actually don't know what that means, what I mean is place you over to the custody of the UN." "I'll take that", he said gladly.

"You seem eager for that, what do you know I don't know?" "Nothing, I do know once my people find out what happen to me, they'll seek revenge on you."

"Really so what you're saying, an eye for an eye, what about balls for balls?"

"I didn't say that, as the beam above began to buckle, as hissing noises could be heard, for Jack to say, "How much do you weigh?"

"Oh give or take five hundred?"

Jack leaves him, to go around and opens the door for Kristy, to say, "Come on, here is your chance at retribution, as he pulls her out as she was getting second thoughts, to say, "You do it?"

"Do what, I have no grudge, with him, although he did threaten my family, what do you propose I do with him?"

"Cut off his balls?"

"You do it", as Jack sees the King flopping around, and just missed a kick, as Jack grabs for an ankle, catches it, zip ties it and then the other, just as the beam creaks some more, he notices a pipe, and then pulls her out, and gives it to her and closes the door, and then goes around and gets in to see the two of them, as she held the pipe up she swung at the King, as he was egging her on, it was like watching a piñata, she connected with him several times, as she motioned for Jack to come, so he put his phone away, and got out, and went over to Kristy to say, "What is?"

I want to hit his dick?"

"Whoa wait mister that's not fair."

Jack pulled his credit cards, and just like a tailor, he cut off his belt, and the pants went to his ankles, as Kristy watched, for her to get riled up, to say, "Take down those shorts."

Jack yanked them down, to see the King's manhood was risen, it was quite impressive in all of its size and girth, as Jack side stepped as Kristy took aim, and connected, as the King let out a moan, as he was crying as she took another direct hit, she caught it again, nearly cutting it in two, as it instantly went flat, tears were flowing as Jack watched, then allowed her retribution, he went back to the vehicle, and on his phone, looked down, and in that moment, the cable broke, and came back to snap and crack the front windshield, he got out as it was too late, King Huffa fell on Kristy, her head was bent back, instantly killing her, Jack rolled the King off of her, his penis was severally mutilated, Jack rolled the King on his back, pushed his now open legs apart, went over and picked up the iron bar, adjusted the grip, went to the king's waist, bent over and yelled, "Tee up?"

Jack swung that pipe, it connected with the King's balls, as Jack drove them home.

The big King was out, as Jack called in Lisa, waited, instantly vehicles swarmed him, got out and Jack saw Lisa, to say, "It over and all is done, the retribution is clear, he is all yours."

"Well actually he is not, he belongs to you, we will take him to the hospital to get stitched up it's a shame for her, she had a promising career being your wife."

"Yeah, I know, it's a loss, I guess the whole Enzo Bonn is over?"

"It is in fact over as everyone now knows it was Jack Cash is in town, and people are scattering, we will call you when the King is ready for pick up."

Jack took one last look at the body of Kristy whose head was on her back, for Jack to say, “She died instantly.”

Jack saw a ride for him as he got in, and the car took him back to Police HQ, where a big van was out front, and those that were taken, were led in, to include Pacifica, she was in a robe, along with six of the other slaves, seeing Jack riled them up as he made his way in, to a standing ovation, led by Jared the desk sergeant, as Jack said, “You got my truck keys?”

Jared threw them at Jack, he caught them, and went out the door, as he stopped as Pacifica said, “This won’t be the last you see of me, mister Jack Cash, or whomever you are?”

Jack received a text, he answered it, as it read, “All secure here, what is next?”

“He put, “Find the trailer with a plans of some building drawings.”

Jack saw another one come in, it to say, “We are ready four strong, four hours my house how long, till we see you?”

Jack looks at his watch thinking what if, only to see it was ten minutes away, to say, “Thirty minutes, as he headed to his home in the garden district, went into the garage, it went down a level, he turned it over to Jim, and went into the basement up the stairs, to see Jaime, he had a frown on his face, as she came to him, he embraced her, as she too got a whiff of him to say?”

“Don’t ask, I’m afraid to tell that your sister is gone.”

“What I just saw her an hour ago?, how why, who.”

Jack held her to say, “It was an accident, a huge car fell on her.”

“What are you saying?”

“Exactly, yes, she died instantly.”

She cried, hysterically, till she came to her senses, to say, “Then let me go see her?”

“Sure, come on,” said Jack.

“Wait what about the children?” asked Jaime.

“Let’s have one of them care over them?” said Jack leading her down, to see Jim, who over heard all of it, to say, “I’ll personally watch over them, go along.”

Jack held the door open for Jaime, she got in, and put on her seat belt, and then Jack got in, and drove into the elevator, up to the top it opened he drove out, and back to Police HQ, not more than five miles away, to the morgue. Jack parked out front, the two went inside, as all was quiet, except the ME, was waiting as Jack had texted her he was coming, she met them, and led her into the outside room, to stop and say, "Careful what you will see is gruesome, are you ready?"

"I guess I just want to see my sister?" said Jaime.

The ME pushed the door open, and led Jaime and Jack in, for Jaime to see Kristy's head on her back, she hid her eyes and wept, to say, "She was right, you'd find a way to kill her."

Jack took her out, to waiting room, for her to say, "I want to get out of here, and I'm taking the children with me?"

Jack nodded and said "I'll drive you back."

"No, I don't ever want to see you again." She sat and cried, as Audris, appeared and swooped in and helped out as Jack left. Looking at his watch it was thirty minutes tops, as he drove into Susan's parking space, got out several other cars in front, and across the street. The door opened, to see Susan, which led him to the kitchen, where Jack saw tonight's participates, from the left side, was a scantily clad blonde, who said, "I my name is Stephanie, next to her in the middle, was a sharp dressed woman in a three piece suit, classy lady, to say, "I, my name is Sarah Hoffman, I'm married, and lastly on the right was a younger girl, a bit shy to say, "My name is Melanie Keller, but I think I need to go, and just like that she left.

Susan stepped in to say, are we still on, with the three of us?" as Stephanie also was losing interest, for her to say, "I guess I could stay and watch?"

Sarah stepped forward to say, "I'll let you lick me but no penetration."

Jack looked at them and was about to leave, when Stephanie said, "Wait, I'm down, let's go in there and show these old broads how to fuck."

She takes Jack's hand, and into the spare bedroom, while Susan and Sarah trail behind curious to see what is this all about, Stephanie pulls off her tube dress, to show her boobs, and then pulls down her panties, lies on the bed, spreads her legs, and as Susan and Sarah both watched, as for Jack he said, to them two, "Strip, take off everything", then that was the moment of truth, it resonated with them, and they slowly stripped as Susan, took off her top, then popped her bra, squeezed her tits, then her pants, and finally her panties, and went in on her friends muff.

Sarah was excited and horny as she unbuttoned her blazer, and then took it off, next was her top, she pulled it off, she too had a push up bra, and popped that off, she undid her skirt, allowed it to fall, and finally, she took down her panties, to reveal a thick bush, Jack was naked, and putting on some protection, as he was huge, much to Sarah liking, who went down on that slick cock, and began to polish it off, for the first hour it modest foreplay, and Stephanie was the main attraction, Sarah was on her back licking Stephanie, Susan sat in front kissing Jack as he was deep inside of her, stroking to his heart's content. She was losing steam as Jack lined them up next to each other, and sampled each of them the next hour, then it was individual hour with Susan, then Sarah who willing gave in to Jack, and finally Stephanie, Sarah was texting to Melanie, the time she was missing out.

The final hour was collapse and exhaustion, as Stephanie the profound party girl collapsed first, followed by Susan, still holding herself not wanting anymore, she collapsed, a wreck. The surprise was Sarah, the wife of someone with pent up feeling, Jack had his way with her, every which way, and in every place available, till he let loose and she did the same, he convoluted inside of her, she said, "Let's do this again, you were fun, I got to get home, she got up quickly and took a bit of him with her.

Jack reviewed the carnage, and then went in and took a shower, dried off, got dressed, and went outside, only to receive a unknown caller, which came up Melanie Keller, so he answered it, to say, "This is Jack how may I help you, "This is Melanie, the girl from earlier, well I talked it over with my boyfriend, and he has allowed me to participate in this, is it still going on?"

"Nah, it's over, as it is now, as I'm leaving."

"Is there any way I can make it up to you?" said the sweet innocent voice. Jack thought about it, thinking how cute she was, to say, "Alright, what do you have in mind?"

"Well you can come over to my apartment, as she gives him the address, he looks it up, and then says, "There is a hotel, right around the corner, get me a nice room."

"Are you bringing any reinforcements?" "Like who?"

"Any more guys?"

"Not needed, you'll have your hands full, so text me the room, and I'll see you in ten."

Jack got into his truck, and off he went he drove slow as the night was thick, the fog was in, as he made it to the hotel, and parked in a parking spot next to it, got out, locked the door, and went inside, as he received the text, as the lobby was busy, he took the elevator up to the fourth floor, got off, and went down to her room, knocked on the door, instantly the door opened, to see a beautiful young women, in a sunflower sun dress, and bare feet, as she say, "Come in, I picked us up some fruit platter, and for your appetite and a huge muffletta sandwich."

Jack looks it over and at her, and says, "What do you want to do first?"

"Can I see it?" she said grasping for his manhood, she felt him rising, for her to say, "And you just went four hours, I'm barely lucky to get ten minutes tops from my boyfriend . . ."

"It's really all about mind control, so what made you decide to go through with this?"

"It wasn't me per say, it was really John's idea, you know to spice up the whole adventure, as she unzips him, and pulls it out, she went back to the floor and said, "Wow that's a monster."

"I told you would have your hands full".

She sat back up, as she stroked it with her hands, for Jack to say, "If it was his idea, where's he at?"

"He is in the bathroom, he wanted to watch?"

"Really, have him come out?" as he watched her take a portion in her mouth.

"No, not yet, allow me to give you pleasure first, he is a bit of a jerk, if you know what I mean, as he excitement was increasing, as Jack had his eyes closed, enjoying the pleasure, only to feel something in his back, and a whisper," Alright Jack Cash, I got you your worth 20 million dollars, cash, so put your hands up, Melanie stop doing that as she fell back saying, "No, No, No, all your suppose to do is watch, you asshole."

Instantly Jack turned around and punched John in the adams apple, he went down in a fetal position, crying, Jack took the toy weapon, and threw it at the wall, Jack pulled out a zip tie, and did his wrists, then to his ankles, he himself was sporting a hard on, as Jack zip tied John's mouth, got up, and went over, and picked up the frightened Melanie, and helped her up, turned her over, her willingness over came her fear, as she was ready to receive him, he put on protection, and lifted up her dress, ripped off her panties, in haste and put it in slowly, as it was an extreme tight fit, but her enthusiasm, was making it better and the fact that she saw her boyfriend looking at her, as Jack rammed her from behind, Jack was out of the view for John, as his eye was going a mile to a minute, Jack had his hands all over her firm body, as she was trying to pull her dress over her head, while still holding him back, her hands firmly on the bed, but was sliding, inch by inch pulling the dress with her free hand, she went to her elbows, giving her hands free, to find her shaven spot, with one hand, her fingers finding their way in, and feeling Jack's manhood coursing inside of her, after a solid thirty minutes, she finally was able to pull the dress over her head, as Jack had a better access to her breasts as she said, "Pop the bra, looking over at her man, on the floor, made her even hotter, as she saw his eye going in a rapid fashion, as she reached back with a single hand, and undid her bra, it fell away, and for Jack it meant he could now hold on to them, as he continued to stroke her, still fully dressed, he was getting hot, and began to shred his wind breaker, next was his holster and gun, his shirt and then pulled off his t-shirt, he undid his belt, and unbuttoned his pants, and let them fall away, as his hands went back to her breasts, as she cleared her head, she turned towards her boyfriend, to smile, as she did a push up, to straighten out her back, and making it easy for Jack to continue to stroke her.

It was actually getting easier as time went on, she was young, but extremely sexually charged, as pleasure was on her mind, as her fingers were inside of herself, feeling the shaft, of his massive size, she was opening to allow this to happen, she was now moaning with pleasure, as Jack switched to holding her hips, but kept on going, she was letting loose, and dropping fluid, as the friction kept it going, at one point he held her head down, to go even deeper, it was if it were a perfect fit, her orgasms were coming closer, and it was building to a huge final explosion, she soaked him, and he was still stroking her, for her to pant, and say, "This has never happen to me, you got to be kidding, you got some stamina, are you into Orgies as well?"

"Yep, just as long as it is with girls?"

"You got it, my sorority sisters will be all over this?" "Stop talking" said Jack getting bothered by her, as she said, "How about we switch?" "Why's that?"

"Actually I don't care if you ram me all night, I just want to get up and put a sheet over John, you know I want our alone time?"

"Will you shut up then?" asked Jack.

"Yes, you can even duct tape my mouth."

Jack slowed his pace, till he stopped and pulled it out, and with it fluids, her gaping hole was flowing with fluid, as her panting was ever increasing, contemplating if it was the right decision or not, she turned to see how purple and throbbing he was, as she turned, to actually, put her whole hand rolled up as a fist inside of her now gaping hole, she pulled it out, as Jack went over to the fruit platter and began to forger.

She rolled over again, tried to get up and collapsed, several times she tried to get up, but she was spent, finally, she made it up, she was extremely turned on, as she, pulled the top cover, and placed it over John, to say, "Now we can fuck in privacy."

"Your boyfriend seems pretty charged, you sure you don't want to do him now?"

"Nope, never again, she said, sharing fruit with Jack, to say, "Look at my body, this is the most I have ever been turned on, and

I'm ready to go again, what about you, it seems if I get you off, will you rise again?"

"Absolutely" said Jack proudly.

"Well then lover, How about I make you cum, so we get all that blood out of there, cuz right now it looks like it's going to explode."

Jack was led by Melanie, to say, "Shall I call in reinforcements?" "Not necessary I actually like the fact I can be inside of you for roughly an hour."

"Hell you stay inside of me all night if you like, I haven't ever been fucked like that, you're bringing this to a whole new level, so come her lie on the bed, eat your fruit, and I'll get you off, then, you can mount me, and stay in me all night long, I promise." Jack took his fruit, and set it down on the bed, she helped him prop up some pillows, she wore a pearl necklace, that she took off, as she waited for Jack, to lie down, and then she knelt over his right knee, and placed her box, on his knee cap, and took that thing with both hands, and her mouth out wide, and began to go up and down, for Jack to ease back, and close his eyes, as she easily got his overly excite, and he blew, she coughed and allowed it to escape as it was a fountain of spray, she wiped it all over her breasts, as she came up and laid on his side under his armpit, she placed her leg over his and said, "There, now when you hard again, put it back into me, and if you're out, I have some protection in my purse, Jack reaches over, to find her small purse, and opens it up, as she felt him rising again, to say, "Oh my god, you're not kidding, her let me help you with that." She took her purse from him, and the two she had, she put on one and rolled it down, as she climbed up, and lowered herself on it, she was squatting and going up and down, to say, "This is what we do in yoga class, but your much more fun."

"Hush", said Jack, as she shut her mouth, and continued to work, for her to say, "Go ahead as you let rip, my goal for you tonight is for you to get it all out of your system, I know I'll be quiet."

Jack continued to allow her on top, as he supported her breasts, and pinched her nipples, she orgasmed, to a point, she just collapsed, on his chest, while he was still pulsating inside of her, finally she was through and rolled over on her back, as Jack mounted her, and continued to stroke her.

The next morning, Jack was still inside of Melanie, but off to the side, as he had her one leg up, and he was still pulsating her, she awoke, to say, "Oh my god, are you kidding me, you had that thing in me all night?, this bed is saturated, she cozied up to him, to allow it to go in and out more freely, to say, "How long can you go?"

"I don't know."

"Well from my estimate it's been 12 hours, I'm seriously getting a great work out, but I do need to go?"

"Why's that?" asked Jack.

"I have school today, actually in a hour." "Or you can stay here."

"Or I can stay here, how about, if I go, I can bring back reinforcements, and we pick this back up tonight?"

Jack continued to stroke her, and to say, "Its up to you."

She felt him, and herself, and thought about it, to say, "I really would like a break, and tonight It will be you and I, and three of my sorority sisters?"

"Suit yourself, if you got to go, go then."

"Oh no, I'm not going anywhere, that's what I'm liking about you, you're so non-judgmental, you just keep it going as long as you like, I'm more than willing to get all that blood out of there, I'm helping you, as she moves up on top of him, to take her hands and cup his face to say, "From this point forward there is only going to be your cock inside of me forever, will you marry me?"

"Sure." Said Jack . . .

"Seriously, I can plan a wedding?"

"Yep." Said Jack as she kissed his face, and pulled back, to say, "Your making me the happiest girl alive, from now on, you don't need protection, I'm ready to have your babies, as she lifted up and grinded against him, to say, "You can have me anyway you like."

"Shut up" said Jack, enjoying the moment as it lasted till noon, then his phone was ringing, as she climbed off of him, and went down with her mouth to finish him off, as the two of them erupted together this time she took all that Jack had to offer, for another ten more minutes, till he finally went soft, for her to say, "There all the blood is gone, now you can have a great day, she extracted herself off of him, tried to stand and collapsed to the floor, she took her time getting up, she went over to her former boyfriend, to pull off the blanket to see he peed himself, to say, "You have been naughty, but I don't care anymore, you have today to get your shit out of my apartment, or I will sic Jack cash on you." She went up past him, and into the shower, meanwhile Jack finished off the fruit platter, then swung around, and got up, stepped over John, semi hyper ventilating, and into the bathroom, where Melanie, was all soaped up, as Jack was bobbing, to show her he was again ready, she motioned for him to come in.

CH 13

Criminal cleanup

James had been trying to get in touch with his sister all morning long, and that of Enzo Bonn, after a night of what they went through this morning was one for the records book, in from the hospital, was the King Huffa, and paraded through the precinct, it was one of those moments that defined and put New Orleans on the map, as for Jack Cash, everyone knew now, he was the same, as Lisa Curtis gathered up the HQ, and said, "I have an announcement to make, as director of the Central Investigative Group, I will tell you, your HQ is credited with freeing over two hundred captured and tortured individuals, and taking down a one King Huffa of South Africa, as led by our man Enzo Bonn, but most of us know him as Jack Cash."

"I told you", said a confident Roxy.

"Now Jack Cash, has the authority to detain, arrest, and kill anyone, who stands in his path, he is the only one, that can do this without consequences, so if you have a case that is lingering, give it to him and he will put your criminal away, over to your left is two agents from the United Nations, they'll carry out Jack Cash's will, do not approach them, they are here solely for one reason and one reason alone, all for Jack Cash's processing of criminals, and the first one is King Huffa, and his attorney Jess Thomas, and I'm sure there is going to be more that follows, I will say, I imagine there will be some retaliation, so be on your best behaviors and help to support our man while he is here to clean up your city, now I'm going to turn it over to your Captain Ernesto Bryant."

Ernesto came to the podium, to say, "Great job all of you, for last night, I want JL to still be working with Enzo, or Jack."

"Whatever he wants to be called, I'd say Enzo, just to keep his cover safe for a while" said Lisa.

"Will do, it will be Enzo Bonn, and for back up "Abby and Roxy, cover the night shift with them two, Miz, your on mornings", said the Captain. Jared raised his hand, "I'd like to go out and help arrest these people?"

"Alright I'll see what Enzo needs, now go back to work," said the Captain, who saw Lisa to say, "So where is our boy now?"

Lisa.

"No idea, probably resting it off, just give him a call?" said

"I don't have his number?"

"Sure you do, dial 000-000-0001"

"Now that is easy, that's his cell phone number?"

"Yep, it is actually the White House switch board, as you can imagine dialing a zero instead on a one."

James was going frantically trying to get a hold of his sister, meanwhile Jack went to Café Bonnet, and had some Beignets and chicory coffee, all the while checking his phone, and from one number there was fifteen messages, all from Melanie, from I love you to I'll be walking with a limp for the rest of the day, don't worry I'm going shopping, and I need to talk with three of my sisters, bye lover."

Jack saw that James called, so he called him back, he answered to say, "Where have you been, seen my sister?"

"Yeah, you left me there, why?"

"Well she isn't answering her phone?"

"Well she was pretty out of it last night, she is probably sleeping it off, I imagine, she will be calling you soon."

"Really, where are you at so we can hook up?"

"On a stake out, actually, I'm here at Café Bonnet on the esplanade."

"Do you need back up?" "Who do you mean?"

"Well Roxy and Abby are here?"

"Sure bring them along." Said Jack as his two o'clock arrived, she sat down, with her hat to cover her face, beads around her neck, and sunglasses to cover her eyes, to say, "That was some night?"

"It was indeed, what is your friend Carter up to?"

"He has some job, to steal some plans, actually, it was those plans you wanted me to find, are we still on?"

"Absolutely, find the plans, divert your boyfriend." "Listen he isn't my boy friend, I got a new lover, as she touched his hand. He pulled away, to say, "Go find out what he knows, and get back on that ship, and find those plans, now leave I have more pressing business."

Meanwhile back at Tulane university, was Melanie walking like she was wounded, as it was all over school, John blabbed, that he was taken down and zipped tied by the famous Jack Cash, International Bounty Hunter, but that was it, no mention of Melanie, except he was no longer her boyfriend as he was capitalizing on his new success. She struggled to sit in her classes, and as the bell rang, she decided to skip the rest, as her mind was on tonight, as she saw her BFF, Caroline Bray a tall blonde, came to her and said, "Darling I just heard?"

"Heard what?"

"That you and John are over, that must have been some wild night."

"More than that, I think I found the stud we have been looking for?"

"He has to be better than John, the last girl was so frustrated she quit, I think we now have an enduring line up, so tell me what is he like?"

As the two took a bench, for Melanie to relax, as she said, "You know when you find that guy that is just perfect but can't reach him, well Enzo is just that and much more, it all started yesterday, I was at the agency, and my boss received a call, from her friend, that she needed reinforcements."

"Reinforcements what is that?"

"Its girls he needed, to give this Enzo pleasure." "Wait are you saying, he took on four girls at once?" "In theory, yes, but I bowed out."

"Why, this was a perfect opportunity to find the stud we have been looking for?"

"Precisely, so I told John about the encounter, and he suggested we role play with him, and he could watch?"

"Now I'm really getting excited, what happen next?"

"Well I guess you could say, he finished up with my boss and her friend and some other girl, and then I waited the four hours out."

"Wait what's four hours have to do with it?" "That's his requirement."

"Seriously, four hours, what do you do in that period of time, it usually lasts ten minutes tops."

"He calls it Sport Fucking."

"Sport Fucking, are you kidding me, it's like we have access to our own porn star, you hit the jack pot, so what else happen, because you weren't there how do you know about what he can do?"

"That's just it, I called him four hours later, he said he was just finishing up, and told him I was ready whenever he was?"

"What did he say, Ooh this is getting me super wet." Said Caroline, licking her lips.

"I suggested he come to my apartment, and he said, go to the Bourbon street hotel, get a room, and text him the number, so I went got the room, took John with me, put him in the bathroom, and told him not to come out till he was banging me, to watch."

"Oh girlfriend that is some kinky stuff."

"I figure he could do me in front of John, and if he was that much of a stud, then I wanted to see it first hand, well guess what happen?"

"What tell me" as the bell rang for the next class, for Melanie to say, "I'm going to round up some reinforcements and prepare for tonight's events, are you going to come?"

"Yes, count me in, but tell me what happen?"

"So Enzo came to the door, I let him in, as he backed me up to the bed, I wanted to know what was it all about, he guided my head down, so I got on my knees, and pulled it out, I have to tell you this, it was massive, and that was still after four hours of fucking, so I made it my mission to get it down, that was till John came out of the bathroom, and stuck a toy gun in his back, and told him to put his hands up."

"Hot, super hot, tell me more."

"So I went to a corner, and in that instant Enzo turned around and punched John in the throat, and John went down, he used some plastic ties to cinch up his wrists and ankles, and one on his head to keep him quiet, then I allowed him to do whatever he wanted to do to me, and he started from behind to allow John to watch."

"Oh my God, that is so hot, what was it like?"

'it was like your huge dildo, and a salami stuck in there, it was wave of ecstasy, I had at least thirty orgasms, and when he blew, it was like a fountain."

A smile formed on Caroline's mouth to nod her head, to say, "Count me in, and when did it end right away?"

"Nope, he was ready to go again."

"What, that's unheard of, how long did it go?" "That's it."

"That's what, when did it end?"

"It isn't, he could have went all day, we went all night twelve hours and it was in me all that time."

"Oh my God, that's why your wrecked."

"Yeah, imagine our sorority sisters, if he did that to me, what will he do with them?"

Caroline put her hand to her mouth, to say, "Your right, you have found a stud, so what does he want?"

"What do you mean, what?"

"Like cash, do we pay him, like we offered other boys?" "Nah, I don't know, All I know is I've found my next husband."

"Are you serious, you're going to marry him?"

"Yep why not, he satisfies me sexual, so what is there left, I'm rich, and we could actually live on love."

"Wow, I'd say he wrecked you, if he is so great, why are you sharing him with others?"

"Well you know how I like girls, and he has a huge appetite, so why not feed him and I get what I want, and he gets to live out his fantasy."

"Come lets go recruit reinforcements" said Caroline, helping her friend up, and she walked gingerly.

Meanwhile in Port of New Orleans, was the Parthian Stranger, led by Mark and Mike and the rest of the crew, Sara had called to say she would be in town tomorrow, and the rest of the wives were going back to Cuba, Jack monitored his phone, and the surveillance at a warehouse, when James arrived, took a seat, to say, "You had some secret, why didn't you tell your partner, now what?"

"Now, what cases do you have you can't solve, James slides a file over to Jack, as another helping of Beignets were served to him, by a pretty young girl, named Tia, who smiled back at him, to say, "Shall I refresh your coffee, Mister Enzo Bonn?"

"Yes", said Jack, as he looked in the folder, for James to say, "As you . . ."

"Hush up, come next to me and sit, your blocking my view." Just then a stunning black haired woman, came out of a shop, in a black dress, and sparkling jewelry, for Jack to say, "I bet she is hot, literally, and spending her husband's money while he is away?"

"Who are you talking about?" asked James.

"She is or her name is Pacifico, and leader of some girl prostitution ring, do you want to follow her?"

"Yeah, who wouldn't?"

"Well I'm not stopping you, follow her, she probably is going back to their compound, set up and I'll be there shortly."

"Now?" asked James.

"Yes, go now, or you may lose her, in that case here is her address . . . ." Jack gives him a napkin, which was blank.

"Wait, let me get something to write with."

As Tia, hands James a piece of paper and a pen, as she bent over, and whispering into Jack's ear, "How about I get off and you and I go . . . ."

She was interrupted by two women, for Jack to say, "Maybe later", and Tia drops a small piece of paper, Jack takes it, in his right hand, to say,"2645 E Dauphine Street, in Chalmette, as they watched Pacifico take off in a sleek black escalade. James scurries away, as the two women take a seat beside Jack, for Roxy to say, "So I heard about, you and Abigail?"

Jack looks over to the smiling girl, to say, "Yeah, It was fun, so what's up?"

"How about you and I recreate that?" said Roxy.

"I don't know it was hot then and now not so much, but maybe if you surprise me, what do you have in mind?" as he looked at her and away from a recent text from Melanie, "All thing almost ready, be at my apartment for dinner at six."

Jack closed up his phone, to say, "So what cases do you have for me?"

"First let's talk about you, and how, we can get you into bed?" asked Roxy.

"Just the two of you?"

"What not enough for you?"

"Nah, I was thinking what I would be doing the next three in half hours?"

"Wait what, how long?" asked Roxy.

"Yeah, when I go I need at least four hours tops."

She looked at him, then said, "What about the wash room,?" "I was being rushed and prefer, that long, but I'll do it anywhere, what do you have in mind?" "Tonight my apartment?" "Who's all there?"

"Well me and Abby?" he saw Abby smiling.

"And who else?" asked Jack, looking at Roxy, for her to say, "How many more do I need?"

"For starters at least four, and maybe from the looks of it up to ten?"

She looked at him like he was crazy, to say, "I don't know, I don't know that many girls, let alone see me in the nude, Abby maybe, what about just the two of us?"

"I don't know, it's just like I was getting started, so if you both can go four hours, I'd say, we could try it, I was only thinking of your sake?"

She leaned in to whisper, "Oh honey, you need not to worry, "I'll go all night with you?"

"Perhaps, but you may need to line up some reinforcements just to be on the safe side, so when you come up short, you'll be able to call them in to back you up?"

"Now your beginning to scare me, Abby said your big, I think I know when I can . . ." she stopped seeing Abby, signal her, to stop, for Roxy to say, "Alright, I'll try, I know a paramedic, who is super cute, I'll talk with her, so what do you call this four hour session?"

"Sport Fucking" said Jack proudly, as she and Abby perked up for Roxy to say, 'Sport Fucking", as Tia, over heard and said, "I'd be down to joining you?"

Roxy looks up at Tia as did Abby, to nod her head in agreement, as Jack said, "There you go, Now there is three of you, as Tia, bent over she whispered, "I know several girls who might be game for this?"

Roxy took a deep breath, to say, "You are cute, I'll give you that?" "Its just pleasure right?" asked Tia.

"Yeah, alright "said Roxy, as the two exchange numbers, for Roxy to say, "When can you secure the others?"

"I could get off in a hour, go to my Sorority, and recruit the girls, how many would you like Mister Bonn?"

"As many as you can?" said Jack, not even thinking, he was smiling, and looking up at Tia, she went in, and kissed Jack on the lips parted his lips, to touch his tongue, and held his head in her hands, and after a minute, released him, for Roxy to say, "Now you're getting me wet."

Tia, takes Jack's plate, and leaves, for Roxy to say, "Alright looks like we're on, tonight then?"

"Nah, can't tonight, I have another arrangement, but text me when you have your group in place.

"What all this build up, and let us off" said Roxy.

"Get your team together, then I'll text you the where and when's, so what case do you have for me?"

"The same one for me," said Roxy. As she slides a folder over to him, he opens it up, to see serial rapist Greg Rice, to say, "Alright I'll pick him up and what do you have Abby?", he looks at her and trying to remember what happen earlier, as she slide him over four files, as Jack places them on the other to say, "What are you girls up to now?"

"We're at you're beck and call?" said Roxy.

"Alright I got a job for you both?" "Sure what is it?"

"Follow around Carter Grimes, known thief and if he does something, take him in."

They both shake their heads, and look at Jack, who say, "Off with you both."

They leave, and Tia comes back over, to take a seat, to say, "I just got off the phone with my sorority girls, and they said, you're welcome any time, so when can we expect you?"

"Oh maybe tomorrow, what's better for you?" "For me personally it's in the morning?" said Tia. "So say, four in the morning?" said Jack.

"Yeah that should work, you'll get all the girls, you could ever want."

"How many to be exact?" asked Jack.

"Over eighteen?" said Tia proudly.

"Really, and I can just come over and they are down with this?" said Jack who was rising just thinking about the encounter.

"Yep, you see were all pent up, and most of the guys are gay around here, and so, most of the girls are Virgins, so this would be a refreshing change from doing nothing?" as she stretched her hands around his head, to say, "You got to be the most handsome man I have ever seen, and you're a cop, that's hot, not to mention your name and what you did in New Jersey, you're like a serious protector, and that brings me to a point we have a sorority sister who is being harassed by a stalker, he literally raped her the other night, she is scared for her life, can you take care of him?"

"Got a name?"

"Yeah, it is Greg Rice."

"He is on the top of my list, "I'll have him today."

"Really, she stood up, and kissed him again, to break apart to say,

"You do this and you'll have a friend for life, thank you, can you text me when it's done?"

"Sure?" said Jack, looking over his phone, for her to say,

"Care for anything else?" smiling at him. Nah, I'm full, what do I owe you?"

"Nothing it's on the house", she said, as she got up, backing up showing her hands, and running into someone, to say, "I'm sorry, as Jack pulls out his wad of cash, and pulls a 100 dollar bill, and sets it under the powered sugar container. Gets up, and goes over to his truck, gets in and drives off.

An excited waitress comes to Tia, to say, "Look what your rich guy left you, showing her the 100 dollar bill, to say, "You must of done something special to receive that?"

"No, not yet, but tomorrow morning, I'm going to give him the ride of his life."

"Oh you're so bad."

Jack met up with James at the precinct, and Jack said, "Lets go pick up some criminals, do you have a van we could use to collect them?"

"Yeah, but it's the police sergeant's, and their crew's." "Fine get them involve."

"What are you going to do?"

"Just go up to their door, and take them into custody." "How convenient, your able to do that, we'll have the city cleaned up in no time?"

"That is my objective." Said Jack as he followed James in, and tossed his keys to Jared, who had a smile on his face, as he was handing out vests, as Jack went upstairs.

Meanwhile, Abby and Roxy, met up with Roxy's friend, as she had texted her, she wanted to meet, as they met, at an intersection, as she got out and Roxy, said, "Listen I got a proposal for you, I got a guy I really like, but he is an endurance man, and needs some help, would you participate with us?"

"Who you and Abby, that could be hot, I'd be game, what do you want me to do and how long are we talking about, ten minutes or so?"

"Oh no, I said endurance, try four hours plus" said Roxy.

"What, when, that would sum up my entire sexual experience in one night, four hours, are you kidding me, they call that something, you know what I'm talking about?"

"Hold on, you know about the four hours?"

"Yeah, we had a call earlier from a woman who was wrecked, she participated in what she called sport fucking, some guy drilled her for that time, and it was a mess, and now you got something like this, it is probably the same guy, I don't know?"

"What happen to her?"

"He spread her wide, it was a huge gaping hole." "How old was the girl?"

"Twenty something?"

"Oh shit, maybe I should reconsider this?"

"To tell you the truth he is probably a criminal for what he is doing to those women."

"Really you feel that way?"

"No, but I'm actually kind of excited about all of this, I guess you can say I'll be game, just text me the time and place."

The two hugged and then kissed and lingered, to break apart, as the ambulance took off, and Roxy got back into her car.

After a run to the store to get supplies for the evening, Melanie and Caroline made it back to the sorority, Sigma, sigma, tau, or SST for short, as they met with the other two seniors, up in Cheryl's room, to see her Melanie said, "I think I have a solution to the Virgin problem?"

"Let me guess, you found a stud?" "How did you know?"

"Its all over school, how some guy pony fucked you last night, as your boy friend watched, so, how was it?"

"Rather good, that's why I'm here." "To do what?"

"To recruit reinforcements." "So what do you need?"

"Tonight, at least two more girls?"

"Who do you have now?" asked Cheryl.

"Well Caroline is coming, and she volunteered Lindsay, and I just need another?"

"Take your choice, from Tiegan, Mary, or Claudia."

"I or we were thinking we would ask whoever wanted to go" said Melanie.

"Alright, I can see where this is heading, if he Is half as good as John is bragging, then count me in as well?"

"No, in time, I don't want to bring in all the pros now, and overwhelm him" said Melanie.

"What's there to overwhelm, all he is going to do is fuck you, besides I've got to get the girls ready for their big trip in a couple of days, I'm taking, Virgin Regan, Virgin Darla, and somewhat experienced Paula, so go and have fun, and give me all the good details later."

The two girls made it down stairs, to see all the girls had assembled, as those were giggling, and listened as Melanie began "Listen up girls, I have finally found a stud, who will wipe away your virginity, and for those who have some experience, he is a pro, so who wants' to be in tonight, as they looked around the room, to see Lindsay, Caroline's girl, a young lady, with a petite figure as Melanie saw Kara a sassy blonde, nearly perfect body, she was a freshman, to say, "Alright I'll try it."

For Melanie to say, after today, I'll expect full cooperation, so I put up a sign up sheet, place your name down and I'll be back tomorrow and the next day till were through everyone, any questions?"

A big breasted Claudia raised her hand, to say, "What was it like to have that thing in there all night?"

"Think of your dildo and the wettest it has ever been, jammed up as far as you can take it, to taste it."

"Wow" said Tiegan, with her hands to her face, for girls getting ready for the trip to Honduras, they were told by Cheryl, "You'll all have to do a session before you go, so I signed up Myself, Paula, Darla and you Regan, tomorrow."

They all just shook their head in acknowledgement.

Jack heard the whooping and hollering, as it was getting close, to leaving, he went down stairs to see Jared had a group of his officers, who said, "We are ready to be your ride, care to take the passenger seat?"

Jack followed them outside to see the van, Jack got in, to a air conditioned vehicle, as Jared took the driver's seat, and the rest of the team went in the back, as Jack said, I first want to go visit a house on North Miro in Mid city, on the eight block, 807.

Jared drove a short ways, onto that street, to see a single house in the middle of the street, as Jared was looking in his GPS for it and who lived there, he stopped, and Jack set the files up on the dash, and went out up the way to the front door, as everyone waited.

Jack knocked on the door, and waited till he heard, "Hold on."

The guy opens the door, to see Jack, to say, "What do you need?" "I'm with the police department, and we have discovered a guy who says you were part of a heist four years ago, is this true?" "No, I don't know anything about a heist, how much did they get?"

"20 million dollars."

"Really, and what do you want me to do?"

"I D one of the guys, and clear your name, and then it will be over."

"Sure why not, it could be fun right?" said Roger, to add,

"Hold on let me get some shoes on, to add, "You said your name was ?"

"Enzo Bonn."

"Aren't you gonna ask me my name?"

"Nah, I have it here, as Jack took a picture of him that said,

"Roger Hays", career criminal, armed and dangerous."

Jack escorts Roger to the van, Jack opens the back, for Roger to see the cops, to say, "Whoa this is a party."

"Nah, were on for the ride, said Jared helping Roger in the back. He got up front, to see Jack cross him off the list, to say, "Now onto the Cajun country, and a place called Good Hope, and gave Jared the address, and Jared drove, he got onto the free way, and out past the airport, and off hwy 61, into the little quaint town, as Jared says, "So what are you gonna tell this guy, he'll see this police van a mile away."

"So we will go in and I'll ask him and his family to come along peacefully." As Jared shook his head in disbelief, he slowed to the gate, it was closed, so Jack said, "Stay here, I'll go get someone to open it, and let you in,", Jack was out, before, Jared could offer some assistance.

Jack scaled the fence, and walked up the road towards the house, on both sides was huge oak trees line the path, at the doors end, stood a red haired woman, as she made out Jack to say, "Mister you are trespassing, if you come any closer I'll shoot."

Jack continued onward, as she went back in and got a shotgun, came out to say, "Hold on their mister, come any closer and I'll shoot you dead as to where you stand, I have a right to defend our property."

Jack finally spoke up, to say, "I have a paper here, to bring in your daughter Linda, is she available?"

There was a pause, as she turned, back in, then another figure emerged, for the new woman to cry out, "Who says are you?"

"I'm Enzo Bonn NOLA police department, would like you and your mom to come down to the station and clear your son of any wrong doings he may of caused, is he there right now?"

"Are you alone?"

"Yes, look around who else do I have, said Jack as he got closer, to about the shotgun range, and for Jack to see how ugly the sister was, for Jack to say, "Says here you vandalized a one Bradley Bolton's house, did you do that, Linda?"

She paused, then said, "Yeah, so what?"

"Well he has pressed charges and would like you to come in and see what we have for you, can you do that?"

"I guess, hold on."

Jack waited, to only see Linda come up to him, as Jack said, "You carrying?"

"Nope, it is just questions right?"

"Yep, alright, come on, as Jack led her to the gate, she opened it, and around the bend was the cops, for her to say, "Is this an ambush?"

Jack put up his hands, to say, "No, No, No, it's just a ride, their all along for the ride, as he helps her in, he goes back to the house, and this time knocks on the door, Betsy answers it, to see Jack to say, "What do you want now?"

"I changed my mind?"

"How so?" said the bitter woman. well."

"After I thought about it, I decided I'd like to take you in as

"Why?" she said taking a long drag off of her cigarette

"It was something you said, that threaten me", said Jack as she went for her shotgun, and Jack had his weapon out, to say,

"Continue going for it and or I'll smoke you."

Out of the basement, came Greg, as he caught Jack and the two went down as Greg said, "You will not hurt my mamma."

Jack held Greg in such a way, he was cutting off his blood supply to his brain, till he experience sleep, and just like that he swung around and zip tied his wrists, and ankles, while his mom watched, then, his head, as he got up and motioned for her to do the same, as Jack dialed up Jared, to bring down the van, for two more to pick up, as Jack looked at his watch to see it was getting rather late. Jared and the team gets them on board, with out incident, for Jared, to say, "All aboard, now where?"

"Oh back, and step on it" said Jack, seeing he was going to be late for his next appointment.

Jack got in, and Jared drove while Jack rested his eyes, back to the precinct, the police ushered the criminal inside with Jack's help, to the glass door, that read, "International Terrorist Group", Jack knocked on the door, and Gene appeared to say, "Ah, you have us some more, lead them in, the four filed in single file, and the door closed, Jack asked Jared, "Do you have my keys?"

"Yep, here you go?"

Behind the door, those were getting a firsthand look at the UN, one by one they filed in, to a sea of United nation's people, first up was Roger, who came to the first station, and a young girl said, "Strip off all your clothes."

He said, "Do you know what is going on here?"

The young lady said, "Your going someplace that will seem like a vacation to you but actually it will be paradise, all in support of what you did." She said with a smile, as she stuck him with a set of shots.

Meanwhile Jack got in his truck, and drove to the apartment that Melanie texted to him.

CH 14

Jack's a stud and the world knows it

Jack went up the stairs, and saw her number and knocked, the door open, to see his new girl Melanie. Looking around at the quaint living room, then one by one, a girl came out, first it was Caroline, who said, "Hi my name is Caroline, her cute smile was infectious with her bleached blonde hair. Next up was a girl who was innocent, who said, as she used her dainty hand, to allow him to touch hers, "I'm Lindsay", another cute blonde, and finally, another blonde, to say, "I'm Kara. They took a seat in the living room as Jack saw what was going on, to say, "I hope they can keep up."

"They may not, but you know I will, so how will all this work?, do you take each of them back, and deflower them as you go?"

"Wait what, did you say?" asked Jack, looking at them.

"Deflower them" said Melanie.

"So there all virgins?" asked Jack.

"Is that a problem?" said Melanie? Jack ready to go, to say, "Lets go?"

"Whoa wait, don't you want to get to know them, you know who they are, and . . ." said Melanie.

"And when and where they're going to take my dick" said Jack bluntly. He looked around at the three looking innocent.

"Well you got a point there, I made dinner, its spaghetti, let's sit down, I need to prepare the bed."

Jack sat, as Melanie served him and the rest, to motion for Caroline to come with her, while Kara and Lindsay sat with Jack, each looking at him as they all ate, from the looks of it, Kara had the firmer body, and she sure smiled a lot, as Lindsay was quiet and reserved, till she said, "What do you do?"

Jack looked at her, to say, "I'm a International Bounty Hunter."

"Wow that's cool, so you go to different places and what bring back prisoners?"

"Yep something like that, as Jack got up, and went to the refrigerator, found the milk, but also looked in, to see the other two had stripped the bed, and put on a plastic sheet, then he went looking for the chocolate, found a can of it, used a can opener, and poured some in a glass, then the milk, as both girls saw it to say, "We please, would like that", as Jack was to hand Kara the milk mix he made up, she said, "No the chocolate", and she got up, unbuttoned her shirt, to her bra, and dipped some between her breasts to say, "Will you lick it off, please."

Jack was ready, and began to lick, it was sweet, she smelled divine, as she held his head, at her chest, as she pulled off her shirt, and with a flick of the wrist, off went her bra, it fell on his head, as she pulled it off, Jack had his hands on her tits, as Lindsay was getting hot watching this, came over and knelt down, and reached for Jack's manhood, she unzipped him, and reached in, and pulled it out and went at it like a pro, no complaining, as Jack moved down to Kara's pant's undid them, and she pulled them down, turned around at the table, bent over as he was fully risen, and positioned her, and slipped on protection, then he went slowly in, she received him, at first it was stuck, as she turned around to say, "That happens to my dildo, and then Jack was doing his thing, in and out, as Lindsay, was trying to lick his balls. It wasn't till Kara let out a scream, did it get Melanie's and Caroline's attention, only to see one of their charges getting drilled, for Caroline to say, "One down, one to go, as the two of them watched, as the minutes went by, it was getting on, as Jack held onto her hips, as he continued to thrust, at one point Kara said, "Are you ready to go?"

"Nope, I'm good" said Jack as he continued to enlarge her hole, her orgasm's increased, as she was the only nude one, as at one point Jack grabbed her tits, and was biting the back of her neck, as both senior girls made up a plate, and sat and watched, as Lindsay joined them to say, "When do we get naked?" Melanie looked over at Jack who was still into Kara, to the first hour, to say, "I guess anytime is the right time, as Lindsay stood, closed her eyes, and began to unbutton her blouse, she let it fall away exposing her firm bra, not really thinking, she popped it off, and with one hand pulled it away to show them and Jack her perfect breasts, as she danced, she undid her shorts, and wiggled out of them, and then finally, she pulled down her panties, to say,

"I hope he has plenty to fuck me next."

She went into the bedroom, as Melanie looked at her friend, and back over at Kara who was in full pleasure mode, legs spread, her juices were all over, then in a quick, motion, Jack pulled out, and spun her around, picked her up onto the spaghetti, and laid her down, and then mounted her, it slid in easily, as she took him to her hilt. She was loving it as she picked up the spaghetti and began to rub it all over her breasts, her legs were wide spread, as he did all the work, in and out and kept up that momentum, meanwhile Caroline, looked over at Melanie to say, "Are you ready?"

Caroline stood up, unbuttoned her blouse, and pulled it away, then quickly popped her bra, and then unbuttoned her jeans, and slipped them off, and then slid down her panties to reveal a brown patch, for Melanie to say, "Your sure getting wild down there."

"What about you, your still dressed?"

It took Melanie seconds to shred her clothes, to show her friend she was clean shaven, and proud of it, as Melanie came over to Jack to say, "When you get done with her we will be in the bedroom?"

Jack continued on, sliding it in and out, and orgasm after orgasm, till she couldn't take it any longer, he pulled out, and she went down to her knees, and took his cock, till he exploded, and she took it all. It was over for her, as she got up, and went to the sofa, curled up, and Jack laid a blanket over her, and went into the bedroom.

There was a frantic pace of texting going on between Roxy and Tia, Roxy assured she had Abigail and her friend Janet, who did she have?"

"I have the entire sorority house, including the house mom who said she was down, so when are you coming over?"

"3 am?"

"No he won't be here till four am, use the back door, and I'll bring you into my room" said Tia, as Roxy was getting worked up by all of this."

Back at Melanie's, Jack entered the room, ready to go again, this time he had stripped off all of his clothes, and stood, proud, while Melanie was in between Lindsay's legs, and Caroline sat on her face, the three were in a world to themselves, but that didn't bother Jack, as he placed on new protection, and came in from behind Melanie, spread her legs a bit, and slid it in, and held her hips as he stroked her, she came and gushed him, she moved out of the way, so Jack could mount, Lindsay, who was preoccupied, till it started to go in, and then she held on for dear life, as it was extremely tight, and at one point Jack considered turning her around, but it popped and it was in, and that was it, as Jack slid it in and out, as she held onto his hips, soon her legs fell to the sides as he was doing some damage, she too had an orgasm, with some blood mix, but Jack kept on going, she came again, and then again, and as Jack continued he just stayed where he was at, he constantly was pushing her legs up as he held onto her thigh's, her body was sweated, as the third hour had past, it was so tight, he let loose, and laid on her as she stroked his hair, to say, "That was good lover, can I go rest now?"

Jack pulled it out, as Melanie helped her man out, as Lindsay, walked gingerly to the sofa, and climbed in next to Kara.

Jack laid down, as Caroline was on one side, and Melanie was on the other, both taking their turns licking and sucking Jack's cock, while he fingered their wet box's. It went on till they both came, it was cruising to 11o clock, five hours in, and now it was time for Caroline, as he had Melanie put on protection for him, Caroline lowered herself on Jack's cock, a wave of emotion took her over, as she orgasmed, and then began to cry, tears rolling down her face, as she continued to grind him, her wet pussy was a mess, Jack had his hands all over her natural breasts pinching her nipples, as she continued to come, as the tears stopped and a smile was on her face, as she came once again. She rolled off of Jack, pulled off his protection, as she began to take him in her mouth easily, he couldn't hold it any longer, and let go, she choked on it and then swallowed it, she too got up as Melanie, came to Jack, put on protection, and she mounted him, laid down and went to sleep, on his chest. She was tired, he too went to sleep, he awoke, with his alarm, he set on his watch, it buzzed, it was 3 30, am, he rolled Melanie off and covered her up, took off his protection and went into the shower, cleaned up, and went out and got dressed, he got another helping of cold spaghetti, and out the door he went.

The drive over to Tia's was on the other side of the city, it was ten till four, as he knocked on the door, and it was opened by a young girl in a robe, it was open, to see she was nude, for her to say, "Who are you going to see?"

"Tia?" said Jack looking at her, wide open as she led him in, she turned to say, "You must be the stud?"

"Yeah, I can carry my own, why what do you need?" "What you got, as she pulled him close, and the two kissed, she tasted sweet, as, he allowed it to last, as he pulled the robe from her body, and his fingers went into her wet box, she was ready to gush, as he worked at a feverishly pace, then she tensed up, and climaxed, he broke the embrace, spun her around, bent her over the back of the sofa, pulled it out, slipped on protection, and entered her easily, much to her delight, he had her hips, and pulled her hair all the while still going in and out of her. This lasted till Tia said "India, is that you and turned on the lights, to see her friend getting plowed, and it all instantly stopped. Jack stayed inside of her as he just kept on going, as she was trying to cover up her tits, to say, "Do you mind Tia, I'm getting fucked." Jack took that moment to strip out of his clothes, and then resume the action. Tia watched her friend take Jack for the next thirty minutes and then went back to report to the girls waiting, to say, "It looks like it may be a few more minutes, but he said, go ahead and get naked, he will be here soon?"

None of the girls did anything, as Tia, wore a robe, and thought, I'll go back with Jack and India. She left them, to go to the rec room, where a line had formed, to see her other sorority sisters were waiting, for Tia to say, "No, he is mine, next, go back to your rooms, give India, some privacy, except one girl left, a black haired beauty, who was mesmerized, to say, "Can I be next?" "No Taylor, he is mine, wait your turn?"

Jack saw her and her beauty was immense, she had a pout for a smile, and said "Come on over, as Tia watched, as Taylor came over to Jack, Jack took his hand and touched her robe, she undid it, and allowed it to fall, her nude body was taut, as he pulled her in closer by grasping her butt cheek, and inserting his fingers in her wet box, in one motion, he guided her downwards, and pulled out of India, and inserted it into Taylor, who took him easily, she was dripping wet, as he went at it, while Tia opened her robe and began to play with herself stroking her pussy with her hand up to playing with her breasts, as she caught Jack's eye, her friend India, was passed out still lying over the sofa, Tia moved over to stand in front of Jack, and shred her robe, and played with herself, while Jack fucked Taylor. Till Tia had enough, and came over next to Jack and bent over, to be next, as Jack heard Taylor scream with ecstasy, and Jack pulled out, she too collapsed over the sofa, and pushed down on Tia's back as he inserted it into her, she took it easily, even though she was a solid foot lower than him, he was widening her with each stroke, till she climaxed, multiple times, she was screaming with delight, as the line reformed, each girl was now nude, a pair of sisters were next, as finally the panting was turning to "No, please stop, yelled Tia, as Jack pulled out, and then a taller girl was ready, and he pushed her down, and inserted into her, it was wide and open, for Jack to say," Ah experienced, as he held onto her hips, down the hall the whole sorority was up now, as it was apparent what was going on, as the three women who were waiting went to the door, to see Jack plowing each girl, took their turn, as it was hot, for Roxy, as she had never seen that before, as one by one, a girl would get in line, then bend over and Jack would stick his dick into each one, and after the entire sorority was plowed, Jack smiled over at the three of them, each shaking her head "No, and left". They slowly walked through the carnage, as Jack himself found a shower, took one, dried off, got dressed, and Jack left too, and went back to Melanie's apartment, went to the door, it was locked, he pulled his pick set, and unlocked the door, went in, to see the three girls on the sofa, and went into the bedroom, to see Melanie still curled up in a blanket., Jack took off his clothes, and got naked, and slid in behind Melanie, as she said, "What have you been up to?"

"About eighteen?"

The next day Jack awoke, the place was empty, he got up and took a shower, dried off and then dressed, it was 2pm, and he thought of roll call, but shrugged it off, he saw he missed some calls, and then made a call to James his partner, who answered, "Where you been?, a lot has transpired, you know that Roger hays you took off the streets, it has set off a chain reaction, and the Mob is warning, professional killers are in town, all looking for Enzo Bonn, are you sure you want to keep up that title?" "Sure, let them come at me, I'm ready."

"Also there is some talk, that you self could be liable for some sexual charges on those women you put in the hospital?"

"What are you talking about?"

"Yeah, I guess you went to some sorority party last night, and seven girls went to the hospital, boy I wish I was there."

"Roxy and Abigail was there watching."

There was a pause at the other end of the line, for James to say,

"Really, I did not know that."

"So ask them what happen, I'll see you later, I'm going to see my CI."

James slid his phone shut, to listen to the Captain, "Put any men needed to assist Enzo, the next few days are gonna be worse." The Captain, went to his office to see a stunning brunette, who extended her hand, to say, "I, Captain, my name is Erica Meyers, I represent Jack Cash, or you may know him as Enzo Bonn, I was summoned when I got first wind of this whole thing of you thinking about charging Jack for sexual battery, where are you at on that?" His hands were up in the air, to say, "I don't know a concerned father phoned in the sexual battery, and I sent two detectives over to assess the damages and to see if we need to investigate further."

Roxy looked over at Abigail, as they got firsthand look at Jack's work, as the doctor, said, "The vagina was stretched from a 1 to a ten in probably in less than minutes, causing internal bleeding, ripping and some damage, it may take weeks to a month or more to heal, and she is just one of six more just like her?"

"Was there anymore involved?"

"Don't know, just what came in last night."

"Really" said Roxy, as she took Abigail aside to say, "That could have been you or I last night, we may have to keep this on the DL."

"Oh I already forgot about it."

"So what of your fantasy now?" said Abby.

"No way, ever." Said Roxy.

They stood outside in the hall, and saw, an out raged father, who was screaming about revenge, as Roxy went on the offense, and confronted him, and said, "I'm with the police department you need to calm down", and just like that he pushed her into a wall, and she went down, wobbly, and then passed out.

Moments later she came to as she was being helped to, her partner Abigail was helping her up, she had a bloody nose, she sat down, she was crying, as she opened up her phone, and called Jack Cash, he answered, to say, "This is Jack Cash, how may I help you?"

"This is Roxy, I was just assaulted?" "By who?"

"He was one of these angry parents of the women who are in the hospital."

"This is the first I've heard of this, where are you at,?" as Jack saw it on his phone, and changed course, and drove over to NOLA university hospital, parked out front, to see some commotion, a guy was just assaulted, as Jack was on the move, gun out, he said, "Stop, turn around, so I can see your face."

The man turned to see it was a undercover something, for Jack to say, "Now inter lock your fingers, and kneel on the ground, just then two guys appeared one with a gun out who said, "You can't talk to my boss like that" as Jack held a gun to him, to say, "Drop your weapon, or I'll drop you."

"Listen to what he is saying, Dean, or I know he will kill you."

Jack motions for the pair to do the same, to say, "Interlace your fingers together, and on top of your head, and now kneel."

"Mister your making a huge mistake, I'm with the Riordain family?"

Jack holstered, and zip tied the older man, to say, "And I don't care."

"Dad, there just gonna kill him." "Hush up junior, don't provoke him."

Jack zip tied, the large son, and his friend, as he pulled him along, to the back of his truck, and wheeled him in, he rolled, and then the other two, he said, "Get up there and lie down, as Jack took a picture, of all three men, to say," Alright, I have a career criminal, in one John Spikes, looks like you have a huge rap sheet, next to you is your son, Francis the fighter, well this is gonna hurt your fight game, and Dean Saad, another criminal, so all lie down" as Jack zip tied their ankles, and each of them zip tied their heads shut, until he reached the father who said, "I want my attorney?"

"You can have him join you, your now my property." "Who are you?"

"Enzo Bonn, International Bounty Hunter."

The father said "Ohh." As Jack put him face first, and zip tied his head. Jack hopped out, and went to the front seat and found a cable, he zip tied the end, to the back frame, and then passed it through, their backs, feed it through the back bumper, and back to the front, as the rain let on, as he jumped out of the back, and went inside.

Jack reached the third floor, as a police officer was there checking ID's, Jack showed him his from the NOLA police, as he put the picture back in his pocket. Jack down the hall, to see a lineup of rooms, clear glass fronts, as Jack took the first room, a very beautiful women, first one being, Michelle Newsome, as Jack took a picture of her, everyone connected to her showed, she was clean, as she smiled, when she saw him, he opened her door, and went in, to her bedside, to say, "I'm sorry I did this to you?"

"It's not you, it was all me, I'm the one who stood in line, I bent over for you, the good thing is I'm not a virgin anymore, and I don't feel all compacted, it's like I'm flowing free, come here closer." she takes his hand to say, "You can come back and visit me whenever you want, now or in the future, she kissed his hand, her warmth was inviting, for her to say, "Its unfortunate what happen, but I'm glad I did it."

Jack left, and the next room was just like the last, enclosed in glass, he took her picture, it came back, Dana Anderson of NOLA, young coed, he choose not to stop, next glass room, was a older man and younger woman, he took her picture, and then one of his, it went through his data base, it came up with a red flag, espionage, detain., her name was Heidi Becker exchange student from Berlin, he was Helmut Starling, famed German arms dealer and scientist.

Jack knocked, the older man saw him, and opened the door for him, as Jack said, "Can you place your hands behind your back?" Jack said sternly.

"What is this all about, I'm a German citizen, I have Diplomatic Immunity", Jack cinched him up as his daughter was screaming, "What are you doing with my father, Hey I know you know, you're the one who raped me?"

Jack pulled out his gun, and said, "If you ever lie again, I'll canoe your head." Instantly she stopped, as Jack wheeled Helmut to the floor, the zip tied his wrists, and his ankles, and then his mouth, he got up to say, "Sorry you feel that way", Jack was ready to go, when she said "Wait, I was wrong, but is sure hurts."

Jack turned to see her crying to say, "What are you going to do to my father?"

"Your both going to the UN?" "Wait what did I do?"

"According to my records, your visa expired last semester." "Oh about that" said Heidi.

"Yeah about that, sorry about what I did to you, but I got to do what I gotta do."

"Who are you? she said in anger, as Jack left the room, and went to the next, isolation glass room, next up was Christine Cooper from Michigan, Coed, blonde blue eyed, he knocked, she waved him in, and he popped his head in to say, "Sorry I did this to you."

"No, don't be, I feel so much better, it was like a big clomp."

"TMI", said Jack as he went to the next room, snapped her picture, it came back as Taylor Spikes, from the man down in his truck, and her brother, he entered, she smiled at him, to say, "Come closer, she had a wild look in her eye, pulled a gun, and shot at Jack, he took the first one in his badge, and the second, and the third, till he grabbed it from her hand, and it hit the window, she looked at him, as he zip tied her right wrist, to the rail?"

As she exclaimed, what about I have to go the bathroom?" "I guess you'll have to wait, you just tried to kill me." "Yeah so what, you opened me up like a can of sardines with that big cock of yours that thing is dangerous, I had internal bleeding, I'm gonna sue you for damages."

Jack left as the sound proof door closed, next room up was a younger gentleman, who Jack took his picture, it said, 'Flynn Socorro, of the Socorro family of NOLA, his trade was enforcer, Jack came in to see the girl, India Reynolds, came up, as Jack stepped in, caught Flynn off guard, spun his hand behind his back, and collapsed down on top of him, and was able to zip tie his wrists to hear, "What are you doing Mister, I did no wrong?"

Jack zip ties his ankles, then at his head, Jack says, "Now stick in your tongue, and then he zip tied his mouth shut, and let him be, as he got up and went to her bed, he touched her hand, and she woke, she smiled, and said, "Who knew a encounter, would lead to all of this, have you seen my brother?"

"Yeah he is lying on the floor" said Jack with a foot on him, to see her looked in a puzzled way, then said, "But I don't regret it, and would consider doing it again?"

"Perhaps, but what can you tell me about your father?"

"Well not much to tell, I lived with my mom, in Baton Rouge, and then I came here for schooling, I know he financed me through school and he is a mobster, but that's about it."

"That sounds alright with me, I will see you later." "You can count on it" said a surprising India.

"Go get some sleep, as Jack turned out the light, and left to see in a room catty corner from this row was Roxy sitting on the edge of the bed, he came in to say, "What happen to you, I saw you didn't participate last night?"

"You mean this morning, and how could I? There was a line up."

"Sounds like your jealous?"

"A little maybe, you sure did some damage, and the kicker is their all clean?"

"What do you mean, clean?"

"No STD's, nothing, usually on something like that, you'd get something on their genitalia, but nothing."

"How do you know?"

"I worked vice for several years" said Roxy.

"What was your job?" "Decoy, and entrapment?" "Ever get naked?"

"Yeah, once and twice I was practically raped, but nothing like what I saw you do to all those poor girls."

"So that means you're out?"

"Well I didn't say that, but this will stick in my mind for some time to come."

"So it seems your Okay, well so where are you at on, Carter Grimes?"

"He is working for some guy named, Charles Rand, a defense contractor out of Algiers, and all I could get out of Carter was the Shadow Project."

"Really where is Carter now?"

"Oh in lock up, he was all over Abigail, so I arrested him, and then your girl can be free of him."

"Good job, said Jack as he moved in and touched her thigh, she smiled to say, "Maybe I will allow you to do what you did to them, as he turned back, to see Tia was on the end, and from her bed she motioned for him to come to her, so he got up and turned to say, "Oh by the way, I took down an angry old man outside, I hope he isn't the one who accosted you?"

"I don't know, but I'll check."

Jack left her room, to walk over and open Tia room door, she smiled as he came in, and the door closed.

Jack stood by her bed side, to hear, "Thank you for this morning, if I could I get up, but I have stitches in me. Jack took a picture of her, as it came back Tai Riley from Naples Italy, all work current, for her to say, "Did you take that picture to have a memory of me, or when I get out, you'll be coming back over."

"I don't know maybe both, that was crazy" said Jack apologetically to her.

"That was a mere glimpse of a growing epidemic in this country."

"How so, what do you mean?" asked Jack.

"Well its simple, most young girls get to college, a virgin, they would like to hook up, but it ends up three ways, they are either raped, abused or kidnapped, did you know that New Orleans, next to Miami is the capitol for coed trade in the world?"

"No I didn't know that" said Jack.

"So all of those girls you did this morning were elated by having a stud clean them out, and now they can get back focused on their work, school and the desperation, goes away, just last month a girl friend of mine, hooked up with some guy who was homeless, but just because he showed her some interest, she did him, come on, it's a war over eligible men, especially a stud."

"What's that" asked Jack honestly.

"It's a guy who is hung like yourself, whose mission is to just fuck, and so when a sorority house can find a guy, he becomes their guy, and would be willing to pay 100k a pop, anything less, then they're not in the game, and the stud, will be taken by the highest bidder, so when I recruited you, as you said you into Sport fucking, that was a perfect shoe-in, for our Sorority." "So it's not about a guy?"

"Yes, your right, it doesn't matter, it's all about what you could do for them, and you're a stud, heck you put down over twenty, we had two girls on a sleep over that you plowed, and now they may pledge to us, No you're a commodity, and I hope your still on board with visiting us at least once a week?"

"Sure I'm game with that, except Heidi won't be joining us." "Why's that?"

"Her Visa has expired."

"Come on we need her, is there any way you can get it extended till the end of the year?"

"I'll check on it, what about you said something that women get abused?"

"Oh about that, its mainly drug trade?" "How so?"

"Well girls fall into traps, for sex and drug trafficking, they'll find a stud, and the stud will enlarge them, so that they can stuff cocaine in their uterus, and bring it back from Mexico, you have to think about all the colleges in this area some thirty, then over 100 thousand girls are virgins, and the rest well either their good or their bad, and will find a way to do something, you gotta remember a lot of them do it for the money, but it all starts with a stud."

Jack was thinking of Melanie, and that she said something about a daily line up, as he thought to himself as he got up and said, "I hope to see you at the Café soon?"

"Well I should be able to go home tonight, then be ready in a week to do this all over again?"

"In the mean time?" said Jack.

"Probably sleep alone?"

"Sounds like you need company?"

"Well your always welcome" said Tai as Jack was out the door. Jack was on his phone, as he applied for Heidi's Visa, it came back approved, and it said for indefinite. He went back and pulled Flynn from the room, and swung her curtain closed, then went down and pulled Helmut, and saw Heidi was crying, for Jack to say, "Don't fret, you're here indefinitely, but you owe me?"

"Really, yeah sure, you want it right now?"

"No, I want you to get me everything on your father, and present it to me later."

"Yes Sir." She said with a smile. Jack noticed a girl sitting in some chairs, with a cap on covering her eyes, as he drug those that he had, to a Gurney, and set them next to each other, as she got up and jumped Jack, her arms and legs were wrapped around him, as Jack was swinging elbows, he reached in and got his gun, turned it around, and struck her in the head, with the butt, instantly it shocked her, as she let go, he holstered, then, took a picture minus the cap, came back, Michelle Wayne from Slidell, last known job, working as a investigator, as she had made inquiries into Helmut Starling.

CH 15

King Leon, King of the Gangster's

A week had past, as the dust settled, all the girls were discharged and back to class, Tia was back at her job, as for Taylor Spikes, Jack swung by the sorority and picked her up, and took her in for shooting at him. As for Melanie, since that night, he hasn't saw her, he went by her apartment several times, to see it was the way she had left it, other than that she had no affiliations, he thought he should of taken their pictures, but it did give him a hit, for a one Kelly Hill, not in the college data base, criminal data base, shop lifting, under 25 dollars, and on campus, as those files, were open for his viewing, he began to see patterns growing, and a lot of counter espionage was going on, as several Professors were the subject of all of this, a pattern was forming with Jack and criminals, every day he would pick up several he was cleaning up New Orleans with his partner James, who has since been distance with Jack as his sister is even different after their encounter, she too isn't excited to see Jack either. His house in the garden district is now full of coed's who come to him to lose their virginity, as sent to him by Tia, and the girls from SST.

Every night he comes in after a day of rounding up criminals, to a house full of helpers, and every night at least one or two stay for Jack. This night, Lacy Huffman, a freshman, was ready, as Jack laid down, both nude, and he held her for the first time, and they both fell asleep, in the middle of the night, Jack got up, to push one out, but did it with the lights out and the door part way closed, to hear a noise, as he quickly finished up, he heard, "Swoop, Swoop, Swoop, all from rounds shot from a silenced weapon, Jack came from the bathroom, and rushed and knocked the shooter off balance, Jack took down the shooter, and wrapped his arm around his neck, as the two went to the floor, Jack cinched up the rear naked choke hold, till he put the shooter out, then let him go, scrambled to get up, he went to his coat, and pulled a zip ties, went to the guys wrists, as the guy was face down, he zip tied his ankles, then to his face, he enlarged the tie, and then cinched it down, he searched him to find his phone, he saw it had a code, as Jack looked over to see Lacy was done, so he covered her up, and took the shooter's phone to swipe the face of his phone, and saw the info, as his phone, that sent a virus in to destroy any trace of records, Jack threw it aside, he opens the file, to see the phone directory was vast, to include e-mails, sent to Marcus, to assassinate Enzo Bonn, so then Jack went into the UN directory to find, how to deal with an assassin, it came up, remove both sets of the tips, the digits of thumb and fore finger, and he will never be a threat to you ever again. Jack closed up that file, and thought about it, then decided to use the Parthian Stranger the boat once again, so Jack sent out a blast e-mail, from the last reporting agent's signature, Marcus phone, IS, and sent to over 2200, names in his directory, and surprising there were half women, as Jack thought, he was way behind him, if he was in fact a stud or also doubles as an assassin. The E-mail, said, RSVP, the deep sea fishing trip, the first response was from Leon, to say, "Is he dead, Cut off his head, and bring it to me right now, so we can feast on his eyes, a, Ha, Ha, and I have your ten million dollars". Jack responded, "Yeah, on my way." Jack dressed, and went down stairs, and into the basement, whereas he saw, Jim, who said, "We saw it, and we tried to get to you, sorry."

"No worries, do you have a pair of hand pruners, and a torch?"

"Yeah, what are you going to do with that?" said Jim. "Oh some handy-work, can you take care of the body?" "Yep" said Jim, as two people handed Jack the tools, he went back upstairs, to see Marcus was gone, zip ties all that remained, as a window was open, Jack looked through it, to see a van start up, he pulled his weapon, and pointed it at the van in the distance and fired, the round was losing its trajectory, as it hit the rear outside tire, as the driver was spinning the tires, as it became flat, Jack was on the street, running towards them, to the passenger side door, it was unlocked as Marcus was trying to pull his weapon, as Jack struck the window, with the butt of his gun, it shattered, all the while holding on, to say, "Pull it over or I'll canoe Marcus's head." The guy slowed the vehicle, to a stop, and heard Jack say, "Now you put your hands, on the wheel, as Jack took, Marcus weapon, as tossed it on the dash, to say, "Now place your hands in front of you, Marcus did as he was told, as Jack cinched Marcus up, through the safety bar on the dash, as Jack said, "You're not very good at being an assassin."

Jack made his way over to the other guy, and said, "Get out, and repair your rear flat, the guy exited, and went to the back and began the process, he found the jack, lifted up the van part way, and then cracked the nuts, then lifted it up all the way, enough to pull off the shredded tire, and pulled the spare, mounted it. The guy tightened the lug nuts, then lowered the jack, then tightened the nuts to finish, for Jack who had picked up Marcus's weapon. Seth Guzmon was his name, the driver, as Jack took Seth's phone, to say, "I want you to drive, take me to this Leon." "Gladly, then there will be plenty of them, to kill you."

Jack got in the back, as Seth spun out the tires sending Jack back, he fell into the rear door, he got up and went up to the front, put his gun to Seth's ear and whispered you do that again, and I'll cut off one of Marcus's fingers, pulling out a pair of hand shears, and holstering his weapon, as Jack sliced off the tip of Marcus's right thumb, as Marcus let out a cry. Jack zip tied Marcus's head to the seat, at his Adam's apple. Seth was super silent as Jack, went back to his ear, to say, "You drive to this place, you make a noise, you flash your lights, you do anything out of the norm, and I'll canoe you and your father, Jacob, you think your tough, I'll not only go after you, but your family in Sicily, he looked over at Jack to show he meant it by allowing a tear to flow down his harden face. He then saw, Jack use a small torch to cauterize the wound, the smell of burnt flesh, knocked out Marcus, and Seth was in fear. The ride was short as it was out in the famed Chalmette district, to a large compound, high walled fence and barbed wire on top, the gates open, and allowed the van in, Jack had texted to his friends, the strike team, Black ops from the air, as he arrived, they jumped from the plane, and from the air, they descended.

The van drove to the back, and parked, as a huge party was in full swing, that was until Jack zip tied Seth to the steering wheel, and then popped up of the side, with guns out, and the party instantly stopped, it was a bit of a stand still as Jack yelled, "Everyone on the deck, you in the pool, out."

Just then a shot rang out, as Jack took it in the back, as Jack turned to see a young kid in a hoodie, as Jack returned a shot, that hit the kid, in his head, and went down, to turn to see a pair of high kicking, twins, as one kicked the gun Jack had out of his hand, but not his signature gun, it was going off, as the kicks and punches were being thrown, it was a fight, as two identical brothers, were squaring off with Jack, as Jack holstered his weapon, as a crowd got up to watch what was happening, Jack took his credit cards out, uncapped them, and held them in the ready position, as another fury of attacks occurred, and this time Jack was cutting and slashing, he swung in, and caught the one in the stomach, till it stuck and he lost it, as one twin went down, holding his stomach, his brother was outraged, as he rushed Jack, Jack sidestepped him, caught his head, and spun it around, to snap it, the twin fell to his death, Jack pulled his gun, to yell, "Everyone on the deck", just as helped arrived, and a few shots later Jack and his help had the compound. Jack called in the Calvary, Lisa and her crew, as Jack took pictures of his prey, the young kid came back, Martin Reece, known drug dealer, the two brothers, Mike, was the one with the broken neck, his brother was Fredrick Wexell, captured, he took pictures of all the coed's to include Michelle Newsome, who smiled, to say, "My father is gone, but he did ask me to tell you he is going to get the meanest bad ass assassin to kill you."

"How do you eat with that mouth, as Jack turned her around and zip tied her up, to hear her say, "What you'd that for?"

"Your my prisoner now, and you can tell that to your dad." "I will, if you let me go."

Jack looked at her naked body, and decided, "Alright I'll play along", as he cut her wrists loose, to say, "You have till Friday, have him at the dock on pier 13, or I'll come get you and . . ."

"And look at me, I'll place a voodoo curse on you", she said as she blew some dust at him, he closed his eyes, and she was gone. He wiped off the remains with a towel, he made it through the palace, and went downward to the basement, to come up on some familiar faces, hung by their wrists were Melanie, Kara, Lindsay and Caroline, along with twenty others, as she smiled to say, "Are you here to rescue us?"

"Yep, as he took a key ring, and began to loosen them up, as Roxy, and some other female officers came down to assist Jack, as he held, Melanie, to say, "I came back and you were gone?"

"Yeah, about that, because of what you did, we were next to go to Honduras, and make a drug run?"

"What, a drug run why?"

"Mainly for the sorority, but as you can see King Leon had other ideas for us", as she pointed to Lindsay, to say, "She got the worse of all of us, she was taken like clockwork, once they found out she wasn't a virgin, and was gang raped, repeatedly, as for myself, I endured it, and Kara, Caroline fought it, and she was whipped for it, as he could see the real marks on her body, Jack was thinking, "This Leon will get what is rightfully his, tonight."

Jack allowed Roxy to take Melanie, as he texted Cassandra, he had found Kelly Hill, she is going to the hospital, here in NOLA." Jack went over to a set of rooms, marked VIP, and inside was a woman, naked arms spread out and tied to the wall, and legs apart, blood, under them, he tried the glass door it was locked, he moved to the next it was the same, as Strike team came down, and shattered all three doors, and Jack followed them in, to snap a picture of each, the first was, Marlene Riordain, family business., second was Daphne Nicoletti, whereas Jack thought so that is where you're at?, she wore a fish net one piece that covered her body, and the last girl, was bloodied in the face, body abused, came up, Lieutenant, Peyton

Reilly, Coast guard, as they took her out. Jack noticed on the far wall three girls were left as a policeman, dressed in blues, was in their faces, as Jack watched their body language, so he went up to the first one, took her picture, it came back Miranda Yates, a tall brunette, nude, as she whispered to Jack "Can you get me away from him."

"Hush up Miranda, I got eyes on you?" said Sherman.

"Officer are you talking to me?" asked Jack looking at him to say, "When are you going to release them, instead of gawking at them, and just like that, LT Casey puts Sherman on the ground, to say, "He has a bomb", as Casey fell back to allow Sherman up, a single shot rang out from Paul Clark, and Sherman's head was bleeding, as he slumped into the wall, and just like that Sherman blew up.

Jack took the next coed's picture Lisa Parks, a hot brunette, covered in some blood and pieces of flesh, but the worse was Riley Zane, a small petite, brunette, whose body was limp, she was taken down, and hauled off as Miranda spilled the beans, and said, "Eric Sherman was a regular, and that the three of us were his play thing, and that they would make runs to Honduras, to take heroin back, all the girls participated in this venture all for the graces of the King, as she continued, she said, "Oh one more thing, about six months ago, a few coed's escaped, but instead of running away, they went upstairs and mutilated the Kings genitals, and thus has but a hole left to piss out of." She said with a smile.

"Was that you?" asked Jack.

"Yes, and next time, I would of used that metal pipe on his skull."

Jack looked at her and said, "You might get that chance later." As the rest of the girls left, on the bed, in the VIP room, Daphne was asking for Enzo to come to her, as Jack was at the door, all cleared out, as he approached her she said, "You know you saved Me and all these girl's lives?"

"How so?"

"I told them that I was you girl friend, and that you would come and rescue me, and here you are, rescuing me, so now what?"

"Now you go home." "What if I don't?"

"Then stay here."

"What about what I said?" "About what?" asked Jack. "About you being my boyfriend?"

"Perhaps we shall see, it's all up to you, but for the meantime, your off to the hospital, and then I'll come and see you."

"You promise?" said a smiling Daphne. "Absolutely, I need a date for tomorrow night?" "Really where are we going?"

"Oh a little birdie told me a big ship is having a party and I want to be there to shut it down, as she was up and hugging Jack, she kissed him on the cheek, to say, "I hope I don't run into your wife?"

"Oh don't worry about that, I'm a widower now?" "She's dead?"

"Yep . . ."

"Oh that's a shame, I knew you really loved her."

She left with an escort, as Jack assessed the carnage, and now his new mission was to find this King Leon and actually exact some revenge and retribution.

Jack left to go see Sara, as he took the van, as he turned left onto hwy 39 what he didn't realize was he was going south, as he came upon a turn off for Polydras, and a further left to English Turn, the country club, he took that, then it was a bit weird, as he slowed through Caernarvon, it was a ghost town, except to a road south, where a plain looking fence, ran for quite a distance, he used his phone, to look up in this area, it showed the recovery from the last hurricane, some construction was fairly new, and the lake measured one foot deep, then Jack got to thinking, why would they spend that kind of money, to have a hundred thousand acre lake, so Jack turned and went south, as he past the open gate that said St Bernard state park on one side, and lake Plaquemines, which stood just above the flood plain. Jack stopped halfway down, he got out, and went to the lakes edge, to see that the lake was flat, but what was odd, was the runoff, there was none, it was like looking at an optical illusion, he took a picture of the anomaly, and saw something that was square, about 100 by 100, thinking "That is odd," as he went to the records and tried to pull up any construction permits for this place, and a history of the lake, then got in the van turned around, and drove to the right towards Polydras, then north, past King Leon's palace, and into town, namely over to the cooking school. Jack got out and went inside, where people all dressed up in white jackets and top hats, as he came upon the receptionist who said, “How may I help you?”

“I came to visit Sara Sanders.”

“Alright I can page her, as I think she may be on break.” Moments later she appeared, to say, “How are you?” as he steered her into a private room and closed the door, she was kissing him, and he was reciprocating, till she broke it up, due to the baby she once was carrying, to say, “I have discomfort from time to time, so tell me what have you been up to?”

“Oh you know, just out recruiting potential wives.” “And how is that going?” said Sara smiling.

“Oh not bad, I think I might have four solid and as for the rest I’ll let you decide on Friday.”

“I will, just as long as you’re here for the competition and graduation” said Sara, for her to add, “I waited for you to pick me up, when you didn’t show, I was worried, but Lisa Curtis, had someone drive me here, so I forgive you.”

“Sorry, I was busy, I will be here for you, can I bring a guest?”

“Sure but let me know how many, so I can put it down.” “Just two?”

“Are you sure, let’s make it four” said Sara, as she was up and opening the door, to see the administrator not happy, as they went past her, he went out, and she went back to class.

Jack checked over messages, to see he received a weird one, so he opened it up, it was from, India Reynolds, who spoke, “Hi Enzo, I wanted to let you know that the big four are having a meeting in your honor, and would like you to be there at 11 am sharp. at the Commanders’ place. Jack hurried up as it was close to that, using his phone as a navigator, it led him, right to it, he parked outside, and went in through the door, he first saw India who lit up, and embraced him, as he saw three other extremely beautiful women, waiting, as India led Jack to where the big four sat, each stood, to shake his hand, to say, “You have been a busy boy, please sit, you have nothing to fear from us, I know a lot has happen, first off I want to introduce myself, I’m Henry Toussaint I’m what you say is the old guard of New Orleans, I was once a professional assassin, now retired, on my right is Dick Silas, he runs all of south at Algiers, next to him is Robert Saad, you had a run in with his son?"

"Is that true?" said Robert.

Jack shook his head, "Lastly, he runs the garden district, where you have a house, and your wife or someone was just Killed by Marcus the resident assassin, and lastly on the end, its India's father Jimmy Socorro, which runs the airport, which I don't believe you used, so Mister Enzo Bonn how did you get into our city?"

"By plane, by boat, or I just simply dropped in?" "Who is supporting you?"

"The US government?" said Jack calmly.

"No wait, you're a cop, just say the police department, spoke the angered Jimmy."

"Pipe down Jimmy" said Henry, to add, "Were not here to harass you, but merely tell you how we feel, and reward you with our greatest possessions."

"Alright I'm listening" said Jack as he pulled his phone and took each of their pictures, then put it away, remembering Lisa handing him two new credit cards and a new stack of cash, thinking he was thirsty, he pulled out his hose and took a clean refreshing cool drink of water, to hear Henry continue, to say, "As I was saying, I want you to enjoy a feast I'm having the entire kitchen prepare everything on the menu, then you eat as much as you like to your heart's content, Then let's talk business."

"No", said Jack, to say, "Let it all spill now, I don't have time to eat, I'm going after this, King Leon, if you know where he is at?", he looks at each mobster one at a time, each shaking their head, till he looked at Henry, who for the first time he himself showed fear, by saying, "He has a little safe house, up by lakeshore airport, but there are traps, I believe my daughter would know, she use to grow up there as a child, Maria, please come here."

She rose and went to him to say, "Yes Papa?"

"That place you grew up, how can this man get inside?" "Its really hard to find the way, I guess I could show you the way?"

Jack looked at her as she looked at her father, who said, "That brings me to why you're here in the first place, for your efforts in taking down King Huffa and King Leon, I want you to borrow this, as he motions for someone to bring a case, they set it down, and Henry gets up, to say, "This is mine, a special rifle designed just for me, in a collaboration with the Russian-French in 1999, 55 inch barrel, muzzle brake, a signature grip, brass stock, mahogany wood, Infer-Red, 20 times scope, painted pure gold, with a marking of TOUSSANT 1, this is yours boy, I'd have it engraved, Mister Bonn, but that's not who you are, is it?"

Jack looked at them who looked back at him, to say, "Your right it isn't, I used that as a cover, as Jack takes it, to hear, wait, so who are you?"

"Jack Cash, International Bounty Hunter."

Jack closes the case, and was ready to go, when Henry said, "One last thing, as a gift from us, we would like you to have each of our first born, for me, it's my girl, Maria."

"But Papa, I'm married for the last fifteen years, I have four children."

"Enough" said Henry, "Respect me", and for Robert, who motioned for his daughter, to say, "This is my beloved Jen, who extended her hand, Jack looked at it, then it was Dick's turn, he stood, to say, "Tessa, come here honey. This is Tessa-Jackie, I want you to marry this man?"

"Alright Papa, as she stood by Jack, to see Jimmy, smoking a cigarette, drawing it down to say, "Oh alright, here is mine, India."

"Yes Father?"

"Your now a property, of this man, who are you anyway?" "Jack Cash, International Bounty Hunter."

All was silent, as he left them, as the four women followed, to the door, as Jack looked at them to say, "Your free to go as you wish." said Jack as Maria, held his arm, to say, "No, it doesn't work like that". "Were yours till the end of time, what do you want to do with us?"

Jack saw she was serious, to say, "Alright, tell me about yourself?"

"Alright, I'm married to my husband of fifteen years and have four children, and work here for my father."

"Alright stay here, wait, you said something about how you know about this place, can you show me?"

"Sure, can I go change?"

"Can I watch?" asked Jack, as she looked at him, to say,

"Sure, I'm all yours now?" "Go on, who's next?"

Tessa rose her hand, to say, "I'm a house wife, I live in the south, do you want to just come live with us?"

"No, I guess, go home and pack your things", she left in tears, out the back, that came to the two young girls, a short brunette, with a pretty smile who said, "my name is Jennifer, I go to school, to be a attorney, what do you want me to do?"

"Go back to school, you too India."

They left and Jack waited, with case in hand, to see two of them, to hear, "Sorry, my youngest sister, wanted to come along, Jack this is Isabella." Jack took to immediate liking, as she was extremely cute, as he pushed the door, open, he sees the van was gone, and his Mercedes was there, he spoke, "Open, it did, as Maria took the large passenger seat, and Isabella waited, for Jack as she fit in the small space in the back, with case in hand barely he got in, set his phone in the dash, for Maria to touch his arm to say, "My father once told me, I was a mere pawn, used and needed when the time comes, to repay him, and this is my time, so I'm all yours, whatever you want to do with me?"

"Are you into sport fucking?" said Jack.

She looks at him, as the car started and off it went, as Jack punched in the coordinates, she said "No, never heard of that?"

"I have Mister Cash" said Isabella excitedly.

Maria looks back at her, seeing there was easily a twenty year difference, for Isabella to say, "Come on sis, sure you know what it is, it's the rage now."

As Maria looked over at Jack to say, "I guess I'm in, what do I have to do?"

Jack looked over at her and just smiled, as the car, was heading towards, the lakeshore Airport, he even passed his old van, as they were going 200 miles per hour, as he slowed to see another compound, for Maria to say, "Use the east side, and turn off, and drive to the south part, is where the tunnel is at, he stopped and parked, he pulled his phone, and felt his arm pull, to see Maria say, "I want to go with you, your mine now to protect."

"No I'm not, tonight your going back to your husband."

"Only with you, you see it's all about principle, I was the property of my father and he gave me to you, evidently you have value to him."

"Yeah, he wants to be safe, from all prosecution." "How so" asked Maria.

"What I'm entitled to is unlimited amount of wives." "Really, so this isn't something new for you?"

"Nope, I already have five, I mean four, one just passed away."

"Alright, so I was wrong." "About what?"

"About us over whelming you."

"Not at all, I do the craziest stuff, so if your mine now, I'd say lead the way, so why is your sister along for the ride?"

"She had hope you'd choose her over me?" said Maria.

"So what you're saying, to fulfill your father's request, instead of choosing you, I'd take Isabella?"

"Yep, that's pretty much it" said Maria.

"Let me think on this one, how do you feel about this?" said Jack, as he looked at her in the back, as she was cramped in.

"I'm okay, I'll take one for my sister, but I need to know, are you really, Enzo Bonn?" said Isabella, enthusiastically.

"Yep that's me too?"

"Oh my god, you're the stud, at the SST house", exclaimed Isabella.

"The one, in the same." said Jack proudly.

She was overly excited, as Jack let her out of the car. Maria was in the lead, as Jack then Isabella, for Jack to say, "Stop, why this way?"

"Because the grounds are booby-trapped by the lizard" said Maria.

"Who's the Lizard?" asked Jack.

"A bomb expert, who like to see things blow up, this is his actual house, said Maria, found a hidden light switch, for Jack to say, "No we don't need this."

"Yes we do, this isn't even accessible from the palace?" "How so?" said Jack.

"It's a secret, my dad built it for a backyard escape, come this won't take too long, I promise, then I want to have my way with you and uphold this new contract."

The walk was short as they were under the main house and basement, stairs between the wall, they went up as all was quiet, as men spoke below, "Listen no man can make it on the front step, I'll blow them up, your safe here, relax watch DVD's, or visit the Coed's, I don't care, as Maria led Jack up to the attic, whereas a trap door opened, that allowed Jack up, as she and Isabella went back down.

Jack went down the stairs to see the King, without makeup, a sinister goatee, eplets on his shoulders, he wore a crown, for Jack to Jump him, Jack launched himself into this little man, the momentum, took them to a wall, as Jack got in several rabbit punches, and was finally able to put him down, pull his hand free, as the King began to cry, Jack hooked him up, and zip tied his wrists, as he put him down on top of his face, and held him there as he zip tied his ankles, and then pulled him into a closet, and shut the door, he doubled back to hear some girls singing, and looked in to see at least four having fun, as Jack thought, either join them or, turn and go back.

Jack turned to see the lizard, a man, dressed as a cat, with fangs from his head, and a claw from his hands, he swiped at Jack, as Jack pulled his weapon, and fired, at his knee, as the cat sailed at Jack, and fell in a huff., searing pain, and just like that behind him, he saw a nude Giant Russian, "Igor", as he was a pretty easy target to hit, but moved like a panther, as Jack watched as Igor, lifted Jack up and hurled him into the wall, the brick broke easily, as the passageway was now exposed, Jack got off a shot, in the knee, and Igor toppled, standing in the door way was Michelle Newsome nude with weapon, saying, "Come out, so I can finally kill you once and for all."

Jack recovered, by shaking out the cob webs, stood up, was a bit wobbly, as she waited for him to get his bearings and shot, Jack took the bullet in his heart, spun around, and went down to the floor, he rolled on one side, slowly pulled his weapon up, as she looked down and Jack returned a shot, his bullet, rattled around in her head, as she fell dead right in front of him. Jack took his time getting up, as he zip tied both the Russian, and the lizard, as he took their pictures, then went to the remaining girls. Who staggered out of there, as Jack took a picture of each, face, then one came back Tamara Riordain, as Jack escorted her out, into a room, to get dressed, as did the others, who said they were prostitutes, so Jack asked, "How did you get in here?"

They all shrugged their shoulders and waited, as Jack went to the open wall, and kicked it further open, as he dialed up reinforcements.

Jack told of the booby-traps, to call bomb squad, while they waited, he called for Maria and Isabella to come up and help out, as he took out all those in the house, carefully, with Maria and Isabella's help, while the Calvary drove up, the B support teams was there, as Jack transferred the King and his accomplish, to Lisa team member, as other members went in and pulled the remaining people out, one carried Michelle out for Lisa to say "What happen to her?"

"She liked to play with firearms, so I shot her, oh by the way, meet my new wife or wives, they haven't decided who wants to be it?" the two sisters formed up, as Lisa went to them, to say, "Which one of you has decided to be his wife?"

Isabella was the only one who raised her hand, for Lisa to say, "This is pretty easy, I have this document to sign, and for safety and security purposes, I need your fingerprints and a face recognition, as Lisa took her picture with her camera.

Isabella signed off on the main form, to hear Lisa say, "What do you most look forward to being with Jack?"

"To love him every day I have on this earth, and make my papa proud." Said Isabella, smiling.

"When is the wedding planned?"

"I don't know, I have family in Palermo, Sicily, who would like to come."

"I imagine, he would fly out there?"

"Really, are you serious, that would be great" as Lisa finished up with her to say, "You check out, Its official on our end, where are you staying now?"

"I have a small apartment in the garden district?" as she adds, "Do I need to move, or will he come live with me?"

"We will move you to the house in the garden district." Said Lisa, making all the arrangements, as Isabella offered up her keys, Lisa said, "That won't be needed, all of your stuff will be moved tomorrow."

Jack went to his car, as Maria met up with him, to say, "Thank you for choosing Isabella, she seems to adore you and I need to get back to my family, she will make you a very happy man."

"I was just afraid of the retribution your father was going to give to you, for backing out of your father's wishes" said Jack.

"Don't worry about that, I spoke with my mother, and she said just as long as someone was there to fulfill my obligation that my father would be alright, besides I have a great relationship with him, he'll be fine."

She embraced him, and kissed him on the cheek, to say, you're not half bad. To say, "Do I get a ride with you or . . ."

"Or have Lisa give you one back, I'm going to the hospital."

Said Jack as he embraced his new wife, Isabella, he felt her hips to say, "Hey were you there couple nights ago?" she smiled up at him as the two kissed, and she hugged him, it was smoldering as several people watched, as he pulled apart to say, "Your kiss isn't half bad either." Jack looked her over, to smile and said "I remember now."

"Hush, Mister, I'm a lady" said Isabella smiling. Jack got into his car, and took off, as the two girls looked at each other, then a suburban pulled up, and a handsome man got out, to say,

"Hi, my name is Randy West, Miss Isabella, I'll be your bodyguard, for the rest of your life."

Isabella smiled, then took the passenger seat, motioned for her sister to get in, as she said, "Randy, where to first?, and how much do you know about my husband, Jack Cash?"

He spoke eloquently, "First off, I'm at your disposal, meaning, safety and security, I watch you and when necessary intervene and support you, I will be there in and around you for the rest of your life, as where you want to go, this is your vehicle."

She smiled as she turned to look at her sister who knew she herself would have loved a life like that, as Isabella said, "Tell me about Jack?"

"Not much to say, he is a renegade among agents, he is always first in, and ask questions later, as for his wives, they are his support team, that's why I imagine why he married you?"

"How so, what do you mean?" asked Isabella.

"What I meant was, no disrespect, I was referring to your heritage, your Italian, like from southern Italy, were loyalty is strong."

She smiled at him to say, "Close Sicily, but I feel your drift."

"If I may, I normally won't speak to you, I only answer you, just to let you know?"

"Thanks'", as Isabella, was telling the world, she was Misses Jack Cash proudly, as she looked up, to see Randy, who sat waiting her word, she said, "Will you drive us to our father's restaurant please."

He drove them back to the restaurant, as news had traveled super fast, as it came from Isabella herself, excited to be married, especially that it will take place in Sicily, vehicle stopped out front, and all three went inside, it was in full swing, as Henry saw them, to motion for them to come to him, instantly he changed his attitude, as he drug his eldest by the arm, for her to complain, "Papa your hurting me?" said Maria.

He stopped as he threw her down, to say, "Your are a disgrace to me, I offered you up to Mister Jack Cash, for what he did for all of us, and you repay me, by bringing your sister in the fray, I will allow that union to happen, but as far as I'm concerned with you your dead to me, now get out and I don't ever want to see you again, and don't think you're going home again either."

She showed panic on her face, as she screamed at him, "What have you done with my husband?" it caught the attention of Isabella, who was busy texting all of her friends, the news, she went to the aid of her oldest sister, to see her, on the floor. Their Papa standing over her, like never before, cussing her out and saying mean and hurtful things. Isabella was horrified.

"The same that will happen to you, you'll both be swimming with the fishes."

"No, Papa, No, why . . ." as she cried very loudly, as he had motioned for his second bodyguard, to pick her up and out the back he went did a loop and swung her up into the trash dump. The old man shook out his hands, and went back in. her sister came to her aid, to say, "Maria, Maria."

"In here."

Isabella, looked at Randy, to say, "Will you please get my sister out of there?"

"Yes, Ma'am" said Randy, as he scaled the ladder, and held his hand out for her to reach, as he, hoisted her up, and lifted her out, she was a mess, her shirt was stained, her pants a mess, for Maria to say, "I guess we never knew he would have done that to me."

"Lets go find this Jack Cash, and see if he'll reconsider."

Said Isabella.

Meanwhile Jack was diverted over to and with James, to a death notification, as Jack drove up in his Mercedes, he parked across the street, he saw what appeared to be some topless man leaving the residence from the rear, and over a short fence, down the slope, to a beat up car, Jack took his picture, and that of the car. Then saw James drive up, Jack got out, and the two went up together, and JL knocked and Jack used the door bell, moments later, a door opened just so slightly, and a figure stood, dressed in a robe, it was partly open, as Jack had a full view, she was naked, as JL said, "Are you Miss Caitlyn Sherman?"

"Yes, I am, what seems to be the trouble here?"

"Oh not that much to concern yourself with?" said James, also getting a good view of her glistened wet box, as she said, "Would you care to come in?"

They both shook their heads, "Yes", as she allowed them in, as her robe was open and in full view, for all to see, as she said, "Sorry, it won't happen again."

"As I was saying, My name is James Lancaster, and this here is my partner, Enzo Bonn, we come here today, to notify you that Eric has been killed." They waited a response, then she said, "Well he has since moved out a year ago, I caught him with three girls, all at once, can you believe that, three girls, so I kicked him out, so as far as I know, he is dead to me."

"Well it says here, he left you a Fifty, Thousand Dollar policy and your due his full pension, all I need for you to come down to the station and sign the death certificate." As a smile appeared on her face, to say, "I can do that, shall I go change."

"No, ma'am, that won't be necessary, just do it on your own time" said James, looking for a way out of there.

"Actually, I would love a ride there, can you wait, till I change?" said Caitlyn.

They waited, while she threw on some shorts and a blouse, as Jack said, "Then are you seeing anyone?" "Not that it matters, I'm not."

A whiff of her scent was intoxicating, as she was a serious beauty.

CH 16

The Shadow Project

The ride over was calm, as Caitlyn chose Jack over James and his Mercedes, she cozied up next to Jack. She was flirting the whole time, with her hand on his thigh, and how she accidently opened her blouse, as he parked, she said, "Why did you ask if I was seeing anyone, are you interested?"

"Could be, but I was more interested in the guy that was here before we arrived?"

She looked at him, to say, "He is nobody", as they got out and Jack held the door open for her, as they went into the morgue, as Jack led her through a maze of bodies, to a isolated room, where a box was, a lid over the top, to cover the remains. Jack was left up to interpret, to say to her, as she was trying to figure it out, Jack said, "He was blown up?", as he lifted off the top, for her to peer inside, for her to say, coldly, "I can see that, but how?"

"I guess he had a bomb on himself, but I imagine, he'll be a hero, for using himself other than for others.

She looked at him, then turned away, as Jack held her in his arms, to say, "Now can you sign the death certificate, and your free to go."

She broke away from him, and signed the form, and Jack, said,

"They will send you the check in a week or two." "Wait aren't you going to drive me back?" "What for?" said Jack losing interest in her.

"As a courtesy, and it's a gentleman's thing to do."

"Sure, let's go, as Jack held the door opened for her, she turned to say, "Did you kill my husband, I know who you are, your Jack Cash, some bounty hunter."

"No I didn't, get in or I may change my mind."

She did as she was told, and he went around, got in, to see she held a gun, for her to say, "I want you to turn around, and drive, I'll let you know where and when, so shut up, your my prisoner now." Jack drove, and though of the heads up display, it showed him his features, as he saw pass side sleep, he said, "Sleep slowly", as the gas was disbursed, she still watched him as her eyes fluttered, then she closed her eyes, and she was out, he stopped the car, went around, and opened the passenger door, she fell out, he hoisted her up, carried to the trunk and laid her down, then zip tied her wrists and ankles, then one for her head, then closed the trunk lid. Jack doubled back as he was on the road to St Bernard state park, and he got to thinking, what is so important down here, he pulled his phone, to do a history study on improvements in this area, and send. Jack drove back into the city, and to the hospital, and got out, and went to waiting, there she was Daphne Nicoletti, a real gem of a beauty, she got up and embraced him to say,

"Now where to?"

"On to a shop, I'm buying you a new dress."

The night was in full swing, as cars lined up at the dock, to get into the newest arrival, from the South Pacifica, a three level dance party, and sex and drug club. He put his Mercedes car in valet mode, as he stepped out with his phone in hand, and the other was holding the lovely Miss Nicoletti, they were waved right in, as the bouncer saw who was driving what, as Jack remembered what it once was, and a new guard was in charge, a tough looking guy, and the same old cast and characters, young women, he even saw a few of his coed's, not to mention the stake out team of Roxy and Abigail, out of the corner of his eye he saw CC, she used her eyes to communicate with Jack, so he allowed Daphne to go mingle, as he caught up with Her, as she pulled him into a bathroom, and locked the door, as she pulled him close, to say,

"I've checked 56, and I still have 2500, I need some help."

"Quit whining, this is your mission, so carry it out, I'll see what it will take for reinforcements." Said Jack as he went past her and out the door and continued to mingle, when his eyes lit up, to see Miranda Yates and Lisa Parks, both seemed fine, but Lisa was complaining of a piece of her left breast caught some fragments." As if she was going to show him. He waved her off, it was as if Jack was waiting for something to happen, and then it did, Black Ops and SEAL teams arrived, to secure every door, as everyone was held inside as a team from the precinct made their selves present to Jack, and he went around taking pictures, a quick ID, and he either arrested them or simply let them go, it became easy for Jack, as one by one, he had, a member of King Huffa's crew, as there were mingling with the others, first caught was, Elka, a slave loyalist, who fought but was detained. After that calmed, next was Neci, who Jack somewhat remembered, and flirted with her, she suggested going to the ladies room, he oblige her and once inside, she was ready to please, and Jack was ready, but if it was only another day, time and place, he hooked her up, and zip tied her wrists, from behind as she said, "Kinky, bend over and fuck me, I'm willing?" he saw Roxy come in as he passed her off. Next up was a super hot blonde, as she flirted with everyone, as Jack saw her, he clipped a picture of her, it came back, as Sabrina Stevens, known associate to King Huffa, AKA as Lyric, she was a suppose singer/model, Jack went right up to her, instantly she smiled and said, "What is a guy like you doing in a place like this?"

"I'd say the same for you?"

"Well for me, I just fell in with the wrong crowd", then she knew what was happening, as they were surrounding in around her, as Jack hooked her up, and zip tied her hands, he let her go, as he cleared off the bottom floor. This floor was easy due to the drug intake, but up a flight, it was all different, it was a full blown dance floor, and over 500 people, and this was where all the players, were, so he decided to go up another floor, to a more peaceful surroundings and where the sex was all the rage, there was half as more than the bottom floor, but all of these people were naked, and going at one another, it was individual rooms, open for all to view, room by room he took pictures, till finally, he got a hit, as it came back Jack watched a young lady take it doggie style, as it showed her to be Doreen, Davis a famed Helicopter pilot, and career criminal, he marked her by assigning, Paul Clark to her, as he gladly watched, as Jack continued, he viewed everything imaginable, the use of a swing, some tied up, some were even in a bathtub, "Weird", he thought, as he turned the corner, to see VIP rooms, and continued on with his entourage of enforcers, the first room yield a find, it was a rack of sorts, as a woman was bounded by the wrists, as men took her from behind, as her body was in the rack, he took a picture of her, it came back as Jennifer Jones, Ex-military, weapons woman, and career criminal, as Jack motioned for the next person up to detain her, as it was Lt Casey Morales, he smiled at the assignment as Jack and the others broke the men up, and arrested were made by others as Jack assigned, by either looks, likes or dislikes, some were criminals, whereas others had ties to King Huffa. Jack turned the corner, and saw two rooms, that said, "Private Keep Out, Invitational only, Jack tried the door, it was locked, so he pulled his pick set, and easily, turned the key, and opened it up slowly, he stepped in with his second as being Craig Morris, to see a woman was on top of a man, screaming at him, to, "Do It harder", she was nude, as Jack sided up by her, for her to say, "What the fuck man, this is private, as Jack took her picture, and just like that she jumped off of the guy, and was coming at Jack as Craig stepped in the way, and actually caught her in mid flight, as she was known as Xing Mao, it said she was extremely dangerous, as Craig, changed her flight plan, and sent her into the steel wall, she hit to a thump, and Craig was on top of her, zip tying her up, the man on the bed, was also a career criminal, so the next up was Tony O'Brien, as he hooked up Engine Green, known baddie.

Jack left the room, to go across the hall, another door locked, Jack again picked it, he turned the knob, and slowly opened the door to screams of passions, a guy was between a woman's spread legs, as Jack came over to the side, as he clipped a picture of the guy, it came back, Captain Patrice Norman, an ex-Black ops deserter, and Jack signaled, as Craig Bauer, jumped up on the bed, caught him off guard, and tried to zip tie one wrist, as he put up a fight, tackled him, as the woman, Jack confirmed was in fact Pacifica, King Huffa's suppose wife, she rolled off the bed on the other side as Cpl Spancer tackled her as she tried to pull a weapon, but it was no use, and succumbed to Spancer holding her, he held her while Steve Brooks, zip tied her, her screaming wasn't at all heard, as they zip tied her mouth.

The young Captain, also gave in as several others helped Craig, subdue the Captain. Jack searched the rest of the floor, it produced very little, he did however find King Huffa's room, and a huge wall safe, he left Art Jackson and Scott Mackenzie, to deal with that, as he took the others down a flight, to see the party was happening, Jack was looking for one or two in particular, King Huffa's second and His top enforcer, both had eluded Jack, he searched, as Jack went up to the wheel house, and then he was on to something, as he and his men, put down the crew, stationed in the house, who said, Kurtis is in the operations room, a man stands up, to say, "You need a password, and or that man's hand, and eye scan." The guy was hoisted up, drug over to the door, scanned his eye, and put his hand on the reader, and the door cracked open, Jack pushed the heavy door open to hear, "Arturo, what do you need, as Kurtis, was holding some papers, as Jack said, "Turn around", and he did, as he tossed the papers, and began to run, as Jack calmly, took out his gun, and shot Kurtis in the knee, he spun around and hit the passageway, and was in an intense amount of pain, as he was holding his right knee, to say,

"Cops aren't suppose to just shoot, I have my rights."

Jack came up to him to say, "You have no rights, once you pose a threat to the US, all of your rights vanish, I as a bounty hunter have been given the power, to arrest, detain, maim, or simply kill you at my leisure."

"When has this been in force?" "Ever since 1929."

"Why hasn't this come sooner?"

"I don't know, I think you never had the chance to meet one of us?"

"How many are you?" "Two?"

"All in the US?"

"Yep." Said Jack, hoisting him up.

Kurtis was hooked up, as Jack received via an ear piece that Black Ops team two, has a runner, some Rene Linc, shoot to kill or . . ."

"No, I want him alive, and detain or corral him, I'll be down there." Said Jack as Kurtis heard him to say, "So you have to be present to arrest the people?"

"Yep"

"Wow I don't envy your responsibility." That was the last thing Kurtis said. Jack hurried downward, taking step by steps, down into the very bottom floor, where the massive engines, were, and in the middle was the drug room, it was a sea of white powder, as everyone had to mask up, as Craig Bauer helped Jack with his, as Jack went in, to feel the intense heat as you could feel the warmth of the cocaine, shots rang out, as the man spoke French, and for Jack to say, "Get a cleanup crew, and get me a rocket launcher", the French man heard that, to yell out the "Surrender", in French, Jack said, "Come out", back in French, so said his phone, as he repeated it, loudly, as the Frenchman showed his hands, and just like that he was subdued by Black ops, and taken out. Jack followed them out, and pulled off his mask, and that of Rene's, and then zip tied him up, as he was taken out, as Jack made it up, to the dance floor, as it was nearly impossible to check everyone, so Jack stood at the main door, and snapped pictures of those leaving, and for some he arrested, and others, he simply let go, till the very end, as Lisa and her crew went inside, and vans transported the prisoners back to the precinct.

Jack saw his support in the form of Gene Garp and Roberta Myers, as they took charge of all the capture's, as Jack signed off of them, Roberta took the opportunity to say, "So when do you want Claire back?"

"Claire who?" responded Jack as he found Daphne, the two got into his car, and it was off. It was a short drive to the SST sorority, as he parked, he said, "Stay here and sleep", she was out, as he got out, and shut the door to say, "Secure, and went in from the back door, he walked in, thinking of the last time, but this time it was different, except of some huffing and panting, as Jack opened a door to the cute Dana Anderson's room to see her getting plowed from behind as she was crying and yelling, "Please stop, leave me alone, Enzo will kill you . . ." she pleaded.

And just like that, Jack pulled his weapon, turned it around, and struck, church tattoo man in the back of the head, the shock of the gun transferred, and he went to the floor, in convolutions. Jack zip tied him up, including his ankles and head. He went around and cut off, Dana's bindings, as she fell into his arms, to say,

"I knew you would come to save me."

"It will be alright now, as Jack dialed up Lisa, for a pickup of one, Corey Reid. Jack left her room, as she went to lie down, Jack caught up with his new wife, to be, India, who came up and gave him a kiss on the mouth, and an embrace, to say, "Now what?"

"Stay here till Friday, gather your stuff, and we're all going on a cruise, then you plan out our wedding?"

"What budget do I have?"

"Unlimited, just whatever you want?"

She smiled, to say, "My father, told me this could happen to me, some day, I didn't believe it, I just don't know why?"

"That's an easy one, they want federal protection, from prosecution, what they don't know is that I can still take them down."

"You don't want to do that, and I see what is my purpose now, to keep my father safe."

"Yep, and me satisfied" said Jack.

"So with that said, come into my room, and let's make love, and I want lots of babies."

Jack's eyes lit up, as Jack was texting Jim, he had a prisoner in his trunk, but before he sent it, he deleted that request, for Jack, to say, "Can you hold on, I need to check on something, as he went outside, he saw Daphne, and knew it wasn't the right time or place, so he went back in, he saw India, to say, "Meet me at my boat, slip number 13, on Friday night, I got to go." The two kissed once again, as Jack left and went out to his car, got in, and drove off, back to his house in the garden district. He pulled into the garage, went down a level, as a crew of workers were ready for the car, as Jack said, "Awake", Daphne came to, to say, "Sorry I must of dozed."

"I'd say, you were sawing logs, as he led her out, and showed her to the basement door, as he followed.

Jack led to the stairs, when he heard Jim say, You have someone in the trunk?"

Jack doubled back, and cut off her binding, and lifted her out of the trunk, Caitlyn, hugged Jack, to say, "I'm sorry I was wrong, I learned my lesson." Caitlyn smiled and embraced him, to say, "I'm sorry, it was out of desperation", as he knew she was harmless.

For Jack, to say, "I'll Let you go, and visit the others, as he placed a arm around her to say, "Oh by the way, I caught your man, doing one of my girls, at her sorority."

"What man I have no . . ."

Jack says, "Remember Church tattoo boy who did you just before we arrived to let you know your husband just died."

"Oh him, he meant nothing to me, how about you, do you have any plans for me?"

"Nah, I was thinking of stripping you down, and giving you a bath and then putting you to bed, as it looked like you wet yourself?"

"And I hope that means you'll be with me?" "Absolutely."

Jack and Caitlyn went up the basement steps, as the top door was open, and, there were women all over, there was Isabella, and her distant sister Maria, who came to him, as he holds Caitlyn back.

He saw the girls from the SST house, to include Melanie, who has since sworn off drug runs, smiles at him and of the recent women who has been betrothed to him, to include the two sisters, and their dilemma, Tessa was the house mother now, as the Men down below had brought in some beds for them to sleep on, Jack took Caitlyn by the hand, went upstairs, went into his room, led her in, locked the door, motioned for her to remove her clothes, she took her time, unbuttoning her blouse, she let it fall off of her, with one motion, she flick off her bra, so Jack may get his hands on them, he grabbed them forcefully, as she wiggled out of her pants and waited for Jack to take off all his clothes, and as he finished, a knock on the door, he said, "Who is it?"

"Isabella, I want to know if I could come in and we could consummate our marriage."

Jack unlocked the door, opened it up, for her to see how ready he was, and for her to come in, she stepped in, to see the lovely Caitlyn, and wasted no time in shredding her dress, as Jack closed the door, and locked it, to see Isabella, turn around, and pop off her bra, she pulled it away, and motioned for Jack to come to her, he touched her hips, and said, "So it was you?"

"Yes, and I want this every night." As she handles him, and strokes him, while he pulled down her panties, and placed a finger inside, as he bent over her, while Caitlyn watched, as Jack swung Isabella around, and instantly he went in without protection, and she insisted, as she was on all fours, as Caitlyn, came over and sat down, and laid under her from the side, as the two, kissed each other in a playful way, all the while Isabella held up, to the ramming she was getting, Isabella's arms were strong, and it showed, as Jack, placed his hand down her arm, to her firm breasts, and held on as he increased, so did she, as she let it out, a scream of passion, as she went down, Jack went around to Caitlyn, who's legs were already far apart, that was until, Jack placed on some protection, and held up her legs, and snaked it in, half way, as she was in major pain, as she was screaming not ecstasy but pain, telling him to "Stop, you're hurting me?"

Jack pulled out, as heard another knock at the door, he went over, and unlocked it, to see a line had formed. He said, "Next", two girls, Melanie and Daphne came in, and Caitlyn was taken out, while Jack plunged back into Isabella. The others took Caitlyn, as Melanie, said, "It's a full house tonight, and closed the door, locked it down, to see her new partner Daphne was stripping, as so was she, as Daphne, went next, she bent over next to Isabella, and Melanie was next to her, as he finished off Isabella, he put protection on, and went easily into Daphne, who rose up to the girth, but easily accepted it, and an hour later she collapsed, and waiting was Miss Melanie, with love in her eyes, she held him in her arms, and said, "Lets lie down lover and let's get some rest." Jack nodded with his head, and followed her to the other side of the bed, where she got in under the covers, and Jack followed right behind, and then stuck his dick inside of her, and went to sleep, his other hand cupping one of her firm breasts.

The next morning, Jack awoke to bustling around, he saw Isabella, standing in front of his view naked, drying off the earlier shower, and Daphne and Melanie were drying each other, he just had a smile on his face, he got up past them and into the shower, it was fast, when he got out, the bed was made, his clothes was folded neatly and then he got dressed, to include gun, and holster, and wind breaker, he pulled his phone to see he had missed seventy four calls, as he looked them over, he saw one from Miranda Yates, it said, "I have been recruited to join the Shadow Project, the details are sketchy, but the just of it, is that they target Professors, who target Coed's, and they have a facility down here below caer . . .", and the line went dead.

Jack was pulling resources, as he had a picture of the location, and decided to call up a destroyer, and punched in the coordination's, and authorized code, it came back to the commander of the 7th fleet, Gary Jones, who said, "Authenticate who this is?"

"Jack Cash, put in his ID, which changes every 15 seconds, confirmed, Gary said, "On my mark, and it shall be done, as Jack had checked with all agencies, no one knew of nothing in that location, thermal imaging from satellite, showed it to be a massive metal top of some sorts. The destroyer launched a 20inch round, just as a family of four, spent the early morning at the park, and was driving out, as the rocket roared in, hit the top and exploded, as it rocked the community, as even New Orleans, felt the blast, instantly all the water drained inward, as from the sky and on the ground, over thousand men, swarmed the top, of the facility, in through the top, and downward, they detained people, as it became apparent it was a secret base of some sorts, easily capturing the whole staff of eighteen, and on the lower twenty floor of this self enclosed unit, was the core processor, a uranium nightmare, as weapons grade plutonium was being manufactured.

Jack was on his way, as he left passing all the girls, and took the Mercedes, he took the Hwy down and followed the fire trucks, he arrived, to see the fire department, was laddering people out. and the site secure, as the structure was now visible, Lisa also arrived along with the two UN representatives. Lisa said, "So Jack what have you been up to?"

Jack shrugged his shoulders to say, "Just a hunch?"

Jack and Lisa, went down into the secret facility. The modern facility similar to a large room, the size of, 100x100, and twenty levels, all in a stairwell system, the lighting was hooked to a power generator, but really unnoticed as it was low level energy, but what really powered all the computers on level three and further down was all the servers, each level further down, exposed a huge room ten stories high, that sat the nuclear reactor, and Helmut Starlings name was all over everything, there was no violence except for the bomb that blew the top open, a secret tunnel, led some to a storm drain, by a mall, where some had their cars, but from aside that this secret facility was under no specific nationality nor jurisdiction, as a recovery team was called in, as it was still working, and operational, so the National Energy Foundation, would take it over, and instead of what they were doing was for evil purposes, it was to be used as, for good, and the top would be repaired, and the cooling ducts upgraded, and put it back in use. Several officials, proclaimed Jack as the nation's hero for this find, as Lisa pulled Jack aside, to say, "Your safe house is really filling up with girls that want to marry you, do you have a number?"

"Nah, I don't know, what all that even entails?"

"Well officially they all have to live under your roof?"

"So what if they don't?", like Maria, Alex and Alba goes back to Cuba and Dominican Republic, who says they have to?"

"I don't follow you?" said an angered Lisa.

"Well Maria and Alba went back to Cuba, and Alex is in the Dominican Republic."

"Oh I see, I don't know how all of this works either?" "Can you call someone, to find out?"

"Yeah sure, right now?" said the annoyed Lisa.

She left him, to make a call, a voice answered, to say, ".Yes, Miss Curtis how may I be of some assistance?"

"Jack just asked me what is his requirements for the women he wants to marry."

"There is none, there can be as many as he wants, and oh by the way, congratulations, for that find where you're at."

"Thanks, it was all Jack's idea?, I would have never noticed a 100x100 twenty stories crate, in the ground".

"Yes, we know, and the President, wants to award him the peace prize in conjunction with the Nobel people, can you have him available?"

"Yes, but is he in fact going to be one of the President's representative at the spy conference?"

"Wait one, and I'll confirm that, as of today, we still don't have official word, but the word we do have is that its open to all 178 countries, meaning some 356 agents are attending, what is currently in the works, is a place for women, and if that's the case, Ben and Jack will have to select some women to send?"

"Just them get to decide?"

"They are our only spies, are you suggesting yourself, don't even ask."

"What should I tell Jack?"

"Tell him whatever he wants, if it's a hundred, thousand or a million, he can have unlimited, but now comes the logistics of all this, we may have a problem housing all of them right away, if I were you I'd find a way, if you could suggest ten at a time, so the DOD can process them, the last request for a Isabella Toussaint was immediately approved, I have Randy West there to be her temporarily support, but as far as anyone else, it's a first come first serve basis, but there will be none turned away."

Lisa pondered her next move, when she heard, "He is our most valuable asset, so what he wants, he gets, remember that, you're still technically his boss, which keeping him happy should be your number one priority, I have a long line of others, wanting that role, namely, Samantha Kohl, second at the CIA, so be on your best behavior, and satisfy our man, even if it means yourself."

“Yes Sir” she said as closed up her phone, she walked back over to see Jack to say, “What ever you want, whenever you want, and I guess, all you need is access to them.”

“So if one wanted to go to college.” “Then they can” said Lisa.

“And a restaurant?”

“So they can, they main thing here is so that you have access to them, and they must be available to you as you see fit.”

“Good to hear that, I’ll leave, I got some urgent business to attend to, as he saw the new text he received from Miranda Yates, they were moving her to a warehouse.”, she ended the call to look at her associates, to hear, “Good job, Miranda, now position your warriors at all the entrances, and lets be ready to kill this guy, who has destroyed twenty years of work, I hate this guy” said the boss, Charles Rand, as he squeezed his wife and partner, Vienna, who said, “We should just flee, did you see what he did to the site?”

“Yeah so what, he doesn’t know Miranda is on our side.” “What makes you think he cares, he could have a rocket sent at us?”

“Doubtful, he likes our top performer, and she sold it well, her and Lisa, Parks, No, we’ll be fine, I just hope thirty men is enough.”

Jack was driving towards the warehouse, as he thought, why not send in the teams, first, maybe it’s a trap, he thought, as he coordinated his strike team over to the warehouse, they were closer than he was, and Jack gave the okay, to go in and find, this Miranda Yates, and make sure she was free, was the last thing he wrote.

The strike team, dropped off its people, first it was the sniper group, of Art Jackson, Spancer and Brooks, over to the next building, Bauer and O’Brien, and Morris, to the south, Tim Nelson, was with the team, he and Scott Mackenzie together, as Clark and Morales, all had a door, instantly they took fire, and took down casualties, they were like rats taking down those that had weapons, as they were at the top level, in a matter of moments, as they cleared floor by floor, to the top of the spacious offices, holding the principles at the ready, as team leaders yelled, “Clear, Clear, Hands up so that we can see them.” Jack arrived, he parked out front, all was calm, as the strike team led him up, to the third floor, to see a husband a harden criminal, as Jack took a picture of him, to see who it was, and then of the older girl, who was his wife, Vienna, and of Miranda and Lisa, who both came in, for Jack to hear, from Paul, who said, "They were free to roam, they might be connected."

Jack turned, took another snap shot, and then said, "Allow them to be free, so it says here you're a known prostitution pimp?"

"Yeah, so arrest me, my attorney will have me out tonight." "Really who is he?"

"It's a she, her name is Jess Thomas?" "Sorry, I just picked her up the other day." "Wait I get an attorney?"

"Not right now, for you and your crew, it's off to the UN and appear before the World Council."

"What where, how?"

"Enough on your knees, as the pair went down, Jack zip tied them up, to say, "Bye, bye."

Jack had another issue to contend with what to do with the two Toussaint sisters, and according to his phone, the best solution is to take them both, the old man is so stubborn, that her death is of greater value than the disgrace he will have to endure from his family, and the loss of the youngest, could make up for the eldest mistake, so Jack let it go, as he was summons by JL on a case that he was at a night club, and that the owner wanted to see Jack, so Jack allowed the strike team to hold everyone, as he left, as Miranda asked if she could go with him, leaving Lisa Parks behind. Miranda caught up with Jack, as he led her out, for her to say, "Where are you going now?"

"On to a night club to help out my partner." "Sounds fun, can I come?"

"Well see", as he held the door open for her, as she got in he said, "Sleep". And then got in, and to see she was out, he rummaged through her purse, to see the normal stuff, except a written note, that read, "At all costs keep him away from the dorms."

Jack just shook his head in disbelief, but then he thought, maybe it's a trick, as he surveyed the note with his phone, it was a man's handwriting, DNA of a partial print, came up as one Charles Rand. Jack allowed Sara to drive to the night club. The car arrived as Jack pulled his phone, and got out, to see James vehicle he went in, to see an older man behind the bar and a tougher one at the bar, and JL arguing, they all stopped, seeing Jack instantly the two girls, Marlene and Tamara, got up and came over to Jack and gave him a hug, just as their father spoke, "So this is the man who freed you both?"

"That's what I've been trying to tell you" said James.

"Is this true Mister, Bonn?"

Jack held both of the girls, by the waist, to say, "Name is Jack Cash."

A stunned look appeared, over his face as he said, "So that was what Toussaint was talking about, in a lower voice, then spoke up, to say, "In honor, for this occasion, I offer you one or both of my girls for you to marry, do you understand what I ask?"

"I do, but what's James problem?"

"He is actually professed his love for one of them?" "Which one?"

"Well that's for you to decide, and if it's the right one, then true love will prevail if not, then you Jack Cash will go home the winner, and Mister Lancaster will go home the loser, which will it be?" as Jack wheeled both of them around to look at the pair, Marlene, was tall, slender and very athletic, as for Tamara, she was shorter, a bit more lovelier and had a real sexy smile. Jack pulled his phone took a picture of each, he knew what his partner liked and besides he couldn't stop talking about Tamara, but as cute as she was, she had a bigger smile on her face for Jack, as she was literally mouthing the words, "Pick Me?", now Jack was in a bit of a quandary, ruin his friends hopes and dreams, or . . ."

"I'm waiting Mister Cash, who shall it be, either, or . . ."

Jack spoke up to say, "You choose?"

"Nah, it doesn't work like that especially it's all over town that Henry disallowed his eldest from the escape of his wrath, for not obeying his wishes, so you choose."

Jack leaned in and whispered to Tamara, "Are you into Sport fucking?", he pulled back to see her say, "Yes?", as she bit her lip. Jack did the same for Marlene, as he pulled back, to here "No, Hell no."

Jack said, "Alright I'll take Tamara."

She smiled and leapt into Jack's arms, and hugged him around the neck, to whisper, 'I'll make you feel like a million bucks, thank you, thank you." As Marlene went over to James, he got up and hugged her, for her to say, "Looks like it's just you and I."

As Jack left, went outside, as Tamara, followed, to say, "Wait, we need to plan out our wedding?"

"No you do that, I'll have someone over to collect you and your belongings, were taking a boat out on tomorrow, just be there."

Jack got back in, and said, "Awake", as Miranda came to, to say,

"Sorry I must of doze off, what about the night club?, how was it?" "Oh, you know, the same old thing, so let's talk about this whole dorm thing and come clean, now, as Sara drove the car off, She smiled, to realize that Jack wasn't playing around anymore, to say, "Alright, I know about this Shadow project at least a year ago, I was recruited, to follow some professor, and when the opportunity arose, I had my friend tape, our encounter, then we black mailed him, to do whatever we wanted."

Jack cut her off to say, "So your behind all of this?"

"No silly, just part of the problem I guess", she showed him a fake tear, for Jack to say, "Sorry that won't work on me, but I do have some good news for you, your off the hook."

"What do you mean?" she instantly smiled.

"Yeah, for helping me, to that secret location, and for what you're doing now, I'll let you go, where do you want me to let you off?"

"What happens, if I don't want to be let out?" "What are you suggesting?"

"What if I work for you?"

"In what capacity" asked Jack, she begins to undress, as she unbuttons her blouse, and, then opens it up to allow him to see her perfectly sized breasts, to say, "Go ahead touch them, do whatever you want with them, and me, your quite powerful man, and I want you to be inside of me?"

Jack looks at her, playing with her breasts, to say, "Maybe we can, what do you have in mind?"

"Well I can get you into the dorms, and then watch as you take down those four men?"

"What four men?"

"Oh, I mean the men who run the Coed trafficking?" "And your part of this, maybe I should reconsider letting you off."

"It was either join them or be sent out myself." "What did you have to do for that?"

"Oh you know a little of this and a little of that, but I'm here right now, to help you take them down,"

"Do you know that they're taking fellow girls, you might know and kidnapping them?"

"No they're not." "How so?"

"The program is just this, they follow professors, politicians, and others around, to get dirt on them and entice them to have sex."

Jack looks over at her to say, "So where is all the other 25,000 missing women?"

"I don't know, what are you talking about?"

"Just that, a girl goes missing every day, no let me correct that, ten girls go missing every day that figures to be 25,000 a year, what of them?"

"I didn't know anything about that, honestly."

"I think, this Shadow Project is all a ruse, into allowing you girls to think you're playing an espionage game, where in fact, it was all a game to keep you guessing, where one of your friends is at", he saw she was crying, now, as she knew he was right, to say, "I'm sorry, can I help you, to help stop them?"

"Absolutely", said Jack still looking at her breasts were out, for Jack to say, "A guy could get used to seeing that, can I ask you something?"

"Sure what is it?"

"Are you into sport fucking?" "Absolutely, wanna go around now?" "No maybe tonight" said Jack. "Sounds fun, count me in."

The car came to New Orleans University, as Miranda instructed Jack where to go, he took control of the wheel, to a dorm off the main part, to a maintenance building, and parked, she said, "You'll need key access."

"I have one", said Jack showing her his phone. Jack got out as she did, to say, "Wait I can help?"

"I really think you'll be safe in the car."

She came up to him, and said, "Let's do this together." "I don't think it's a good idea."

As she went ahead of him, swiped her card, and the door unlocked, as she held the door open, for Jack, as he looked back to say, "Secure, with precautions", and went into the building, it was cool, as she led him along, passing several cute girls, till she came to a room, swiped her card, the door was still secure, as she said, "I don't know why, it's not working, just then a older looking guy appeared from around the corner, to say, "So what do you want Miss Yates", for her to say, "I was bringing this man here to see you, as she peeled away, the security guard, tried to pull his weapon, but still had his hand on the gun, as Jack held out his, to say, "On your knees, interlace your fingers, as Jack, lifted up his face, he took a picture, and then zip tied his wrists, it came back Jacob Owlokosky, and it sync up with Marci, the 5-10 blonde, as Jack saw the entrance to the room, with the guard station, as some girls fled, seeing what Jack just did, moments later, Jack was walking in, and off to the right was a conference room, where the three of them sat, arguing, as Jack opened the door, to say,

"I hope I wasn't bothering your meeting?" "Who are you and what do you want?"

'I'm Jack Cash, and I want to know who knows anything about Coed Sex trafficking?"

They all looked at one another, as the attorney stood up, to say,

"As I speak for my two clients, they don't have to say a word?" "Says who?" asked Jack.

"Say's me, I'm Matt Hughes, attorney for the two of them?" "What of your security guy, are you his attorney also?"

"Yes him too, is there something going on I should be aware of?"

"Well actually, your all under arrest, hands out where I can see them" said Jack instantly pulling his weapon.

"That won't be necessary, let me see your warrant?" "Jack looked at him, and pointed his weapon at Matt and said, "I'll say this one last time, hands on the table, or I'll canoe your head first."

Just then Miranda turns the corner, to say, "Hey Jack, that one moved so I put him down."

Just then each men moved, as Markus pulled a gun, and fired at Jack's last position, as the man with the patch, went for the door, Jack landed on the Attorney, a right to the head, and he was out, Jack turned over, and fired two shots, hitting both of Markus's knees, and he buckled and went down, in agony, then Jack turned to see the other guy under the desk, for Jack to motion him up, as he did, as he was told, and motioned for him to come to him, for Jack to say, "Turn around?", he did so, without incident, then Jack zip tied his wrists, and then spun him around into a chair, to say, "Stay here, and someone will take you in."

"Wait, what is this all about?" "Don't you know?"

"Know what?"

"That your part of a group that kidnaps girls and sends them around the world" said Jack.

"What, I don't know what you're talking about, all I do is load manifests, and some logistics, how does that say what you say?"

"I don't know", as Jack went around, and zip tied the attorney, and then tended to the hurt one, when, he saw blood on the glass door, and looked past that, to see, Miranda, her head was cracked open, as she was bleeding out, Jack knew it was too late as her eyes were glossed over, for Jack to zip tie Markus, Jack turned back to take a picture and it came back Scott Tamlepage, for Jack to say, "Now you'll be charged as an accessory to murder."

"Who did I murder?"

As Jack closed the door, he went out to see two coed's at the counter, to say, "Can we see Markus, he promised that we would see Germany?"

"Sorry ladies, he is all tied up, but do come back later perhaps, someone else will help you?"

One looked at the other, as they headed off to say, "That guy is sure weird?"

"Yeah, I wonder why he was there, he is sure driving us away" said the other.

CH 17

Celebrations of discovery

The authorities discovered, over three hundred, thousand women names, places and contacts the single largest discovery of women trafficking in history, as for the Shadow Project all the remaining women, including Lisa Parks, had been arrested, among the arrests were the girls leader, a Denise Slade, with ties to a professor in the name of Sung-so-Lynn, as girls were being sent to Japan, and as more were found out, three professors, to include and more notably, Karl Pelton, a German, who's connections run deep with Helmut Starlings, who sent girls to Europe, and finally, locally, this professor of ethics a Mark Regis, his own wife was brained washed, he went down with a fight, that was till Jack kicked him in the head, and knocked those wire rimmed glasses from his head.

Jack spent the last of his Friday in the precinct saying his goodbyes, and even embracing his new friend, James, who said, "Him and Marlene will be getting married, I want you to be my best man?"

"Sure, how's your sister?"

"Still a wreck, you really did a number on her, but one good thing came of this?"

"What is that?"

"She doesn't call me twenty times a day anymore?" "You think she'll recover?"

"Yep, she'll be fine, as the two embraced, they broke apart as it was Roxy next who hugged him, and gave him a kiss on the cheek, to say, "I want a rain check?"

"Sure, come aboard my boat, were having celebration, tonight, well after this."

"Alright I'll be there."

Next up was Abigail, she kissed him first, then hugged him, to whisper, "I'm sorry, I should have just taken it."

"No worries, you're a good detective, keep up the good work."

"Thanks", she said as they broke apart, for Jack to see the Captain, Jack said, "Thanks for allowing me to help you out." "Your welcome, you just secured my job, till I retire, thank you" said Captain Ernesto.

Jack waved his last goodbyes, and then went down stairs, to see the door that once stood, was down, and it looked like empty offices, as he turned to see the desk sergeant beaming with enthusiasm, as Jack said, "Why are you so happy?"

"That's just who I am?"

Jack waves to him, to say, "See you around?"

"Is that in invitation to come work for you?"

"You want to be on my team?, Jack looked at Jared, to say, "Yeah, alright, be at the Lake shore Airport at 6pm tonight, and someone will get you going?"

Jack went out to his car which was parked in front, in a space, newly erected that said, "Reserved for Jack Cash, specifically, and for those that are doing great things for this precinct", signed Ernesto Bryant Captain.

Jack allowed Sara to drive him to her graduation, at the cooking academy, he was running late, but took the handicap spot up front, got out, and went inside to see it was standing room only, as names were being called out, from the twelve, its class size, then it was Sara who made it up to the stage, to hear, "And this is for your family's sake, I hope my lesson helped you, this is for you Miss Sara Sanders.", she saw Jack and lit up, smiled and waved, and then, was working her way over to him, as others cleared a space, she reached him, as the last remaining girl, rose, went up, to hear the chef say, "And to our highest point getter, she can truly cook, if you would, I'd offer you a placc in my restaurant, but you refused me, so your husband Rick, will be the only one sampling your skills, here's to you, Jessica Weiss, good job."

Sara embraced Jack, and kissed him, to smell the perfume, to say, "You have been busy, come, what no entourage of girls, or boys?"

"Nah, that is later, tonight, It's just you and I"

"Well actually, it will be you and Rick, we only have twelve tables, but some have more than others, so less than one, you're at the VIP table, as Sara takes Jack over to the table, where Rick shakes his hand, as Sara kisses him goodbye, to say, "You play fair."

Rick looked at Jack who took his picture, to say, "Why did she say that?"

"I don't know?"

Just then two other men were escort to Jack's table, a young girl who stared at Jack, as her father sat on one side of Jack, and the other man, whose wife kissed him on the lips, both men, introduced themselves, the older man, said, "My name is Wolfgang Drake, I'm from Germany?"

"What brings you to New Orleans?" asked Jack.

"Oh the fun in the sun, I come every ninety days, as the face recognition came back, "Dangerous known ties to Charles Rand."

And to the other guy, who shook the hell out of Jack's hand to see his watch to say, "That is some serious watch?"

"Yeah, I guess so."

"How much you pay for that?"

"I didn't, some guy just gave it to me."

As the man was frigidity, for Jack to say, "Are you nervous?" "Yeah, it's the first time, I come to this place, as Jack took his picture, discreetly, as man said, "The name is Franz Chadbourn, from Bonn, Germany?"

"Really", said Jack holding his excitement back, to say,

"Ever heard of a man named, Gunther Schecter?"

"Yeah, are you kidding me, the Schecters are my next door neighbor."

"Seriously" said Jack.

"Yeah, but Gunther has since past, from what we were told, he was captured and killed, but his mother and sister still lives there, or maybe, their broke now and is going to be forced to move."

Jack typed all that in, but it still came back nothing, so he put away the phone, and waited for the five course meal to arrive, in between bites, Wolfgang kept hounding him, "What is your name?"

Jack thought about Enzo, or his name, back and forth, until Wolfgang, received his own word, and the news, for him, to say, "Please excuse me I must go?"

He got up and went down the hall, as Jack followed, till he was at the door, as Jack had his weapon out, to say, "Hands up, and turn around?"

For Wolfgang to say, "Who are you?"

"The name is Jack Cash, International Bounty Hunter, now, on your knees, as he does what he is told, as Jack zip ties, his wrists, gets him up, and outside to the rain, for Jack to say, "Open trunk", he tossed Wolfgang in, and then zip tied his ankles, then one for his mouth, then closed the trunk and went back inside.

The meal was over, as the graduates, congregated, Jennifer Drake was asking anyone, if they had seen her father?

Jack said, "He got a call and had to leave." "Oh it figures he always does that?"

"Well you can come with us, on our boat and celebrate with us if you like?"

She saw Sara and Jessica, and Sela, who said, "Me and my husband are on a flight out in two hours, back to Germany."

The meal was officially over as Jack was carrying Sara's suitcase, and led her out, to the car, the rain was fierce, so he helped her to the passenger side seat, to say, warm to 90, forced air, and he took his time, with her suitcase, as he opened the trunk, and put the suitcase on top of Wolfgang, he got in as Rick and Jessica were going to follow them. Jack got in, to see Sara was soaked, as the forced air, wasn't doing anything except fog up the window on her side, as she admired his car, he put his phone in the dash, and then Sara roared to life, and off they went, as the Weiss family followed. They reached the slip he was at, the big Parthian Stranger stood proud, as his crew was busy with her, he parked in the makeshift tent that was set up, and a bridge that was covered, to the deck which was loaded down, and a huge tent covered the deck, to keep all the rain out, Mark was there to help Sara out, and up the ramp, Jim appeared, to see Jack, to say, "Were all set" "There is a gift in the trunk, I'll call Lisa."

"Not to worry, I'll see her soon, go have fun."

Jack had his phone in hand, as he exited, and went around to the trunk, it opened, and pulled the case, and closed it on Wolfgang, and went up the bridge, to the deck. Instantly a whole slew of women came out, as Jack said, "I need you to form a single line, as Sara took a seat to say, "What is going on here, Jack?"

"These are the new candidates, to be my wives?"

"Really what brought that on, alright, I'm game, do I get a vote?" said the curious Sara.

"Yep, you first, then I'll decide, as he saw Roxy and Abigail away from the girls, as they turned to see, a guy say?" Is this the right vessel, going out tonight?"

Roxy looks at him to say, "Your name please?"

He looks at her, to say, "Jeremy Tyler, I'm a diver, will we be driving, as Jack moved around, and hooked up Jeremy, and took him below, as Sara was interviewing the potential new wives. Rick and Jessica arrived, got out of their car, also Jennifer Drake was close by, as Roxy led them to the tent.

Jack came back to hear Roxy say, "What are you doing with your guests?"

"Taking down some, if they look shady detain them, open and free, let them in the tent?"

"How do we know how many will show?" "Will be here till seven then were off."

Next up the bridge was a heavy breasted black haired girl, as Jack took her picture, it came back Kitty Lane, known bounty hunter, as Jack signaled for her arrested, but Roxy had to tussle with that one, till she put her in a choke hold, and subdued her, Jack hooked her up, and took her down. Jack watched as Sara was taking her time, as Mark blew a loud warning, and just like that those still on the dock appeared, instantly both knew it was wrong, as Roxy took the nearest Mexican, and Jack rushed the other, and right there, both were subdued, Jack drug them away, as the next guest was an evil looking guy, a picture confirmed who it was, A Dustin Birch, ex-Navy, and Jack took him down, as he wrapped up his arm behind his back, and zip tied him and led him down, and lastly a bearded man, with a back pack, and dark glasses, then it was serious as he showed a switch he had, as he was at the edge, as Mark, threw it in gear, and the sudden rock, took him over hitting the dock, and an explosion was heard, as the boat left dock, and down the Mississippi river, all was calming down, as Jack took the other two, nationalist, one was a guy named Barlow, that had no ties to a Juan Aureole, which was the other, and took them all to a room, enroute was a Coast Guard Cutter, as Jack made it up to the wheel house, to see it coming, and he told Mark, to find a slip to park, and asked Mike and Timmy to help out, but looked again, as it was Jared, to say, "Where's Timmy?"

"At school or for something, we found a new replacement on the boat." Said Mike.

"I can see that, but I was thinking of the team?"

"Oh I don't know about that", as Randy West appeared, to say, "Do you know when they'll serve chow?"

"Don't know, but I imagine there is someone in the galley, said Jack as he led him, to see the boat was parked next to the huge cutter, as Jack and Jared, and Mike all took a body and helped it along, to the receiving porter, at the edge of the ship, as it was Lisa, directing the men, one by one, till all five were loaded, and for Jack to say to Roxy and Abigail, "I guess this is a good bye?"

"Who say so?" said Roxy.

"Well I thought you two might want to get back?"

"Where are you heading?"

"Back to Mobile and I thought you wanted to go home?" "Well you thought wrong, this is your time for that rain check? As Jack waved up to Mark, who got the wave off, from the Coast Guard, as he powered the Parthian Stranger back on course, as Jack put his arms around the two detectives he walked them back to the tent. And let them go, to take a seat, next to Sara, to say, "What do you think?"

"Now who and where will they stay?"

"We have the room, but DOD has limit me to only ten at a time, and as Jack looked them over, he points to the one on the end, to say, "She is already in, that is unless you object?"

"No, she is alright", said Sara as Jack waves Isabella off, for Jack to see the other sister, for Jack to say, "What of her?"

"Yeah, that older lady, would be alright" said Sara, as Jack motions for them to come to him, as he said, "Now you know, what this entails?"

"Yes", said Maria, and walked off with her sister Isabella.

Next up was the twins, Cara and Christina.

The outgoing twin, Cara, said, "Yes we have all been briefed, and know, we live with you for the rest of your life and produce as many babies you want, no problem."

"Then I guess your both in, go over there?" said Jack. Jack went back over to Sara, to see the next one, a Samantha White, a gorgeous brunette, she smiled, and her enthusiasm was evident, as Sara said, "I like her too?"

"So do I", as he motioned for her to come forward, she did, as Jack said, "Your in", she smiled and kissed him, as he went back into see Kendra Killian, as Sara said, "I don't care much for her, she seemed bossy, as Jack looked her up and down, she smiled at him, and realized it was time to make a decision, so he motioned for her to come forward, as he told her the news, she took it well, and went to the party, as Sara choose Lindsay, and Jack agreed, as for Tia, it was definite for them both especially Sara when she found out what she did for her man. As for Melanie, Sara didn't care as much, and Jack, he told her she was already, next out was Kara, Paula, he didn't even really know, neither Cheryl, who was already half naked, Tiegan, and Mary. They took it alright, Tamara was really undecided, she thought it out and wanted off, as Jack let her go, and now it was the mob girls, both Jack and Sara said really said No to Tessa, who was really on the fence with all the others, it was down to five for three slots, both choose Daphne, and India, that left two for one spot, and Jennifer Saad, was undecided to drop out, that left two, a very unhappy Maria, Sara wanted was Jennifer and so it was made, Jack chose them both.

Back in Mobile, all had settled and Jack was resting, Jack awoke the next morning, as Mitzi came to him with good news, "Jack, Jack, as he turned in his master bed, with Sara next to him, and the very pretty Tia, on the other side, she held the pamphlet as she handed it to him, to say, 'Read this and sign the back, you're going to that spy summit.", the reading was quite fascinating from his standpoint of what countries needs are and if they specifically ask for. Each person will get a minimum of ten million dollars, to unlimited, also the freedom of unlimited travel with military support, in addition all the treasures found are the property of your to keep, do with it or assign it to others, the last few forms dealt with the conference, whereas the top two Spies for each country have been asked to participate, for a total of 356, where as the top twelve will emerge, and receive the title of Super Spy, and with it share ideas and learn from each other, then ever quarter they will meet depending on schedules to have a summit, during this visit to Geneva Switzerland, you may take one additional persons to go with you, all diets and foods to your liking will be available to you. Jack smiled and signed the form, and turned back over and held Sara and Tia.

The End.